JUSTICE

MADALYN MORGAN

Storm

Ebook ISBN: 9978-1-80508-264-4
Paperback ISBN: 978-1-80508-266-8

Previously published as *Shadow Sleeper*

Cover design: Debbie Clement
Cover images: Arcangel, Shutterstock

Published by Storm Publishing.
For further information, visit:
www.stormpublishing.co

ALSO BY MADALYN MORGAN

Sisters of Wartime England Series

Foxden Acres

Destiny

Betrayal

Redemption

Legacy

Reckoning

Confessions

Secrets

Obsessions

Justice

Justice is dedicated to my late parents,
Ena and Jack Smith.
And to my late friend and author, Helena Dennie.

ONE

Ena unlocked the street door to Dudley Green Associates. As it closed, she crossed the lobby to the main office, which she shared with her colleague, Artie Mallory. She unlocked its door and pushed, but it resisted. She pushed again, this time harder, and it gave way swinging back on its hinges. She reached for the light switch and flicked it on. Before her eyes became accustomed to the light, the door flew back at her with contrived force and knocked her off her feet. Someone was behind it. Instinctively she raised her arm to shield her face and slid down the wall. With her eyes shut she waited, hoping that whoever was in the office would think she was unconscious. She felt heavy fabric brush the top of her head as the intruder stepped over her and switched off the light.

Her throat was dry, she was desperate to swallow, but the lack of movement told her that she was being watched. After a long silence she heard the sound of heavy shoes on the stone floor of the entrance lobby. The man – for Ena was sure now that it was a man – had a long stride and a heavy footfall. Keeping her head low, she opened her eyes a little and looked down from underneath her eyelashes. From her position on the floor the man looked like a giant. At a guess he was over six feet tall and thickset with broad shoulders. She was unable to see the colour of his hair as he wore a trilby.

Ena watched him pull open the door to Mercer Street. At the same time a dark saloon car left the car park opposite. Neither the car's headlights nor sidelights were on. The only illumination was from its brake lights. They flashed an orangey-red as the car free-wheeled over the tarmac. Crunching chips of loose gravel beneath its tyres the car bumped over the pavement onto Mercer Street. Ena closed her eyes as it coasted to a standstill.

She sat motionless straining her ears. She heard the passenger door slam and a second later the green Ford Zephyr that she had seen when she parked the Sunbeam, accelerated away.

Ena stayed slumped against the wall for some time; her eyes shut, her senses heightened. She felt a draught. It was only slight, but it told her that the street door was open. She had heard the car leave, but someone could be in the doorway, or watching her from the pavement. She had sensed there were two people in the office, but there could have been a third person outside, keeping watch. When there had been no sound for what Ena estimated was five minutes, she opened her eyes. The street door stood ajar, but there was no one beyond it and the lobby was empty.

She lifted her left arm and groaned. A searing pain shot from her elbow to her shoulder where the office door had slammed into her. She lifted her arm again, slowly. It hurt less this time. She was able to move it a little, which was something she thought. At least it wasn't broken. She tried to rotate it, but quickly stopped. That did hurt.

With her back against the wall, she exhaled with relief. She was alive and whoever had broken into the office had gone. She leaned to the right, allowed gravity to pull her upper body down, before using her right hand as a lever to push herself up into a kneeling position before scrambling to her feet.

On stiff and shaky legs, Ena hobbled into the lobby. She pulled on the door handles of both the waiting room and the cloakroom, before kicking them open and putting on the lights. When she was satisfied that there were no intruders lying in wait for her, she limped to the main door and out onto the pavement. There was no one in the street and the only vehicle in the car park was her Sunbeam Rapier. Supporting her left elbow with her right hand to ensure her forearm and wrist were as comfortable as possible against her body, she returned to the door. Crouching down until her eyes were level with the lock, she saw it was intact. There was not a scratch on it, nor on the door or doorframe. 'Lock picks!' she said, under her breath. Closing the door and locking it, Ena returned to her office.

'The files!' she sighed. Why else would the office be broken into? The files were the most obvious reason. Crossing the room, Ena's heart began to pound. The filing cabinet drawers were closed, but no longer locked. She pulled open the top drawer and walked her fingers across the plastic labels on top of each file. No client names or job titles were missing. It seemed at first glance that nothing was out of place. If they'd removed any files, they'd been meticulous in putting them back in the right order. She then opened the second drawer. Just like the first, nothing appeared to be missing. As she pulled open the third drawer her stomach lurched. The file on her late friend and work colleague, Sid Parfitt – Berlin, pre and post 1936 – had gone.

Ena pushed the cabinet drawers to, went over to her desk and took a key ring with a dozen keys on it from the top drawer. There was little point in locking the filing cabinet now, but she did anyway. Dropping the keys into her desk drawer she slumped down in her chair. A thought suddenly struck her. The intruder hadn't locked the filing cabinet. She was sure they would have done if she hadn't disturbed them; everything about the break-in – from being knocked down but not hurt – apart from her arm, which was accidental rather than intentional – smacked of the intelligence services.

Ena sat perfectly still. Only her eyes moved as she quickly scrutinised the room. There was nothing to see on or above the picture rail. She got up and went over to the window, pulled on the catch, but found it locked. She ran her hand along the top of the window frame and then the blind. Nothing. Turning round, her back against the windowsill, she scanned Artie's desk. She couldn't swear to it as she hadn't taken much notice, but it appeared to be as he had left it. She looked at her own desk. Everything was the same as she had left it too; blotter, pen, notebook, diary and telephone... Or was it?

Ena pushed herself off the windowsill and crossed to her desk. Sitting in her chair she mimed picking up the telephone. Something wasn't right. Was it the handset? She caught her breath. The handset was the correct way round on the cradle, but... She sat back. The cable was on the far side of the telephone, hanging down the outside of the desk. There was no earth-shattering reason for it, it was just a habit of Ena's that she always placed the cable on the inside, so it wasn't visible to clients sitting opposite her. She shuddered. Until eighteen months ago she had worked for the Home Office as Head of the Cold Cases department. She hated the lies, the dirty tricks, spies and traitors – and having to continually sweep the office for listening devices.

The deciding factor for Ena leaving the Home Office was when her friend, Sid Parfitt, was killed on Waterloo Bridge by a spy he had known in Berlin when he was a child. When she had exposed the woman and the spy ring responsible for her colleague's murder, she resigned.

Special Branch and MI5 were as bad. Worse. They didn't only bug people's workplaces, they bugged their homes. MI5 had bugged her previous flat. Anger bubbled up inside her. She had thought those days were in the past. Looking at the telephone, she realised she was wrong.

Getting up, she crossed the room to leave. At the door she reached out to put off the light but looked up and sighed with frustration before flicking the switch. If there was a bug in the ceiling light it could stay there until tomorrow. She opened the office door and bent down to scrutinise the doorframe and lock. Similar to the front door, there was no sign of forced entry. The lock hadn't been tampered with. Ena switched off the light, closed the door and crossed the lobby to the street door. Before leaving she looked at the lock once more. Not a scratch. There was no point getting the locks changed. Ena knew from experience that a professional in the intelligence services – British or any other nationality – could get into any building they wished. And this intruder, Ena knew, was a professional.

TWO

The following morning, from the door of the small hall on the ground floor of the flat above Dudley Green Associates where she and her husband Henry lived, Ena intercepted her colleague, Artie Mallory. Before he had time to put his key in the lock, she grabbed him by the arm and wheeled him into the hall of number 8a.

'We have a problem,' she whispered. 'A couple of pros broke into the office last night.' She put her forefinger up to her lips to stop Artie from commenting. 'I've been in every room and I'm certain it was only the main office they were interested in. So be careful what you say, I'm almost certain we've been bugged.'

'Bloody hell. Right,' Artie said, keeping his voice low, 'we'll do the good morning, how are you, routine, while we look for devices.'

Artie unlocked the office and Ena followed him in. While Artie went into the kitchen, Ena went to her desk, sat down, and opened her diary. 'Not a lot happening today by the looks of this,' she said, slamming the diary shut.

From the kitchen Artie, shouted, 'Coffee?'

'Yes, please. Make it strong.' Ena jumped up and joined him.

'No bugs in here,' he mouthed, opening one cupboard after another, moving jars and bottles, and silently running the flat of his hand under each shelf. He then pulled open the cutlery drawer with a tug and its contents rattled. He gave Ena a cheeky grin. 'Fill the kettle, will you, while I get the coffee tin?'

Ena turned on the cold-water tap. As the water hammered through the pipe she crossed to where the kettle was plugged into the wall. Bringing it back to the sink she rinsed it to prolong the noise and block out their conversation. 'Well?' she whispered, filling it.

Artie shook his head. 'Nothing in here.'

'Good,' Ena replied, not with a smile, but a deep frown. Sid's stolen Berlin file cast a black shadow over everything. 'Being bugged is the least of our problems.'

'Why?'

Ena shot Artie a worried look. 'Whoever broke in last night took Sid's file, his day diary that he kept in Berlin in 1936 and the letter he wrote to me just before he was killed.' Ena felt tears prick her eyes. 'Whoever is blackmailing Rupert Highsmith will now know as much about the work he and Sid did in Berlin as we do.'

Artie scrunched up his shoulders and bit into his bottom lip.

'What is it?'

'I'm sorry, Ena. I know I shouldn't have, but whoever broke in here last night doesn't know anything about Berlin in '36. Not from Sid's file anyway. I took it home with me.'

'Thank God!' Ena exhaled, and then exclaimed, 'You did what? I don't know whether to kiss you or sack you. I should sack you for taking top secret material home with you.'

Artie took the file from his briefcase and handed it to Ena.

She rolled her eyes. 'On this occasion it's a good job you did take it. But,' she said, her frown deepening, 'don't ever take sensitive material out of this office again! Do you hear me?'

'I won't, but we do need to find somewhere safer than the filing cabinet to keep it.'

'We do, and we will. As they didn't find the file last night, it'll be safe here for the time being. Okay,' she said, flicking through the file. 'I'll go back to my desk, you come in and say the milk's off.'

'I'll suggest we go up to Café Romano for coffee and pick up some milk on the way back.'

'Good idea to get out of the office, but we shouldn't talk business in public, especially about Berlin in '36. I'll agree to us going to the café, but we'll go upstairs to the flat instead.'

'Even better. We'll check it for bugs before we discuss the file.'

THREE

'Hello, Rupert.' Ena got up from her desk and motioned to a chair on the nearside of the large, oval, conference table. She walked to the other side and sat down opposite him. Artie pulled out Rupert's chair and when he was seated, joined Ena.

Rupert Highsmith, the man who had once had the ear of Prime Minister Stanley Baldwin, and was instrumental in bringing about the downfall of Adolf Hitler, had a chequered past. As a young man, he had worked in counterespionage. The intelligence service's gossip-mill had it that he was a double agent. Something that was never proved – or disproved. Could it be that the author of the anonymous letters that Highsmith had recently received, which Artie had told Ena about, were sent by someone with a grievance from those days, someone who thought Highsmith had betrayed the country? Or maybe it was an ex-lover who Highsmith had betrayed. If what Ena had heard was true, Highsmith had broken the hearts of many young men. She was sure that there were any number of spies and ex-lovers waiting in the wings to see Highsmith get his comeuppance.

Highsmith took three white envelopes from his briefcase

and put them on the table. Ena noted that they were the type of envelopes that anyone would use to send a letter to a friend or family member. Nothing unique or noteworthy about them. Ordinary envelopes that could be purchased at any stationer, corner shop or Woolworths.

He lined them up. 'The order in which they arrived,' he said.

Ena had known Rupert Highsmith for many years. She had always thought of him as something of an enigma. She looked from the envelopes to his face. His brow was furrowed. His hair was lacklustre and his eyes, usually sparkling with confidence – and often arrogance – were dull with dark rings under them. He looked exhausted. Like him or not, Highsmith had been a confident man with a brilliant mind. Now, Ena thought, he was no longer sure of himself. He was no longer in control of his life. The onslaught of written malice had a hold on him. Something else he wasn't used to.

Highsmith looked at Ena. Despair showed on his face. She smiled at him reassuringly. 'This,' he said, his face as white as a sheet as he took an A4 manilla envelope from his briefcase, 'came this morning. It contains photographs that were taken in Berlin, in 1936.' He pushed the envelope across the table to Ena with the flat of his hand.

Ena braced herself in preparation of what she might see and reached for the envelope. Highsmith didn't let it go. 'They were taken after the Olympic Games had finished, after Parfitt had flown back to London.'

Ena brought to mind her late colleague, Sid Parfitt, and the diary he had left her recounting his time in Berlin and his schooldays at boarding school. Sid's father had been in the Diplomatic Corps in Berlin, and his mother a lecturer in Politics and Humanities at the University of Berlin. It was because Sid was fluent in German that he had been sent to cover the Berlin Olympic Games by *The Times* newspaper – and it was because of his background that British Intelligence had recruited him.

The XI Olympiad in August 1936 was commonly known as Hitler's Olympics. It had been Rupert Highsmith who her friend and colleague, Sid Parfitt, reported to. Highsmith, as Sid's superior in the secret intelligence services, was his handler. Suddenly aware that Highsmith was speaking, Ena pushed the sad memories of Sid to the back of her mind.

'... I had no idea that anyone had taken photographs. I've wracked my brains and I don't remember seeing anyone with a camera on the day I met the boy.'

The boy? For as long as Ena had known Highsmith, she'd known he was homosexual. Everyone knew and most people accepted it. Highsmith had a way about him that in social situations people warmed to. In his job he had earned respect. Even those who looked down their noses at queers, ignored Highsmith's leanings. Ena knew when Highsmith was young he had an unsavoury, some would say iniquitous, reputation, but a boy? She couldn't see him then, or now, with a boy.

In Ena's line of work everything about a client was relevant – their day-to-day activities, their work and their social life – their future plans and their past – especially their past. It was all relevant, all necessary. She was sure she'd learn unsavoury things about Highsmith, but whatever they were, she vowed not to let them bias the investigation. She needed to keep an open mind, remain impartial for Artie's sake, and for the sake of truth. Now photographs were involved, blackmail would no doubt follow.

Ena took a breath and exhaled slowly. She should, and would, put everything she knew about Highsmith's misspent youth out of her mind and concentrate on who it could be that was sending him anonymous letters and photographs.

Highsmith finally let go of the envelope.

Taking out the photographs, Ena laid them on the table. She

looked inside the envelope, put her fingers in, but it was empty. 'Was there no accompanying letter?'

Highsmith, avoiding eye contact with Ena, shook his head.

The first photograph was of a youth, a good-looking boy with black curly hair and big brown eyes. He looked terrified. He was standing in front of a boarded-up café that had anti-Semitic slogans painted on wood covering the glass in the doors and windows. Ena moved the photograph to the side and looked at the next one. The boy again, grubby, his hair thick with brick dust, was standing in the foreground of a row of derelict houses. She picked up the photograph and looked at it closely. The boy was crying. Tears had run down his face, leaving his cheeks streaked with dirt. She put the photograph down with gentle reverence.

The boy reminded her of the many East End children whose families had lost their homes in the Blitz. 'How old is the boy in this photograph?' she asked Highsmith.

'He did tell me, but I don't remember. I think he was about fourteen. And,' Highsmith added, 'before you jump to the conclusion that whoever sent these photographs wants you to jump to, nothing improper happened between the boy and me. Nor the boy and anyone else while he was in my care in Berlin.'

Ena could see sincerity in Highsmith's eyes, pain too. She exhaled with relief and nodded that she believed him, though in truth she wasn't a hundred per cent sure. She picked up the first letter. On it were two typewritten words – *Remember Berlin?* She opened the second envelope. The message, also typed, was longer. *You were very friendly with that boy in 1936.* Ena put it on top of the letter on the right side of the boy's photograph and opened the third letter. *You danced with the devil.* Ena folded the letter in half so only the typewritten words were visible and placed it below the boy's picture.

The next photograph was taken from some distance away; a rear-view shot of Highsmith with the boy. Highsmith had his hand on the boy's shoulder, as if he was guiding him through an open door. Ena held the photograph up to get a better look. The door was the entrance of a hotel called the Berlin Stadthotel. Given the Olympics were in August, the dim glow of a street-light in the distance told her the photograph was taken in the late evening.

The next was of Highsmith and the boy leaving the Berlin Stadthotel in bright sunshine. The photograph was clearly meant to convince anyone looking at it that it was taken the next morning and that the boy had spent the night with Highsmith. The final photograph was of Highsmith speaking to a swarthy looking man of indiscriminate age wearing ill-fitting clothes. The man was short and thin with unkempt black hair and a black straggly beard. Highsmith, bending down, was leaning conspiratorially close to the man and giving him money.

Ena lifted up the photograph. 'I presume the reference to you dancing with the devil refers to the man in this photograph who you're giving money to?'

Highsmith nodded.

Ena laid the photograph on the table in front of her and, after scrutinising all of them again, looked up at Highsmith. 'How did you meet the boy?'

'A couple of days before I was due to leave Berlin, I received a message to meet a British agent. Who the agent was has no relevance to...'

'On the contrary, Rupert. I think *who* the agent was could be very relevant.' It was the first time Artie had spoken during the consultation.

Ena also thought the agent who had sent Highsmith a message to meet him was relevant. She cast her mind back to what Sid had written in his diary the day he left Berlin, or was it in the letter he wrote to her. It didn't matter. What mattered was what he'd said. *My cases were packed and I was ready to leave when Highsmith turned up with my plane ticket home.*

Someone was taking my place as an observer, he told me. Someone not from The Times, *but from British Intelligence.*

'Sid Parfitt told me the person who took over from him when he came home from Berlin in '36, was from British Intelligence.'

'MI5. But I assure you that it was not him who sent these letters and photographs.' A look of desolation spread across Highsmith's face.

Artie laid his hand on Highsmith's arm, tilted his head towards him and smiled encouragingly. Artie's smile, Ena hoped, would persuade Highsmith to explain.

FOUR

Highsmith took a deep breath. 'The agent who took over from Parfitt in Berlin could not have sent these letters because he's dead,' he said at last. 'He was killed on the day he asked to meet me. The official line was he got drunk in a bar in a town on the east side of Berlin called Köpenick. A couple of local men threw him out of the bar and while he was walking back to his hotel he fell into the River Dahme, and was drowned.' Highsmith flicked back his head. 'Huh!'

'But you don't believe that's what happened?'

'No, I don't. The agent asked me to meet him in a café in Berlin, so why would he then go to an out-of-the-way place like Köpenick; a one-man, one-horse town where he had no business to be, which, without a car, he knew would mean he'd have to walk ten kilometres to get back to his hotel in Berlin's Mitte District.'

Highsmith looked all in. He put his head in his hands.

'What is it, Rupert?' Artie asked affectionately.

Highsmith lifted his head. 'Don't you see? The information the agent had for me must have got him killed. I don't suppose I shall ever know for sure, but...' He sighed heavily. 'What was the man thinking? What was so damned important that he abandoned our meeting and went all the way to Köpenick?'

Ena had hoped Artie would take over the interview, but she could see he was too upset on Rupert's behalf. She needed to move the conversation on. 'So, to clarify,' she said, 'you received a note to meet Sid's replacement at a café in Berlin?'

'Yes. His name was Michael Crosier and for whatever reason, he didn't show up. From the side entry of a shop on the opposite side of the road I watched the boarded-up café for more than two hours before I left. It was when I was walking back to my hotel, I stopped to light a cigarette, and I heard a child crying. I went to investigate and found the boy in the photograph in a derelict house. He was cowering in the corner of a room on the ground floor, rocking backwards and forwards, and hugging his knees. I approached him and asked where his parents were. German is a language that I speak badly, but understand moderately well. He must have grasped what I'd said because he told me that the house was his home. He said his mother had sent him to the shop to buy milk and bread, but when he had returned with the food, his family, mother, father, brothers and sisters were in the street, lined up with their neighbours. Soldiers were pointing guns at them and ordering them into the backs of lorries. The soldiers dragged his sick grandmother out of the house and threw her into the back of a lorry with strangers. He said he didn't know when that was, or how long he'd been sitting in the empty house.'

'I'm confused.' Ena pointed to a photograph of a boy outside a boarded-up café. 'Wasn't it there that you were meant to meet the MI5 agent, Michael Crosier?'

'Yes.'

Ena knew from the account Sid had given in his diary that the café had been shut down by the Nazis and the Jewish woman who ran it had gone before he left Berlin. 'Was the boy in the photograph there when you arrived to meet Michael Crosier?'

'Briefly. A second, no more. He was peering into the café through the narrow gaps in the boarded-up windows when I arrived. As soon as he saw me, he ran away. It was after that, when I was heading back to my hotel, that I saw him again in the empty house. He told me each day he walked the streets of the old quarter until it was dark and then he returned to the house.

'On the afternoon the soldiers took his family away he had watched from a distance. He said he waited until he was sure the soldiers weren't going to return before going into the house. He ate some of the bread and drank some of the milk that night and again the next morning. He hid what remained of the food and set off to look for his parents. When he didn't find them he went home, finished the bread and milk and waited, hoping they'd come back for him. I estimated that he'd been hiding for almost a week.'

'Did he say why he was at the café where you were meant to meet the MI5 agent?'

'Not when I first saw him. He told me later that he'd gone there to ask the lady who ran it if she'd give him some food. The child hadn't eaten for several days when I found him. He had no money to buy food. Money and anything of value that belonged to his parents – anything that he could have sold, or traded for food – had been taken by the Nazi soldiers.'

'Were these photographs taken later that day?'

'Yes. I waited until it began to get dark, so the boy would look less conspicuous, and I took him to the hotel.'

'I can see it's getting dark by the streetlight in the distance,' Ena said, pointing to the photograph where Highsmith had his hand on the boy's shoulder.

Highsmith stuck out his chin. 'I know what it looks like!' The arrogant tone he used when Ena first met him was back. 'I took him to the hotel and while he bathed, I went out and bought him clothes. When I returned to my room, he was in my bed fast asleep. *I* slept in the chair. I hardly slept at all, but that's beside the point. The following morning after breakfast I handed him over to this chap.' Highsmith stabbed his forefinger at the swarthy looking man with untidy black hair. 'His name was Saul. I was never told his surname as my contact said it was safer that way.'

'Who was your contact?' Ena asked.

'The hotel manager. He was one of ours. He assured me that Saul, also Jewish, was a good man and that he would get the boy out of Berlin to safety.'

'And the money you're giving him is for the boy's safe passage?'

'Yes. Saul refused to take money for himself, but I made him take some for the boy's food and lodging.' Highsmith took a postcard from his inside pocket. 'The day I left the hotel the manager gave me this.' He passed the card to Ena. 'It's from a place called Lübbenau. It's a farming area.'

There was a picture of fields and trees on the front of the postcard, and on the reverse a handwritten message in German. Highsmith translated it. 'It says, our friend arrived safely and has been given work and lodgings on a farm.' Looking at the card, Highsmith's face softened. 'Work and lodgings!' he said, as if to himself. 'Lübbenau is on the Spree River about eighty-two kilometres southeast of Berlin. He would have been safe there.'

'Can I keep the postcard for a while?'

'Of course, if you think it will help.'

Ena had no idea whether the postcard would help the investigation, but put it in the folder. 'And that was the last you saw or heard of the boy?'

'Until, this lot arrived, yes.' Highsmith brushed his hand over the collection of photographs and anonymous letters.

FIVE

'Café Romano's closed again,' Artie said, shrugging off his jacket and hanging it up.

'It was closed last Friday morning too,' Ena mused. 'I'd have thought Friday mornings would have been too busy to shut-shop. Apart from the regulars, the market traders and people on their way to work in offices and shops, a lot of people do their shopping for the weekend on Fridays. I hope Emilio isn't ill.'

'You okay for coffee?'

Ena lifted her mug as Artie passed her and went into the kitchen.

'I saw him in the café,' Artie said, returning to the office with his coffee to sit at his desk. 'He was talking to a couple of teenage boys.'

'Customers?'

'I only glanced, but I suppose they must have been. Or they could have been family. They looked Italian. Slicked back black hair at the sides, a Brylcreemed quiff at the front.'

'Then why was he closed?' Ena checked her diary. 'What's in your diary for today?'

'Rupert gave me the paperwork from his time in Berlin. I

was going to go through it, see if any of the spooks he handled over there had an axe to grind. Why?'

'Are you hungry?'

Artie laughed. 'Have you ever known me not to be hungry?'

'Silly question. Okay,' Ena said, 'let's go to Café Romano for an early lunch. We'll go through Rupert's Berlin documents together.'

'Sounds good to me.'

'Emilio?' Ena tapped on the pane of glass in the café's door and watched her friend and neighbour, Emilio Bellucci, pull out two chairs from beneath a table in the window, carry them across the room and add them to a stack of half a dozen. 'Emilio?' she shouted again. 'It's Ena and Artie. Can we come in?'

Turning away from the chairs, Emilio's face lit up when he saw Ena and Artie. Smiling, he made his way to the door and unlocked it. He pulled it open and welcomed them with outstretched arms. 'Come in, come in,' he said, ambling over to the counter and taking up his usual position behind it. 'I am sorry. I have no food.'

'But it will soon be lunchtime, Emilio.'

He threw his hands up in the air. 'Yes, I hope to make the food, but for now only coffee. What can I get you?'

'An espresso for me,' Artie said, and looking at Ena, 'cappuccino?' Ena nodded.

'Take a seat, I bring them over to you.'

Artie made for the table with a bench seat where he and Ena usually sat. Ena stayed by the door. 'Shall I turn the closed sign to open, Emilio?'

'No!' the café owner replied, sharply.

Ena was shocked by Emilio's curt response. She wound her way through the tables and sat down next to Artie. 'Something isn't right,' she whispered. Artie shook his head in agreement.

After some hissing from the coffee machine, Emilio brought over two cups of coffee. 'Cappuccino for the signora and for you, Signor Artie, the espresso.'

'Emilio? If the café isn't open, why don't you sit down for a moment?'

'Signora, forgive me, but I do not have the time. I must clean.' He shook his head. 'I must use the disinfectant. It smells, so I must do it fast with the doors open. Get rid of... the smell,' he said, walking away.

'Emilio, what's wrong?' Ena called after him.

The café owner halted, turned and faced her, but didn't speak.

'I can see something's wrong. What is it?'

'Maybe Ena and I can help,' Artie said.

'Rats!' Emilio spat, wringing his hands. Beads of perspiration appeared on his forehead and his usual olive complexion paled. 'I am ashamed, signora.' Emilio shook his head and threw open his arms. 'They saw a rat in the passage to the toilet per signore. They said I will be closed down.'

'Who said that? When was this?'

'Please, signora, I have said too much. Forget I speak, please.'

'Café Romano is always spotless,' said Artie. 'I don't believe anyone saw a rat.'

'Maybe not. But someone only has to say they see the rat and...'

'Was that why you were closed last Monday?'

Emilio looked at Ena, lowered his head and nodded.

'And did someone see a rat last week too?'

Emilio nodded again.

'Was it the same person, Emilio?'

'Yes, the same.'

'Today when I walked past there were two youths in here—'

'Early customers,' the café owner cut in.

'But the closed sign was on the door, Emilio. What's going on? Are these youths trying to extort money from you?'

Emilio dropped into the chair facing Ena and Artie. He took the white cloth from the waistband of his chef's apron and wiped perspiration from his brow before rubbing the cloth over his face. 'They say, give fifty pounds every week and customer don't see rats. If I don't pay them, customers will see rats.'

'They damn well won't see any rats,' Ena said.

'I'll take photographs of them, find out who they are and where they come from. Did they say when they'd be back for the money?' Artie asked.

Emilio shook his head.

'No one will see rats, Emilio. Leave it with Artie and me.'

'Signora, they say I must keep my mouth shut. Not tell anyone. They said bad things would happen to my wife, my family.'

'Emilio, do you know these people?'

The café owner hung his head again. 'The boys are from my country. They are brothers. Sons of a man called Umberto Genovese. I knew some of his family in my country. Umberto is the oldest Genovese brother. He was successful businessman. Something to do with horse racing,' Emilio said. 'I don't know what happened but he was sent to prison. He got out three weeks ago and began working with his father in the family dry-cleaning business in Holborn.'

'Does he still work there?'

'He worked there when he was released, but now?' Emilio shrugged his shoulders. 'Joey Genovese, Umberto's younger brother—' Emilio shook his head. 'Joey is a bad boy. Umberto is always having to... how do you say – bail him out – pay his debts. His mother will hear nothing bad said about him, but Joey is a thug. When Umberto was sent away, Joey took over his business. When Umberto got out, he tried to close the business down. He didn't want Joey getting into trouble, as he had done. But Joey wouldn't have it.'

'You said it was Umberto's business.'

'It was, but Joey had investors. He couldn't give them their money back, even if he wanted to.' Emilio shrugged his shoulders again. 'They fought and Joey put Umberto in hospital. Joey has no... how do you say... *conscience*.'

Ena looked at Artie. A smile played on her lips. 'I have an idea how we can put an end to the young Genovese brothers' extortion racket.'

'No, please, Signora Ena, it is better I pay the money. The boys' Uncle Joey is bad. He runs around with bad people. He is a little crook, but the people he answers to are members of...'

'The Mafia?' Ena queried.

Emilio shook his head vigorously, making the loose flesh under his chin wobble. 'I don't want trouble.'

'And you won't have any trouble, Emilio. Nothing will come back on you. In fact, do as you had planned. Don't give Artie or me another thought. If you think you should give the Genovese brothers money, give it to them. For the time being, do what will keep you and your family safe.'

Artie gave Ena a sideways look. 'Since you used the royal "we", any chance of sharing your idea with me?'

'Yes, when we're back at the office.' Ena smiled at Emilio. 'Now, why don't you open the café? I'd like to order a slice of your home-made Sciachiatta.'

'Signora, for you anything.' Emilio lumbered to the door, unlocked it and turned the closed sign to open. 'Evvia!'

'What about you, Artie? An early lunch?'

He rolled his eyes as if to say, you need to ask me, and nodded.

'Make that two slices of Sciachiatta and two coffees,' Ena called to Emilio who was already slicing the savoury meat pie.

'Mafia? The two kids I saw in here this morning were no more Mafia than I am,' Artie said.

'What's the plan?' Artie asked Ena when they were back in the office.

'First, we find out all we can about the Genovese brothers' dry-cleaning business.'

'It's in Holborn.'

'Good. With a name like Genovese it shouldn't be difficult to find.'

'What? In little Italy?'

'No, in the Home Office records. We need to know if the brothers or any members of the family are in this country illegally.'

'Umberto has a criminal record, so he must be here legally.'

'And if the dry-cleaning company is legit, he'll have paid tax in this country. If it's a front, and if they haven't paid tax, the Inland Revenue would have been alerted when Umberto was convicted. I bet the favourite son, Joey, doesn't pay tax.'

'Hang on, Ena. How are you going to access Home Office records?'

'I still have my Home Office ID.'

'No, Ena, you can't.'

'Yes, Artie, I can.'

'You don't have clearance to access HO files.'

'That's true.' Ena thought for a moment and then said, 'We have good friends in Dan Powell and the recently promoted Detective Sergeant Jarvis at Bow Street, and we both have friends at the Home Office. I think it's time to call in a few favours.'

'What about this lot?' Artie crossed to the table where he had left the pile of folders that Highsmith had given him.

'Everything that Rupert has from Berlin in '36. Which case is more urgent?'

'Highsmith's case, of course.' Ena joined Artie at the conference table. 'Emilio is going to pay the Genovese kids next week, which gives us plenty of time to get information on them.' She took a folder from the top of the pile. 'It's time to find out what Highsmith was actually doing in Berlin in 1936.'

'And who is hell-bent on discrediting him.'

SIX

'A lot of what Highsmith has written about Berlin in 1936 we already know from Sid's diary.'

'It won't hurt to refresh our memories,' Artie replied.

'Of course it won't.' Ena glanced at the first couple of pages which both she and Artie were familiar with.

I received a copy of a memo sent to an employee of The Times, *Sidney Parfitt, who had been chosen to go to Berlin to cover the XI Olympics. He went to school in Berlin and was fluent in German, so seemed the obvious choice. He was to report anything he heard about Chancellor Hitler and the Nazi Party to me* and only me. *His orders were to attend the Olympic Games on alternate days. The days he wasn't at the Games he was to frequent cafés and bars – in particular, establishments where students, militants, extremists and radicals could be found. On the whole, Germans, like all Continentals, don't expect an Englishman to speak or understand their language other than, bitte and danke, the greetings tourists use. Being fluent in German will give Parfitt an advantage. The usual drop was arranged at the Berlin Stadthotel and Parfitt's findings were reported to me. I was in every sense of the word, Parfitt's handler.*

If Parfitt had only been in Berlin as a sports reporter, my first meeting with him would have been cause for concern. I arrived at the Olympisches Gästehaus off Potsdamer Platz in time for our breakfast meeting. He was a no-show, so I went up to his room. He had overslept and was nursing a hangover. He looked as if he'd been dragged through the Grunwald forest backwards. He had been taken out and shown Berlin's rare and rude nightlife and been plied with alcohol until the early hours of the morning, which was what most male tourists did as soon as they arrived in Berlin.

As a rather straight-laced kind of chap, Parfitt was worried that he'd get a reputation for being a drunk. He said he couldn't remember drinking much, which set off a small alarm bell. However, I assured him that no one would notice in Berlin – and if they did, they wouldn't care. Besides, getting drunk in the bars and clubs of Berlin fitted very well with his new character. When a chap has had one over the eight, people tend to ignore him and say things that they wouldn't say in front of a stranger – and definitely not in front of a foreigner – if they thought he understood what they were saying.

Eventually, we went for breakfast. I asked him how long he had known Walter and Frieda Voight. He was shocked by the question, and asked how I knew he'd been with the Voights. It was my job to know, so I told him the truth. It was nothing more Machiavellian than I had been sitting in the foyer of the Olympisches Gästehaus reading a newspaper and drinking schnapps waiting for him to arrive. To my thinking it was a bit of luck that he already knew the Voights.

Parfitt told me that he had been to the same school as Walter and visited the Voights' home, which was where he had first met Frieda. I told him they were the best contacts to have. He had no idea that Walter, having been in the Hitler Youth movement and Frieda the BDM – the girls' wing of the Nazi Party – still embraced Nazi ideology; expansionism, fascism and Nationalism. Parfitt hadn't a clue what his old friends were involved in.

We'd had agents in Berlin since the early 1930s; the Berlin Stadthotel, Embassy and the airport. It was no surprise that Walter and Frieda Voight were there the day Parfitt arrived. The naïve sap thought Walter Voight was his friend. He thought the difference in their beliefs was something he would ignore while he was in Berlin. Not the same for Walter. Walter Voight was predatory. Parfitt was convinced that meeting his old school friend at the Tempelhof airport had been a coincidence. However, Voight had patiently waited at the Tempelhof for twelve hours, just like an animal waiting to pounce on its prey. Walter Voight played Sidney Parfitt from the moment he arrived in Berlin. I don't think Parfitt knew. He may have worked it out later, but by then it was too late. Frieda had stirred his sexual interest and he was back in the heady days when he thought he was in love with her. Frieda had more wiles than Cleopatra. By the time she'd finished with him, Parfitt was a lamb to the slaughter.

I told him to stay close to them, Walter in particular. In the beginning, Baldwin had been keen to appease Hitler. The government believed Hitler was intent on destroying Europe and Baldwin did his best to comply with his demands, for the sake of peace. As far as the Olympic Games was concerned, Parfitt wrote his reports, I read them and if there was anything I thought would provoke Hitler, I amended them before they were taken to the drop and wired to London. Parfitt was answerable to military intelligence. I was answerable to military intelligence too, but my priority, my loyalty, was to the PM.

In the summer of 1936, there was a sinister feel to Berlin. The sun had shone for so long that the earth was baked, the flowerbeds that lined the roads for Hitler's daily arrival and departure were dried up, the blooms dead. The temperature was 86 to 88 Fahrenheit, but a coldness enveloped the people. I have always found Berliners to be warm and friendly, but not anymore. Now they keep their heads bent low as they pass neighbours and work colleagues in the street. They look down as they walk for fear their dull eyes will make contact with other dull eyes. Neighbours fear neighbours. No one knows if the neighbour on their right is a Nazi sympathiser, or the neighbour on the left is a Jew. Unbeknown to the rest of the world, by the time the Olympic Games began thousands of Jews had lost their businesses and their homes, and many of them had been transported out of Berlin.

Fear was etched on the faces of ordinary Berliners and arrogant smiles on the faces of those who believed they were superior because they were members of Hitler's Nazi party.

Hitler's Olympic stadium and sports complex was five miles west of Berlin. It meant I could no longer debrief Parfitt over breakfast. Instead, Parfitt left his report on the Olympics for The Times, along with details pertaining to what he had learned that day, in his room. I scrutinised both before taking them to the drop at the Berlin Stadthotel, where they would be wired securely to England – one report to The Times, the other to Prime Minister Baldwin.

* * *

Parfitt had packed and was ready to leave by the time I arrived with his ticket to fly home. A chap from British Intelligence, Michael Crosier, was taking his place as an observer. Parfitt was pleased to be leaving Berlin. He had seen parts of the city that tourists and sports enthusiasts, there for the Olympic Games, had not seen. Parts that had made him sick and ashamed. He had seen first-hand how the Nazis treated the Jews when he stumbled across a café run by a Jewish woman. She and her husband had *previously owned a popular restaurant in a smart part of central Berlin. She told Parfitt that brownshirts started to frequent the restaurant. They were rowdy, rude to other customers, disrespectful about the Jewish religion – and never paid for their food and drink. The regular customers stopped going to the restaurant and eventually the Nazis took it over. One night the brownshirts beat the woman's husband and left him for dead in the alley at the back of the restaurant. He died in hospital waiting to be seen by a Nazi doctor.*

SEVEN

'I have read Sid's account of the Jewish woman and how she and her husband had been hounded out of their business and home, in the journal he left me. Sid had been mortified by the brutal treatment that Jewish people suffered at the hands of the Nazis.' Highsmith nodded in agreement. If Artie had told him about their late colleague, Sid Parfitt's diary, also written in Berlin 1936, Highsmith didn't say.

'Shops in the streets leading to and from the small Jewish community, owned by Hitler's so called Aryan people, displayed signs that said, *Achtung Juden* – No Jews here.' High-smith shook his head, a look of despair on his face. 'The windows and doors of Jewish shops and cafés had been boarded up. I assumed they had been owned by Jewish people because, *"Untermenschen"* subhuman beings, was scrawled across them and the Star of David had been daubed on the doors in yellow paint.'

He shook his head. 'What I'd seen was upsetting to say the least. I wasn't ready to go back to the hotel so I walked as far as the Potsdamer Platz; to where the woman told Parfitt she and her husband had had a restaurant. It was no longer there. All the buildings looked the same. The Nazi flag flew from every doorway and upstairs windows. Dense white circles with black swastikas at the centre, like the wings of vampire bats, hung in wait to suck the life out of the city and its people.

'I began to understand the shame and disgust that Parfitt had felt because I was feeling the same. I sat for some time in a small square off Potsdamer Platz and watched street cleaners sweeping the rubbish left by the crowds leaving the Games, many of whom had begun to believe Hitler's rhetoric. So many people had been taken-in by the grandeur of the Olympic stadium, the Tempelhof airport, the biggest building in Europe, certainly the biggest airport – and the modern railway station with trains that were said to be the fastest in Europe – and all of it paid for by Nazi Reichmarks in order to show the world that the Third Reich's German Capital, Berlin, was the most wonderful city and Chancellor Hitler the most wonderful leader. The Nazis brainwashed the people with their far-right ideology and galvanised them into hysteria with that dreadful chant, "Sieg Heil!" Hail victory! which they'd adopted early in the 1930s to signal the Nazi Party's obedience to their leader... Adolf Hitler...' Highsmith's voice trailed off and he closed his eyes.

Pulling himself together he opened his eyes and said, in a matter-of-fact way, 'I got back to the hotel in time for a quick lunch, after which I went to my room. There was plenty of time before I was due to meet Parfitt's replacement, so I lay on the bed and closed my eyes.'

'I must have fallen asleep because the next thing I remember was loud knocking at my door. It was the bellboy. Reception had taken a message for me and sent him up with it. He gave me a piece of paper with the words, "RH. Urgent. Café off Sonniger Platz – 6pm. M C."

'MC? The British intelligence agent who had replaced Sid?'

'Yes. Michael Crosier.'

'Michael Crosier wasn't a journalist?'

'No. He had been an architect before joining the intelligence services. Apart from the fact that he now worked for MI5, his cover was real. If anyone questioned him about architecture, he was able to answer correctly. His passport gave his profession as an architect and visitor (Olympic Games). He had a genuine interest in the buildings in Berlin. If he was stopped and questioned as to why he was in Berlin, Crosier was to say that as an architect he was interested in the buildings the Chancellor had had built. His MI5 brief was to visit the sights, socialise and find out whether ordinary Berliners had swallowed the guff the Nazi propaganda machine had spewed out. Berlin's citizens were naturally exuberant because the German Olympic team had won eighty-nine medals. The Americans, fifty something. The rest of the world put together didn't compare.

'Anyway, Crosier was to report back as Parfitt had, but not to me as I was leaving the following week. Another agent should have taken over from me, but the show folded after Crosier was killed.'

'You also said,' Ena read Rupert's words, 'I had met Crosier on half a dozen occasions. Every time he had badgered me to get him a job in the field. He wasn't queer. He just wanted the excitement of working overseas. He was an odd sort of fellow, but I liked him.'

'I did.' Highsmith looked into the mid-distance. 'I blame myself for his death. He wasn't experienced enough. God knows why he wanted the job.' Rupert shook his head. 'It was his first time in the field.'

'You mustn't blame yourself, Rupert,' Artie said.

'Who else should I blame? Berlin in the thirties was a dangerous place. It was for that reason that it was a single man's show. Crosier was married.' He shook his head again. 'I learned some time later that he had a son. I should never have agreed to him coming to Berlin.'

'Who was supposed to take over from you when you came back to England?'

'A chap called Archibald Hollander, a Scotsman. He came out, but not as my replacement. He was sent to handle what military intelligence and the Home Office called the delicate situation of a British tourist falling into a river and drowning after drinking too much strong beer.' Rupert exhaled loudly. 'I don't believe Crosier was drunk and drowned. I didn't believe it then. I told everyone I knew in intelligence, the HO and Parliament that I thought Crosier had been murdered. But I was told that wasn't the case and ordered to keep my mouth shut. The success of Hitler's Olympics must not be overshadowed by the death of an English tourist. Tourist? He was one of us for God's sake.

'In a nutshell, Archibald Hollander's job was to *clean house*; deal with the German police and the authorities and get Crosier's body back to England as quickly as possible. And he did. Hollander was good at his job. He was ex-paramilitary, built like the proverbial out-house, and had once been a lawyer. He wasn't someone I'd want to represent me,' Highsmith said with distaste. 'His legal background was the reason why they sent him to deal with the Berlin authorities. He was a dour Scotsman with no social skills. A man of few words, as far left as they come without actually being Communist, and a tight wad to boot. He looked down his nose at me, probably thought I was going to try and turn him. As if. He was an inverted snob. He railed against what he called "the privileged few", public school education, and titles. He thought the House of Lords should be disbanded, those with titles should be stripped of them, and their houses and lands given over to the poor. He constantly complained that if he'd gone to the right school, the right university, he would have been a QC. Hollander was a sour-puss who openly declared his hatred for Americans and queers.'

Out of the corner of her eye, Ena noticed Artie flinch at Highsmith's use of language.

'And, he blamed Stanley Baldwin for everything from the economic crisis in the thirties to the abdication of King Edward the eighth.'

'Do you know where he is now?'

'No.'

Ena looked at Artie. He nodded and wrote down the name Archibald Hollander. Next to it in capital letters he added, FIND.

Ena wrote on her own notepad Michael Crosier, family and friends. FIND.

* * *

'What do you think?' Artie asked Ena when Rupert had left.

She looked again at the array of letters and photographs. 'It isn't going to be easy to prove who sent this lot.'

'I agree.'

'It shouldn't be too difficult to get hold of Hollander. Give the intelligence services a call – ring round all the agencies until you find him. Start with MI5. Reception, or whoever answers the telephone, will at least be able to tell you if anyone by the name of Archibald Hollander works there. If he doesn't work there now, he may have worked there in the past. The receptionist will know, or be able to find out. If you're lucky and you hit his place of work, ask to be put through to his secretary. And when you're through, make an appointment to see him.'

'If Hollander's there and reception puts me straight through to him, where shall I say I'm calling from?'

Ena tilted her head in thought. 'Would it be stretching the truth too much to say you're calling from GCHQ?'

Artie shot Ena a wide-eyed look of disbelief. 'Stretching the truth? It would be a downright lie. I left GCHQ six months ago.' He thought for a moment and then said with a twinkle in his eye, 'On the other hand, I do still have my ID. I could try I suppose.'

'And while you're trying to get hold of Hollander, I'll try and find Michael Crosier's wife. She may still live in London.'

'It's been twenty-four years. It's more than likely she's remarried by now, so her name might not be Crosier.'

'Rupert said he had children.'

'A son would have the name, Crosier. He'd have to have been born more than twenty-four years ago, which would make him mid to late twenties. With a bit of luck he's got his own place. If he has, he'll have a telephone and be listed in the telephone directory.'

'Maybe.'

'I was living away from home at that age, so why wouldn't he be? Especially if his mother has remarried,' Ena mused. 'But I'm procrastinating.' She jumped up and went over to the filing cabinet. She took the London telephone directory from the top and took it back to the conference table. Opening it, she flicked through the pages until she came to the letter 'C' and then thumbed through until she came to 'CR'. She ran her finger down the columns of names until she found the name, 'Crosier, initial A'. After making a note of the name, address and telephone number she carried on looking for other initials following Crosier. 'There's an M Crosier here.'

Artie was making notes, he looked up. 'Obviously not the late Michael, but it could be his brother. Or his son. Rupert said he had a boy.'

'Brothers with the same initials? It's possible, but unlikely I'd have thought.'

'You're right. Could it be his father.'

Ena did some quick mental arithmetic. 'No, he'd be in his

nineties if he was still alive.' She shook her head. 'More likely to be his son.' She wrote down the address and telephone number. They were the only entries in the London telephone book, but it was a start.

'Tomorrow first thing, you flash your ID at a few receptionists, see if you can find Archibald Hollander and I'll call on Mr M Crosier after I've been to see Inspector Powell and Detective Sergeant Jarvis at Bow Street.'

EIGHT

'Ena?' DI Powell at Bow Street police station was waiting for her, hand outstretched, as soon as she was through the door marked Private.

Ena took his hand. 'You're looking well.'

'Took my mother over to France to stay with my brother and his wife. I did nothing but eat and drink for a week,' he said, leading Ena into his office. 'Take a seat. Jarvis knows you're here.'

Ena sat in the usual chair opposite her friend, Dan Powell, in his familiar office.

'My brother was there in the war,' he continued. 'Went back in '46 and married a French girl. They've got a vineyard. He's a winemaker. Bit different to being a copper,' he said, laughing. 'But seriously, they've got a lovely place. Mum goes over for a couple of months every year. She could live with them if she wanted, but she likes her own home.'

'I can understand that.'

'I can too, but if I was her I'd be tempted...'

There was a knock on the door and without waiting to be asked in, a familiar voice called, 'Hello?'

'I'd know that voice anywhere,' Ena said, turning to greet Detective Sergeant Jarvis who was carrying a tray of refreshments. 'Don't tell me he still gets you to make his tea?'

'No,' Jarvis laughed. 'Well, not as often. This,' she said, putting the tray with three cups of tea on DI Powell's desk, 'is a special occasion.' She took the cups of tea off the tray and placed one in front of Ena, one in front of her boss, and the third on the end of the desk.

'You look well, Sergeant. Promotion suits you.'

DS Jarvis put up her left hand and waggled her fingers.

'Congratulations!' Ena jumped up and hugged the young detective sergeant. 'I hope the ring was given to you by that handsome young man you brought to our housewarming party?'

'It was,' DS Jarvis said, blushing.

'Pull up a chair, Jarvis.'

DS Jarvis took a chair from under the window and placed it at the end of the inspector's desk.

'What did you want to see us about, Ena?' DI Powell asked, taking a sip of his tea.

'I was wondering if you could tell me anything about an Italian family called Genovese who have a dry-cleaning business in Holborn.'

'We know the Genovese family very well,' DI Powell replied.

'I'll get the file,' DS Jarvis said, jumping up and leaving the room.

'The Genovese brothers learned racketeering from some of the best,' Dan Powell explained. 'In '39, when war broke out, there was a huge rise of fascism in Italy and antisemitism became commonplace in London's Italian community. Off the top of my head,' DI Powell continued, 'Umberto Genovese and his brother Joey were interned on the Isle of Man in 1940 along with protection racketeers like Charles Sabini. Being interned with Sabini, whose power rested on the alliance of

Italian and Jewish bookmakers, didn't do either of the brothers any harm.'

'It enhanced their criminal activity and improved their street status,' DS Jarvis added from the doorway, before crossing the room and taking her seat. 'They learned all they could about Sabini's extortion rackets and when he died in 1950 they tried to take over his businesses.' She opened the file. 'Christened Octavius Ottavio, Sabini was better known as Charles Darby Sabini.'

'Or Frank Handley – among other aliases,' DI Powell put in.

DS Jarvis took a sheet of paper from the folder and read, '"Charles Sabini was arrested at Hove Greyhound Stadium in April 1940 and, despite having mixed parentage, was interned. He was released in 1941. However, in 1943, he was found guilty of receiving stolen goods and sentenced to three years in prison."'

'His only son was killed on active service in the RAF in Egypt. It might have been after losing his son that Sabini lost the lust for power and money,' the inspector added.

'His empire was taken over by Alf White – one of the most notorious and vicious London gangsters who terrorised book-makers on racecourses and on street corners. His protection racketing business extended into the West End's clubland – and afterwards by the organisations of Jack Spot and Billy Hill. Sabini became a small bookie himself down in Hove.

'It was after he'd died in 1950 that Umberto and Joey Genovese edged their way into the protection racket.'

'Didn't the organisations that took over Sabini's racketeering mind the Genovese brothers taking a share?'

Dan Powell laughed. 'To people like Spot and Hill, the Genoveses were small fry. I think it was a case of, better the devil you know. But when Umberto began to branch out into other areas of organised crime, like money laundering, which he did through nightclubs in the West End owned by Spot and Hill, an anonymous citizen shopped him. Umberto was sent down for six years. He's only been out a few weeks.'

'And working in the family's dry-cleaning business in Holborn,' Ena said.

'He is now.' DS Jarvis shook her head. 'Umberto's younger brother Joey, who his mother – the matriarch of the Genovese family dotes on – is a thug. When Umberto was sent down, he shut down all his businesses, but Joey started them up again telling people that he'd taken over from Umberto. When Umberto came out, he was furious with his brother and tried to shut his protection business down. He didn't want Joey to get into trouble as he had done and end up in jail. The brother's fought and Joey put Umberto in hospital. Joey has no...'

'Conscience,' Jarvis said.

'That's exactly what Emilio Bellucci at Café Romano told me.'

'And it's because of Mr Bellucci that you wanted to know about the Genovese brothers?'

'Yes.'

'Ena, be careful.'

'It isn't actually the brothers, it's Umberto's sons. The two lads are making the lives of people like Emilio Bellucci a misery, threatening them, trying to extort money.'

'Ena, I think you should let us handle the Genovese family.'

'They're only kids. Thirteen, fourteen-year-olds. I don't intend to cause any trouble. I shall just mention immigration and suggest if they don't want the Home Office looking into the affairs of their grandfather's dry-cleaning business – and the people who work for him – they had better stay in Holborn and not come back to Covent Garden.' Ena checked her watch. 'I have an appointment soon, so I had better make tracks.' Finishing her tea, Ena pushed back her chair and got to her feet. 'Thank you, Detective Sergeant,' she said to Jarvis. 'Again, congratulations on your promotion and on the rock you're wearing on your finger.' A thought crossed Ena's mind. 'You don't wear that out there in the streets when you're mixing with London's less than finest, do you?'

DS Jarvis laughed and stood up. 'No. I wear it on a chain round my neck when I'm not in the station.'

Ena wiped the back of her hand across her brow and blew out her cheeks. 'Thank you for the background on Umberto and Joey Genovese,' she said, shaking hands with DI Powell.

'I'll see you out.' The inspector walked swiftly to the door and opened it for the two women to leave first.

DS Jarvis pushed open the door to her office, which was along the corridor on the right, said goodbye again, and DI Powell led Ena through the door marked Private and out into the warm sunshine. 'You will be careful, Ena?'

She laughed. 'Stop worrying. You know me!'

'Which is why I'm asking you to be careful.'

'I will. I promise.' On tiptoe Ena reached up and kissed Dan Powell on the cheek. 'Put that serious face away, right now!' she ordered.

He put up his hands in surrender. 'I give in.'

'Good. I'd better get a move on. I'll let you know how it goes,' Ena shouted, waving over her shoulder as she ran for the Sunbeam which she'd parked a little further along Bow Street.

NINE

As Streatham Hill Railway Station came into view on the right, Ena turned left from Streatham High Road onto Leigham Court Road. When she had cleared the bus stop, she pulled into the kerb, put on the hand brake and consulted the *A to Z*. There was about a mile to go before she needed to turn left onto Canterbury Grove. She released the hand brake, pressed her foot down on the accelerator and pulled out into the traffic. Artie knew the area and had told her to take the first turning on the left after a big church which was also on the left. St Peter's Church was indeed big. It was set back from the road on raised ground and was easy to spot. Ena pulled up behind a double-decker bus going to Croydon. As people left the bus and others entered, Ena sat and admired the imposing building. Not old, at least not as old as the thirteenth Century, which St Mary's in Lowarth was. St Peter's, she guessed was Victorian. It had been built with bricks of different colours, and had turrets. The windows were in various styles, and a stair turret with a conical roof and a large wheel-window gave the front an asymmetrical but picturesque appearance. It was a shame that it still showed

bomb damage from the war, but it didn't detract from its character. St Peter's Church was an amazing building.

As the bus pulled away from the pavement with its fresh
haul of passengers bound for all stops south until it reached
Croydon, Ena turned left onto Canterbury Grove where she
slowed down again before taking the first right to number three
Orpington Road.

Ena got out of the car, locked it, and passed through the
wooden gate to walk the short distance to the front door. She
lifted the brass door knocker and rapped a couple of times. She
could hear muffled voices inside the house. Then quite clearly, a
woman shouted, 'I'll get it.'

'Hello,' a young woman in her mid-twenties, said. 'Can I
help you?'

'I hope so,' Ena replied, smiling. 'Are you Mrs Crosier?'

'Yes, Annette Crosier. What can I do for you?'

'My name's Ena Green.' Ena opened her handbag and took
a business card from the small pocket in the bag's silk lining.
Handing the young woman her card, she said, 'I work for
Dudley Green Associates.'

Annette Crosier read the card. 'Investigations? Are you a
detective?'

'Private investigator.'

'Goodness,' Annette replied. 'What would a private investigator want with me? Us?' she added, turning at the sound of a
man coming down the stairs.

'Who is it, darling?'

Mr M Crosier – husband of Annette and son of Michael –
was a very handsome man in his late twenties. He looked at Ena
and smiled.

Ena put out her hand. 'Mr Crosier?'

'Matthew.' He took Ena's outstretched hand and shaking it
said, 'What can we do for you, Mrs...?'

Annette Crosier gave Matthew Ena's card.

'Mrs Green?'

'Ena Green of Dudley Green Associates. I'm investigating a case that may be connected to the Olympic Games in Berlin, 1936. Or, to be more precise, the week following the Games, the seventeenth of August, 1936.'

Matthew Crosier didn't speak, but looked inquisitively at Ena. 'Come in,' he said at last. Turning, he walked along the passage and opened the first door on the right.

Ena stepped into the small entrance hall and Annette Crosier stood back for her to pass. She followed Matthew Crosier into a spacious sitting room as Annette closed the front door.

'Take a seat, Mrs Green.' Matthew pointed to an armchair next to the unlit fire. When Ena was seated, his wife joined them. 'Would you like a cup of tea, or coffee, Mrs Green?'

'No, thank you, I had a coffee before I left the office.'

'Matthew?' she asked her husband.

'Not for me, darling.'

Annette crossed the room and sat on the comfortable looking settee under the window. She reached up and gave her husband's shirt sleeve a tug, and he sat down next to her.

'Is your investigation to do with my father, Michael Crosier?'

'Indirectly. Your father was working in Berlin at the same time as my client.'

'Dad wasn't in Berlin long before he was murdered. Not that the German authorities would admit it, nor the British. His death certificate says he drowned. My mother was told when she went to the office where my father worked that he'd been drinking heavily and fell into a river. But that wasn't true. The Germans must have covered up the real reason for his death.'

'What makes you think that?'

'For a start, Dad rarely drank alcohol. A beer, maybe two, if pushed at a party, but never more. And, he was an excellent swimmer. He would have had to have fallen into Niagara Falls to have drowned.' Tears filled Matthew Crosier's eyes. 'I'm sorry,' he said, wiping his face with the back of his hand.

'There's no need to apologise, Mr Crosier. I can imagine how distressing it is for you to talk about your father.'

'I was six when Dad went to Berlin. We were packing to go on our annual fortnight's holiday to stay with my aunt in Herne Bay. The day before we were due to leave, Dad was called into the office and told he had to work. An important job overseas, he said. He told me that while I was having an adventure at the seaside, he would be having an adventure too. He promised that the short time he'd be away would go by very quickly and said he would take Mum and me to the seaside again before I went back to school in September.' Matthew Crosier took a cigarette from the box on the occasional table at the end of the settee, lit it and offered the box to Ena. She declined.

Matthew inhaled deeply and let out a steam of smoke. 'I was never allowed to sit in the front passenger seat of the car in case we were involved in an accident. My father thought it too dangerous. But that day; the day he drove us to the station to catch the train, he said, "You sit next to me, Matthew." I remember feeling very grown up sitting up front next to him. I was so excited to be going to the seaside on a train that I can't remember saying goodbye to him.' Matthew stubbed out his cigarette and cleared his throat.

'Dad carried our luggage to the train and stowed it on the overhead rack above our seats in the compartment. When the whistle blew for the train to depart, he jumped off and walked alongside the train. He ended up running to keep level with us. When the train picked up speed, he had to stop running, but he didn't stop waving. Mum waved to him from the carriage window, although he wouldn't have seen her because of the smoke and steam from the train's engines. I don't know why I didn't wave. That was the last time I saw my father.'

Annette, clearly moved by her husband's recollections, took his hand and held it between both of hers, cradling his hand on her lap. He looked at her lovingly and smiled through tears that he no longer bothered to wipe away.

It was clear to Ena that although it had been twenty-four years, the death of Matthew Crosier's father was still raw. 'I'm sorry to have reminded you of such a sad time.'

'I suppose it's worse because Mum and I were fed lies by the intelligence service that Dad was so proud to work for.' Matthew shook his head. 'Mrs Green, I don't believe my father was drunk, nor do I believe he fell into a river and drowned. I believe he was murdered and it was covered up by the authorities in Berlin, and later by British Intelligence.'

Matthew Crosier looked pleadingly into Ena's eyes. 'Mrs Green, if you find out what really happened to my father in 1936, would you tell me?'

'I'll do my best to find out what happened to your father, but I can't make any promises.'

'I understand.'

The son of the man Ena also believed had been murdered in Berlin said he understood. Did he understand? Ena certainly wouldn't have understood. She held his gaze for some seconds and could see in his eyes that he did not understand. She nodded and smiled sympathetically at him. She needed to speak to Matthew's mother and she needed to see Michael's death certificate. As much as she didn't want to make matters more painful for Matthew Crosier, it was he who had brought up the subject of the death certificate. If she didn't ask now, the moment would pass. 'Could I see your father's death certificate?'

'I don't have it. It was sent to Mum, but I'm sure she'll have kept it.' Matthew jumped up from the settee and crossed the room to a writing bureau. He pulled down the lid, took out a notepad and pen and began to write. When he'd finished, he tore a sheet of paper from the pad and handed it to Ena. 'My mother's address,' he said, returning to sit next to his wife. Ena looked at the name. Audrey Crosier. A. Crosier was the only other Crosier listed in the London telephone directory. She saw no point in telling Matthew that she already had his mother's address, and thanked him. Standing up, she made for the door. Matthew left his seat and joined her. 'I'll call on your mother on my way back to the office.'

'I'd rather you didn't. Not today. She'll want to help you, of course, but she's been unsettled, preoccupied recently. Something is bothering her. She won't tell me what it is, but I expect it's something to do with my father.'

Ena looked sympathetically at Matthew.

Before she could find out more, he continued. 'It would have been my father's birthday this week and their wedding anniversary next week. I suppose two anniversaries within a week of each other has upset her. I'd like to telephone her to tell her that we've spoken, so she knows what to expect.'

'Of course. A much better idea to telephone her first.' Ena wondered if it was his mother who was sending Highsmith anonymous letters and photographs. She was upset about something. Preoccupied he'd said, but why would she wait twenty-four years to take revenge? She hoped Audrey Crosier wouldn't refuse to see her. If she wasn't in a good place there was the possibility that she might not see her, but that was a risk Ena would have to take. Matthew interrupted her thoughts. 'I'm sure my mother will tell you what she knows about my father's death. I shall tell her you know that neither she nor I believe his death was an accident.'

Matthew showed Ena to the front door and Annette followed. Ena thanked them both for their help.

'I'd be grateful to know how my father *really* died. And, if he was killed, by whom, Mrs Green.'

'I'm sorry if I've misled you. I will help if I can, but I am not at liberty to divulge information about an investigation I'm currently working on. I say working on, but it isn't actually my investigation. The lead investigator is my colleague, I'm only assisting him. However, if I learn anything directly connected to your father's death, I'll let you know. I'm sure my colleague will agree to that.'

Driving away from the home of Matthew and Annette Crosier, Ena had an uncomfortable feeling. How did it happen that she had gone to see Matthew Crosier to ask him questions about his father – and inevitably his father's death – and he had turned it around by asking Ena questions, and she had as good as told him that she'd let him know who had killed his father? Still, she had made it quite clear that the investigation wasn't hers. Even so, he had put her in a difficult position.

Recalling what she had actually said, Ena saw a sign for Holborn.

TEN

On the spur of the moment, instead of turning into Wellington Street and driving up to Long Acre, Ena stayed on the Strand and turned left onto Fetter Lane. Bearing left, she went through Hatton Garden and turned right onto Grenville Street. Saffron Hill was off Granville. She may not have been able to interview Audrey Crosier, but she wasn't going to waste the afternoon.

Looking for a dry-cleaner's shopfront, Ena took her foot off the accelerator and slowed to a crawl. There was a lot of traffic which meant the car didn't look too conspicuous moving at a snail's pace. 'Damn.' She arrived at a T-junction. Saffron Hill ran across the top of Granville Street. She was trying to decide which end of the street had the most shops and therefore would be most likely to have a dry cleaner, when the driver of the car behind her hit the horn, twice, emitting two short sharp beeps. Ena looked in her reverse mirror, put up her left hand in an apology, and turned left.

Cars were parked bumper to bumper outside a parade of shops. Ena began to indicate in case she found a parking space, and noticed a small gap between two big cars. After reversing out into the road a couple of times, causing angry drivers to stop and wait for her, she finally slipped the Sunbeam into the only vacant parking space. It was hot, so she wound down her window for some air, leaned back in her seat and looked along the row of shops. There, right in front of her, was a dry cleaners. Above a large glass window was a sign that read, Genovese Dry Cleaners and under it, Shirt Service.

Ena wound up the windows and stepped out of the Sunbeam. Genovese Dry Cleaners was on the sunny side of Saffron Hill. Cars parked on the opposite side of the road were in shade. Knowing how hot the car's interior would be when she returned to it, Ena looked down the road. As far as she could see there were no spaces. She thought about leaving one of the windows open, just a crack would allow in a little breeze to penetrate the heat, but decided against it. An open window would be an invitation for any number of the young scallywags hanging around the streets to break in and hot-wire it.

Locking the door she walked around the front of the car, across the pavement and pushed open the door to Genovese Dry Cleaners. Out of the sun it appeared dark inside – and hot. She stood in the open doorway for a second to give her eyes time to adjust to the shop's dim interior. As she approached the counter a voluminous man with a sallow completion, white hair and dark brown eyes, opened his arms in a gesture of greeting.

'Good day, signora.'

'Hello,' Ena said, smiling. 'I'd like to pick up a coat that my husband brought in last week. The name is Dudley.'

'One moment, signora.' The man, who Ena presumed was Papa Genovese, father of Umberto and Joey and the shop's owner, took a pad and pencil from the right side of the counter. 'The name, signora?'

'Dudley. D-U-D-L-E-Y.'

'And when was the coat brought in?'

'Last week. I'm not sure which day. As I said, my husband brought it in for me.'

'No problem. Last week? Your coat will be ready now. And the colour?'

Ena had leafed through a fashion magazine in the hairdressers a few days before and one particular coat had caught her eye. 'Light tan with black piping round the collar and cuffs. It's straight, there's no belt. Oh, and it has black buttons, which you can't see when the coat is done up.' Papa Genovese's brow furrowed. 'The buttonholes are not on the outside of the coat. They are on the inside.' She watched the penny drop as the man wrote something on the pad in Italian. 'Oh, and it's lightweight. More for a summer evening than for autumn or winter.' Ena was enjoying herself, but hoped she hadn't gone too far with her elaborate description of the non-existent coat.

Papa Genovese who had stopped writing after black piping, drew a ring around the word tan and put up his left hand. 'Tan?' he asked.

'Light brown.'

'Ah! One moment,' he said. Then turning away from her he pushed open a door at the back of the counter and shouted, 'Un cappotto per Dudley marrone chiaro.'

Ena took her purse from her handbag and opened it. 'How much do I owe you?' she asked taking out two-pound notes.

Before the owner could answer, a narrow-faced youth, black greasy hair with sweat running from his forehead down the side of his cheeks, came into the shop from the door behind the counter. He whispered something to the owner who threw his arms up in the air and shouted, 'Ragazzo stupido.' He turned to Ena, 'Scusi Signora. The boy cannot find your coat. One moment please,' he said and chased the boy back into what Ena guessed was the room where clothes were dry-cleaned and shirts were laundered and ironed. A few minutes later the man reappeared. 'Signora, could your husband have said a different name when he brought in your coat?'

'Oh, er, yes, he could have. Green. He may have said, Green.'

'Allora! The boy will soon find the coat. Mi scusi,' he said, and bowing again he turned to the back of the counter, opened the door and shouted, 'Lorenzo? Un cappotto per *Green*! I tell him the coat name is Green,' he explained.

Ena wandered over to the window in an attempt to stop smiling. She stood for a few minutes watching people strolling along in the late morning sunshine. She looked to her right, to where the Sunbeam was parked. The sun was full on the windscreen, and she stopped smiling. It was going to be a hot drive back to Covent Garden. The sound of a door opening caught her attention and she returned to the counter. It was a different boy who emerged this time, younger than the first one, but he had the same sweaty face and greasy hair – and the same message. 'Nessun cappotto per Green,' he said, looking apologetically over the counter at Ena.

'No coat for the name Green,' the old man translated, although Ena had got the gist of what the second boy had said.

She wanted to laugh, but she frowned thoughtfully. 'Perhaps my husband has already picked up my coat. I've been away you see and...' She gave the boy a sweet smile and then, looking back at the older man, continued. 'I'm sorry to have put you to so much trouble.'

Papa Genovese lifted his arms and opened his hands, palms up. Bowing his head, he said, 'It is no trouble.'

'I'll bring my coat in myself next time,' Ena said. Thanking the man, she headed for the open door. When she was sure she was out of sight of the shop window she began to giggle. A man and woman walking towards her gave her a wide berth as they passed. Ena pressed her lips together to stop herself from laughing out loud.

At the car she unlocked the passenger door. As she opened it the heat inside the vehicle hit her in the same way that opening an oven door would. She wound down the window, closed the door, and walked round to the driver's side where she did the same before sliding onto the Sunbeam's hot leather seat. The car's interior was stifling, but she could do nothing about it except keep the windows open. As she drove into the midday traffic, warm air was drawn from the open passenger window across her face and out through the driver's window.

With nowhere to turn the car around, Ena drove north along Saffron Hill towards Lily Place and onto Clerkenwell Road. The route via Theobalds Road and Great Queen Street in Holborn was shorter and, because she was driving at the same speed as the rest of the traffic, she reached Covent Garden in no time. She steered the car into Shelton Street and then into Mercer Street where she parked the hot Sunbeam in the nearest of the two parking spaces allotted to Dudley Green Associates.

As she crossed Mercer Street to the office she brought to mind the faces of the two Genovese boys. She wondered if they were the two extorting money from her friend Emilio at Café Romano. 'Lorenzo,' she mused, was the name of one of them. Papa Genovese hadn't called the other boy by his name. It didn't matter as she knew his face. Ena never forgot faces, and she knew one of the boy's names. She would be able to play one boy off against the other if they were involved in the racket – if she ever got hold of them. Whether they were the ne'er-do-wells or not, she knew the dry cleaners well enough to put the wind up whoever was putting the frighteners on her friend and his wife.

ELEVEN

Ena took off her jacket, put it on the back of her chair and went into the kitchen. She needed to start a file on Michael Crosier and write down everything she had learned from his son, Matthew. She flicked on the kettle and while it boiled returned to her desk and took the key to the filing cabinet from the top drawer. The file headed Highsmith, Berlin, 1936, Ena needed to keep separate from the impending file on Michael Crosier. Her gut told her that Highsmith's anonymous letters and the discrediting photographs were in some way connected to the death of Michael Crosier. What that connection was she would hopefully find out tomorrow when she spoke to his widow, Audrey. She took an empty folder from the back of the drawer and wrote Michael Crosier on the front. Underneath she wrote in brackets (Highsmith, Berlin, 1936). The two files were separate, but would hang side by side. Although she believed they were connected, the information contained in each pertained to two different people. Easier to keep separate files and access each when needed. 'Different clients?' she said, aloud, yet Crosier wasn't a client. Had she given Matthew Crosier the impression that she'd taken on the job of investigating his father's murder?

Not officially, although she had told him that she'd look into his father's death. The other thing; was that a conflict of interest? She had also told Matthew Crosier that her associate was the lead investigator in a case that began in Berlin 1936.

She was now worried that she'd shared information with Matthew Crosier which wasn't hers to share.

She went back to the kitchen, made herself a coffee and returned to Crosier's file. She took an A4 lined notepad and while she drank wrote down everything Mathew Crosier had told her. When she had finished, she glanced through her notes, and satisfied she hadn't left out anything, she returned both files to the cabinet, locked it, put the key back in her drawer and took her coffee mug to the kitchen where she rinsed it under the hot water tap and placed it upside down on the draining board.

* * *

'What did you find out about Archibald Hollander? Do you know where he is now?' Ena asked, as she and Artie sat down to compare notes on the Rupert Highsmith investigation.

'No. No one knows. Rupert said the last he'd heard of Hollander he was working for MI5 out of the Glasgow Office, but there was no record of him having worked at Five, nor at Six. We know he worked for military intelligence in 1936, then there's nothing until 1939. You were at Bletchley, Ena, could he have been at the Bletchley Park?'

'Not in 1936. Hugh Sinclair didn't buy the park until July 1938. It was a wartime base so Hollander wouldn't have been there until '38 / '39.'

'What about the Munich Crisis in the September? If he had worked for the SIS, MI5 or GCHQ then, he'd have been trans- ferred to Bletchley with the rest of the workforce.'

'Yes, but they moved back to London when the crisis

collapsed. Anyway, if he had worked for any of the intelligence agencies, there would be records. So where was he between 1936 and 1939?' Ena mused.

'Who knows? There's no record of him in 1937 nor 1938. And the records I could find were scrappy to say the least. They were Classified Top Secret by the Secret Intelligence Service. Page after page had been blacked out.'

'Which looks like he was working for SIS. What about in the war?'

'Ah-ha! Our Mr Hollander surfaced again in 1945 and worked at GCHQ until 1950 – again, his occupation was blacked out. Then in 1950 he went completely off the radar. Where he is now is anyone's guess.'

'Blacking out his occupation from '39 until '45 means his work is classified top secret, but he could have been working at one of the allied code-breaking centres, most likely Bletchley Park. In early 1939 the SIS set up a twenty-four-hour communications service. Members of Section D also moved to Bletchley in early 1939 to develop sabotage material – incendiaries and plastic explosives.'

'So, if he had been at Bletchley at the time of the Munich Crisis, he might have been recalled?'

'It's possible. When the SIS left Bletchley the code breakers stayed on. Henry was at Bletchley in the war, as was I for a short time. But no one will ever know that either of us were there. My war record states that I worked in an engineering factory, which I did at the beginning of the war. Later I worked on highly classified stuff. Henry's entire war record is classified top secret and blacked out like Hollander's because of Bletchley's top secret status.'

'It still isn't spoken about?'

'I've heard there's still work going on there. Cold war intelligence gathering.'

'So, if Hollander was at Bletchley, there won't be a record of him?'

'I'll ask Henry if he knew him, or can remember anyone named Hollander.' Or, Ena thought, Hollander could have been with the Special Operations Executive. Her sister, Claire, was seconded to the SOE and worked in France with the French Resistance for the duration of the war. But as far as her war record goes she joined the WAAF in 1939 and from 1940 was a clerk in an office that didn't exist.

'Did you try the Home Office records for 1936?'

'No. I'll go tomorrow. I know Crosier worked with Rupert at MI5, but Hollander didn't. Rupert didn't know of him until he went to Berlin after Crosier's death.'

'He could have retired.'

'If he has, he must live somewhere. He can't just disappear off the face of the earth. How old would he be now?'

'He has to be in his late fifties. Maybe even retirement age. I'll ask Rupert if he knows how old Hollander was in 1936.'

'There has to be a record of him somewhere. While you're at the Home Office tomorrow, I'll go to Somerset House. He had to have been born, and if he's dead there'll be a record. If he isn't dead, he may be retired by now?'

'Rupert said he was a dour Scotsman.'

'Then call the Glasgow office. They may have a record of him.'

'Unless he's being shielded.'

'In 1960 – twenty-four years after Berlin? Who would he need to be shielded from, and why?'

TWELVE

It was half past one. Ena scribbled a note telling Artie she had gone to Café Romano for something to eat – adding, 'see you there if you're back in time.' She put on her jacket and locking the doors behind her, headed up Mercer Street. She was pleased to see the café was open. No sooner had she sat down than Emilio was at her table with a menu.

'Signora Green, what can I get for you today?'

Ena perused the menu. 'It all looks delicious, Emilio' – and handing it back to him, said, 'What do you recommend? As long as it's hot and filling,' she added. 'Henry is working out of town for a couple of days and I don't have to cook dinner tonight.'

'In that case, Signora, spaghetti ai gamberi. The prawns, she is fresh from the Billingsgate market,' he said, kissing the tips of his fingers and throwing a loud 'mwah' to the Gods in appreciation.

'Sounds good. Spaghetti with prawns it is.'

'I bring you the bread and the olive oil. And a coffee?'

'I've just had one. I'll have a cappuccino after I've eaten.'

'Perfetto!' Humming to himself, the proprietor of Café Romano threaded his way through the tables to the counter and on into the kitchen. Ena, thinking about what she had learned from Michael Crosier's son, leaned her head against the padded backrest of the bench style seat and relaxed. She was miles away when Emilio returned with crusty bread and olive oil and balsamic vinegar dip.

No sooner had she swallowed the last morsel of the delicious Italian bread when Emilio was back with her main course. He placed a large bowl of spaghetti and prawns in front of her and swept away the starter dishes.

The prawns were as good and as fresh as Emilio had said they would be. She ate hungrily winding the spaghetti around her fork and holding it there by nudging a spoon up to it. When she had finished eating, Emilio cleared the table and brought her a cup of cappuccino and a newspaper. Ena had only taken a sip of her coffee when the café door burst open and a couple of swaggering teenagers entered followed by Artie. Ena lifted her hand, attracted Artie's attention and nodded towards the two lads. Artie raised his eyebrows and instead of joining her, stood beside them at the counter.

The boys turned at the same time and looked Artie up and down. The tallest of the two said, 'We are here on business, old man, private business.' He waved his arm in an arc and looked into the room. 'Plenty of seats. Why don't you go and sit on one of them and Mr Bellucci will take your order when I've finished my business with him?'

'It's okay,' Artie said affably, 'I'm in no hurry, I don't mind waiting.'

'But *I* mind you waiting. So, move it!' the tall kid shouted.

Ena watched the boy square up to Artie. Artie, still smiling, stood six inches taller than the boy. He took a step nearer and looked down on him. The boy's nostrils flared. He was annoyed, but not intimidated. The shorter boy who was first in the queue turned, walked past the taller one and pushed into Artie. Artie shot round as the boy sauntered on to the door of the café, opened it and left.

Nicely done, Ena thought. She got up from her seat and followed the boy outside. She found him standing in the doorway of a building a couple of doors down from the café. With one foot on the ground and one lifted up against the door, he was lighting a cigarette.

'Turn out your pockets,' Ena said, as she approached him.

The boy's lip curled. He took a pull on his cigarette and exhaled, blowing smoke in her face.

Ena sighed loudly. 'Oh, dear. Been watching gangster flicks, have you?' She waved away a second exhalation of smoke. 'If that's how you want to play it, it's fine by me.' She took out her old Home Office ID card and pushed it at the boy. 'Inspector Green, Immigration Department. I saw you pick the pocket of a man in Mr Bellucci's café. I am arresting you for theft.'

'Okay, okay, I give you what I took from the stupid old puff.' The boy took Artie's GCHQ ID card from his pocket and shoved it at her.

The shock of seeing Artie's old ID card must have shown on Ena's face because the boy smirked. She held the ID card up, so the boy could see the photograph of Artie's face. 'Stealing *this*,' she said, menacingly, holding the card close to the boy's nose, 'could get you five years in prison.'

The door to the café opened and the boy who had given Artie lip, who Ena recognised as Lorenzo from the Genovese dry cleaners, came strolling towards them with his hands in his pockets. Ena pushed Artie's ID card deep into her own pocket.

Ena saw Lorenzo's mask of bravado slip. Keeping eye contact with him, she held up her ID.

'She's immigration, Lorenzo.'

'Shut it!' Lorenzo spat. Ena could see fear in his eyes. He wasn't frightened of her, but he was frightened of what

Umberto and Joey would do if they found out he'd been mixing-
it with someone from immigration.

Lorenzo looked at the boy cowering in the doorway and
drew his forefinger across his throat threateningly.

Ena laughed. 'He didn't give you up. He didn't have to. I
know you. I know the Genovese family. I've met your... grandfather is it, who runs the dry cleaners?'

Lorenzo gasped. 'You!' he snarled. 'The coat that we
couldn't find because it was never there in the first place.'

'Well done, Lorenzo. You're quick, I'll give you that. Now,
as I was saying! I know your family.' At that moment she caught
sight of Artie. She shook her head, and Lorenzo, thinking she
was shaking it at him, took a step back. Artie knew the sign was
meant for him and went back into the café. Ena tutted. 'I also
know that your family have no idea that you are discrediting the
Genovese name by picking pockets and working your own
protection racket in Covent Garden.'

Lorenzo looked from Ena to his young partner in crime.
'Look at me when I'm talking to you!' His head snapped back
and he glared at her. 'One word from me,' she continued, 'and
the Genovese dry-cleaning business will have immigration
crawling all over it. Uncle Joey wouldn't like immigration to
look too closely at the Italian men and boys he has working for
him, would he?' Lorenzo didn't reply. 'Would he?' Ena shouted.

'No,' the boy said shakily.

'Nor would he want the Inland Revenue looking too closely
at his businesses. Which,' Ena said in her most authoritative
voice, 'one word from me and they will do.'

She returned her Home Office ID card to her pocket but
said nothing for some seconds. 'So,' she said at last, 'have I made
myself clear?' Lorenzo shrugged and the other lad nodded
rapidly.

'Good, because if I see either of you, or even hear that
you've been back to Covent Garden trying to extort money, it

will be *you who needs protection from me!*' Holding Lorenzo's attention with an ice-cold stare, Ena said, 'Hand it over.'

Staring back at Ena, Lorenzo's dark eyes sparkled with anger beneath their long black lashes as he took a handful of one-pound and five-pound notes from his pocket. Not attempting to hide his anger, he opened his hands and the money fell to the pavement.

Sucking his teeth as he pushed past her, Lorenzo flicked his head at the other boy. 'Andiamo!' he ordered and swaggered off. The boy in the doorway, looking scared to death, ran after him.

With her heart beating like a drum, Ena watched until they had turned onto Long Acre at the top of Mercer Street before she allowed herself to breathe. Shaking, she bent down and picked up the money. Facing down two kids shouldn't have been that frightening, but they weren't ordinary kids, nor was that kind of recklessness Ena's style.

At the door of the café she reached for the handle and nearly jumped out of her skin. Artie and Emilio, watching from the window at the side of the door almost knocked each other over rushing to open it for her.

'Well,' she said, falling into the nearest chair, 'I don't think you'll be seeing those two little wannabe gangsters again. And,' she said to Emilio, taking the protection money from her pocket, 'this belongs to you.'

Emilio wrapped his arms around her and held her tightly. 'Signora Green, you put yourself in danger for me. How shall I ever repay you?'

'With a large espresso,' Ena said, her heart still hammering in her chest.

'Not a cappuccino, signora?'

'I need something stronger, Emilio.'

He laughed. 'The signora wants a stronga coffee, she will get a stronga coffee,' he said over Ena's shoulder to Artie. Still laughing, he let go of Ena. 'Coming up!' he shouted, ambling back to his place by the espresso coffee machine behind the counter.

Artie sat down opposite her. 'I don't know whether that performance with the Italian boys was brave or stupid.'

'Stupid, I expect, but Emilio has got his money. Well, what he gave the little toerag today. For what it's worth, I don't think the boys would have hurt me. They all mouth and Brylcreem.'

'Two large espresso coffees. One for the signora, and one for you, Signor Artie. And signor's lasagne.' When he had placed Artie's lunch in front of him, Emilio went back to the counter. A minute later, he was back with two huge slices of cream Cassatta cake. 'Cassata Siciliana.'

'It looks delicious, Emilio, but I couldn't eat another thing. The spaghetti ai gamberi was very filling.'

'Nor me, not after this lasagne.'

'OK! I put in a box and you take it to the office for the tea break.'

No sooner had they entered the office than the telephone began to ring. Ena gave Artie the Cassata to put in the refriger-ator and picked up the receiver. 'Dudley Green Associates?'

THIRTEEN

'Ena, it's Charles,' Ena and Henry's friend said before Ena had time to ask how she could help.

'Hello, stranger. How lovely to hear from you. How are you, and how's Priscilla?'

'We're both well, thank you. You – and Henry?'

'Henry's fine. A workaholic, like you. And, investigations are coming in slowly for the agency, so I can't complain.'

'I was wondering if we could meet for lunch?'

'That would be lovely. Or you and Priscilla could come here for dinner. We would love to see you both. Henry's away until Friday, but he'll be back for the weekend. How about Saturday night. If you and Pricilla feel...?' Charles didn't reply. 'Charles? Are you still there?'

'Dinner would be lovely and we'll do it soon, but I was hoping to meet with you first; just the two of us? Could you make tomorrow lunchtime?'

A sense of foreboding washed over Ena. 'Is something wrong, Charles?'

'It's a delicate matter, Ena, and one which I would rather not discuss on the telephone. But, if you're busy...'

'No! Not too busy for you, Charles, never. Give me one moment.' Ena opened her diary and turned to the following day's page. As she thought, there was nothing on it for the next day. 'Tomorrow's fine, Charles. Where shall we meet?'

'There's a restaurant near Liberty's. Café Rouge, on Marlborough Street. Would one o'clock be convenient for you?'

'Yes, that's perfect. I'll see you tomorrow at Café Rouge – one o'clock.'

'Thank you, Ena. Goodbye.'

Ena wrote the lunch date in her diary and deep in thought leaned back in her seat. Charles was clearly worried about something. Was Priscilla ill? She wondered, but only for a second, whether her friend was having an affair. No, Priscilla adored Charles. Ena blew out her cheeks. There was clearly something worrying him.

Artie, having resumed the scrutiny of the mound of papers on the conference table, lifted his head. 'What is it, Ena?'

'Charles Galbraith wants to meet me for lunch tomorrow.'

'Huh! It's alright for some,' Artie joked.

'He sounded upset, worried about something.'

'Perhaps the Magpie has been caught stealing again and this time he can't, or won't, buy her out of trouble.'

'Maybe,' Ena said, absent-mindedly. She closed the diary and returned to her chair at the table. 'Now where were we?'

Ena opened the door of the restaurant on Marlborough Street and stepped inside. Charles was sitting towards the back of the room. The moment he saw her he jumped up and, always the gentleman, crossed the room and helped her out of her coat. Handing it to the waiter to hang up, he led Ena to a table for two. He pulled out Ena's chair and when she was seated, he went around the table and sat down.

It had only been six weeks since she had last seen Charles, but he seemed to have aged. He and Priscilla had spent most the summer in the South of France. Even with a full social calendar, which Ena assumed they would have had, she expected Charles to look refreshed and healthy. He looked neither. He was smart and his silver hair was well-groomed, but he looked tired, worried. The waiter, suddenly at Ena's side, handed her a menu. She thanked him and after a courteous nod he moved away.

'You don't have a menu, Charles. Aren't you eating?'

'Yes. I, er, can't have you eating on your own.' He put up his hand and beckoned the waiter. 'I'll have a menu now, if...'

'Certainly, sir.' The waiter made his way to the counter returning seconds later with a menu. The door opened and a young couple entered. The waiter placed Charles' menu in front of him, nodded and crossed the room to attend to the couple who had seated themselves at a table for two in the window.

Ena looked briefly at the list of delicious dishes, decided on Salad Niçoise, closed the menu and laid it at the side of her place setting. Charles did the same.

'Are you ready to order, Ena?'

'Yes, I'd like the Salad Niçoise.'

'A good choice. I'll have the same.' Charles looked across to where the waiter was chatting to the young man and woman. From his body language and the way they were laughing together, he obviously knew the couple.

'Charles?' He looked from the waiter to Ena. 'What did you want to talk to me about? Is something wrong? Are you ill?' He shook his head. 'Is it Priscilla? Is she ill?'

'No, no, it's nothing like that. Priscilla and I are both well. It isn't our health.'

'Then, what is it?'

At that moment the waiter returned to take their order.

'Two Salad Niçoise,' Charles said, 'and,' he looked at Ena, 'Sauvignon Blanc?'

'Lovely.'

The waiter wrote down their food order, added the wine and picked up the menus. When they were alone again, Ena, fearing that if it wasn't ill health, it may be that Charles thought Priscilla was having an affair. Priscilla had a big personality, she was fun, she could be loud, and maybe she occasionally flirted, but of one thing Ena was certain – and that was Priscilla's love and devotion to Charles.

'Charles, what is it that's worrying you?'

'Ena, I know how fond Priscilla is of you, and I wondered if she had told you anything about her life before she met me?'

'A little. She told me she was born in Salford and that although they were poor, her father had a job with the Co-Operative Society. She told me that her mother was from Manchester and had persuaded her father to ask for a transfer. He did, and eventually the family moved to Moss Side in Manchester. Sadly, her mother died not long after moving back to the city she came from. And, Priscilla told me that she had first met you when she picked your pocket at the fair.'

Charles smiled at the memory. It was the first time Ena had seen him smile since they'd been in the restaurant. 'She was tall and slender with long red hair. Her eyes, hazel with green and gold flecks, sparkled with life and energy. She was the most vibrant, beautiful young woman I had ever seen. I say young woman, because both Priscilla and the friend she was with that night were wearing make-up and I thought they were seventeen, maybe even eighteen.' He laughed.

'And she was only fifteen.'

'Yes! I followed her and her friend to the "Shoot a Duck" stall. I put my hand in my pocket to take out some coins and my pocket was empty. It was then that I realised she'd stolen the coins. She'd got away with it, but maybe she wouldn't the next time, so I took a ten-shilling note from my wallet, paid for a couple of rounds – I can't remember how many – and I dropped the change into my jacket pocket hoping she'd take it – and she did. Better she took my money than someone who would call the police.'

'She told me you won a teddy bear, which you gave to her.'

'I did. And she still has it. It's a raggedy old thing now, but she insists that it sits on the chair in our bedroom.'

'She also told me that it was the only teddy bear she'd ever had.'

'Priscilla is sentimental,' Charles said, his eyes glistening with tears.

'And it was several years later that you met her again?'

'More than five years later. My father was a magistrate and I was waiting for him outside the court when I spotted the beautiful girl from the fair come out of the main door. I couldn't help myself. I went up to her. She didn't remember me at first and I didn't know her name. I reminded her about the fair and shooting the ducks, and she told me then that she still had the teddy bear.' Charles smiled at the memory.

The waiter brought their food and the conversation ceased while they ate. The salad was crisp and tasty and the wine was cool and refreshing. When they had finished eating, the waiter cleared the table, returned with the bottle of wine and topped up their glasses.

'Would you like the dessert menu, madam? Sir?'

Neither Charles nor Ena wanted a sweet, but asked if they could have coffee when they had finished the wine. The waiter said, 'Of course,' and left.

Deep in thought, Charles sipped his wine and then said, 'Her father almost died too. Priscilla was a little older by the time he took ill, even so...'

'She told me that she worked in a munitions factory during the war – and that she wanted to keep the house so her father

had somewhere to come back to when he was cured of tuberculosis.'

'Did she tell you that the sanatorium where her father was
took an hour to get to by train and that the cost of travelling
there at the weekends was expensive and she got behind with
the rent?'

'Yes, and the landlord let her pay late several times, but the
debt built up and when she could no longer pay him he took her
to court. She told me that she promised the magistrate to pay
the arrears and took in a lodger to do so.'

'Oh, Ena...' Tears fell from Charles' eyes onto his cheeks.
He took a handkerchief from his jacket pocket, wiped his eyes
and blew his nose. When he had recovered, he said, 'She didn't
tell you...'

'Tell me what? What didn't she tell me, Charles? What is it
that's hurting you so much?'

'My Priscilla was only twenty years old when she got
behind with the rent. Reg Addison, her *landlord,* let her off
twice – and then she was trapped.' Charles looked up at the
ceiling, as if the words he found so hard to say were hanging
there. Then he brought his gaze back to Ena. 'He called in the
debt by abusing my funny, bright, beautiful Priscilla. He forced
himself on her. He told her he'd turn her out of the house if she
didn't *pay him* – and then her father would have nowhere to go
when he came out of the sanatorium but to join her on the
streets. She threatened to tell his wife, but he laughed in her
face. He said his wife wouldn't believe her and she'd still be on
the street.'

'Charles, I'm so sorry. To have gone through all that at such
a young age – at any age...' Thinking Priscilla was distressed,
suffering from depression perhaps, because of the traumatic
experience she had gone through back then, Ena reached out
and put her hand on Charles' forearm. 'What can I do to help
Priscilla? I'll do anything. Tell me what it is I can do.'

FOURTEEN

Charles looked searchingly into Ena's eyes. 'I'd like you to investigate a young woman who claims to be Priscilla's daughter.'

Ena opened her mouth to speak, but could find no words to describe the pain she was feeling for her friend Priscilla.

'You look shocked that Priscilla had an illegitimate child, Ena. Perhaps you would rather not—'

Ena put up her hand. 'Charles, you misunderstand. I am shocked, and I'm angry, but not for the reasons you think. I'm angry that Priscilla was taken advantage of. Raped. For that's what it was. Shocked and saddened that my friend had a child on her own. I presume she was on her own?'

'Yes. As you know, her mother was dead, her father was away having treatment for TB and she had no other relatives. When the women were called up to work for the war effort, Priscilla would have been safer working on the land but she didn't want to be too far away from her father – and land girls went wherever they were most needed. So, to stay in Manchester, she worked in a munitions factory in Telford Park. Munitions work was well paid, which meant she could pay

Addison his rent and she'd keep the house for when her father came home.

'It seemed at last things were working out for her. However, by then she was carrying Addison's child. She confided in a childhood friend, but hid the pregnancy from the other women she worked with in the factory until she began to show. It was dangerous working with highly explosive materials, the fumes were poisonous and she was often ill. She worked on heavy machinery, which, once the women found out she was pregnant, they helped her by swapping shifts and doing the heavy work for her, but working seven days a week took its toll and eventually she was exhausted and too ill to work. She left the munitions factory before she was sacked, hoping that she would get an easier job to tide her over until the baby was born, but there was no time. The baby was born prematurely. The midwife wouldn't let her see the child. Priscilla begged her, but she kept saying she was too ill and that she needed complete rest.'

'But Priscilla did see the baby? Surely the midwife eventually let her see her child?'

Charles shook his head. 'The midwife, if she was a real midwife, kept Priscilla sedated for several weeks.'

'To keep her quiet,' Ena spat. 'I wonder who was paying the midwife?'

'Priscilla said she remembered hearing Reg Addison's voice, but she was so drugged up that she didn't know whether that was immediately after she'd given birth, or several days later. And, she remembered the midwife waking her up in the morning, taking her to the bathroom and then feeding her porridge. It was the same routine at night. This went on for weeks. Occasionally the midwife would say she was sorry. Then, one morning, she told Priscilla she was leaving. No longer under the influence of barbiturates, Priscilla asked to see her baby. It was then that the midwife told her the baby had been adopted.'

Ena thought of her sister Bess and her husband Frank who had adopted the child of a dancer friend of their sister Margot. Nancy's natural parents were both dead. It must be so much more painful to know that the woman who gave birth to you is out there somewhere.

'Charles, will you tell me everything you know about the young woman who says she's Priscilla's daughter?'

Charles leaned sideways, reached down, and picked up his briefcase from the side of his chair. 'I hope you don't think me too presumptuous, but I don't want Priscilla to know you're investigating the young woman. I don't want her to know anything about her yet as I don't want to get her hopes up. I know my wife,' he said, his face softening as it always did when he talked about Priscilla. 'She'll start making plans only to end up with her heart broken. I'm not sure she'd survive another disappointment. So,' he said, taking a large brown envelope from the case, 'I took the liberty of dictating everything I know about the girl to my secretary who has typed it up.'

'Your secretary?'

'Yes. Ruth won't say anything. She's been my secretary for almost forty years. She has no children of her own and treats Priscilla like a daughter. She's devoted to her and, like you, would never do or say anything to hurt her.' Charles gave Ena the envelope. 'All you need to know; all there is to know at the moment, is in there.'

'You said another disappointment? Have you been approached before by someone claiming to be Priscilla's daughter?'

'Yes. Eighteen months ago a girl came to my office. She knew Priscilla was born in Salford, had moved to Manchester when she was a child and that her father had been in a sanatorium with tuberculosis, which was why *her mother* she said, gave her up for adoption.'

Several questions flooded into Ena's mind. How did the girl

know where Priscilla had lived as a child, where her parents had moved to, and that her father had been ill with TB? She made a mental note to check those details first as the girl might have been the child of Priscilla's pick-pocketing friend.

'Ena?'

'Sorry?'

'You were miles away.'

'I was wondering about Priscilla's friend, the girl who was with her at the fair when you first met Priscilla. Do you know what became of her?'

'No. They lost touch at the beginning of the war when Priscilla went to work in the munitions factory.'

Ena nodded. 'Did the girl pretending to be Priscilla's daughter talk about her adoptive parents?'

'She didn't say much, just that her father left her mother for another woman when she was eight years old.'

'And did Priscilla meet her?'

'Oh, yes, and she was convinced the girl was telling the truth.'

'But you weren't?'

Charles shook his head. 'The first time she came to London I met her on my own. She told me she was nineteen, which would have made her the age of Priscilla's child. I thought she looked older, but what do I know? Young women all look the same to me. I thought about it and decided that some people look older than their age.'

'Especially young women,' Ena said, remembering Charles hadn't been a good judge of young women's ages in the past.

'Quite. Looking older than her years wasn't enough to dismiss her as Priscilla's child. So, I gave her the train fare back to Liverpool and I promised to tell Priscilla that I'd met her. I suggested that she might like to come and stay with us in London for a weekend. I thought that way we could all get to know each other, and, more to the point, Mary – that was her name – and Priscilla would have time to get to know each other. She said any weekend would suit her and she gave me her address. I said I'd write to her and from there we could decide upon a weekend that was mutually convenient to us all.

'I told Priscilla that a young woman named Mary who said she was her daughter had been to my office and, as you can imagine, Priscilla couldn't wait to meet her. So, I sent the girl the fare and invited her to London.'

Charles hung his head and exhaled loudly. When he looked up, he said, 'The weekend Mary stayed with us in London, I employed a private investigator to go up to Liverpool. I told him I needed to know whether this girl was Priscilla's daughter. He went to her address and, I'm ashamed to say, would have broken into the house if necessary. I didn't actually ask him to break in, but I made it very clear that I needed something, anything, that would prove without a shadow of doubt that Mary was, or wasn't, Priscilla's daughter.

'I'm pleased to say the private investigator didn't have to break into her house. He found out all he needed to know about the girl calling herself Mary from the next-door neighbour who said she was a *little liar*. The neighbour said the girl's name wasn't Mary but Linda, Linda Bradley, and she had gone to the same school as her daughter. She was in the same class apparently, and her daughter was twenty-two. According to the neighbour, Linda Bradley lived with her boyfriend, an unpleasant character. Neither of them worked, They spent their days lazing around and their evenings in the local pub, often bringing a rowdy crowd home with them. Music blaring out till all hours, that sort of thing.'

'Poor Priscilla. It must have been heartbreaking to find out the girl wasn't the baby she'd had adopted.'

'The baby that was taken from her and adopted without her consent.'

'Yes, I'm sorry.'

'That her baby was taken away from her broke Priscilla's heart. Linda Bradley broke her heart all over again. My darling Priscilla said it was like having her baby taken from her twice, which is why I'm not going to tell Priscilla anything about this second girl.' Charles reached across the table and took hold of Ena's hand. 'I would like to employ your services to find out if the girl who wrote to me this week *is* Priscilla's daughter, or someone else who thinks she'll...' Charles, clearly angry on his wife's behalf, ended the sentence with, 'get money out of her and break her heart all over again!'

It was obvious to Ena that seeing his wife go through so much pain the year before had caused Charles immense pain too. It had also angered him. 'I'll do everything I can to find out the truth about the girl,' Ena replied, putting the envelope in her bag.

'I've never held anything back from my wife, until now. We don't have secrets, but I didn't tell her that I was seeing you today, Ena. Nor have I told her about the letter and that there's a possibility that this girl is her daughter. It isn't about money, Ena.'

'Has the girl asked for money?'

'No. What I meant was, I don't care about the cost. And, if this girl is Priscilla's daughter, she can spoil her as much as she likes. What I will not do is give Priscilla false hope.'

'I understand. I wouldn't hurt Priscilla for the world. Besides, as my client, our conversation is confidential.' Thinking about what she had just said, Ena added, 'I shall of course have to tell my associate Artie Mallory. We work closely together. He'll need to be briefed if I'm to be out of the office on this case.'

'Of course,' Charles agreed. He put up his hand and the waiter brought the bill. Charles covered it with notes from his wallet and thanked the waiter. As he stood up, the waiter pulled out Ena's chair and she too stood. At the door Charles helped her into her coat.

Outside, Charles raised his hand to hail a cab. 'I have a meeting in half an hour, so I'll say goodbye, Ena. Thank you for taking the case on,' he said, worry lines etched on his forehead.

'Goodbye, Charles. If you hear anything else from the young woman, let me know?'

He nodded. 'And don't worry, Priscilla won't get hurt again.'

Ena waved as the black cab pulled away from the kerb and then turned and walked in the opposite direction. She pulled the strap of her shoulder bag further onto her shoulder and held the body of the bag close to her. The contents of her bag could mean a lifetime of happiness for her friend if the girl who wrote to Charles did turn out to be Priscilla's child.

Oblivious to the shops and cafés on her route back to the office, Ena recalled what Priscilla had told her when they first met at the art gallery, and then what she had told her of her life over lunch earlier that summer. There had been a gap when Priscilla told her about her life in Manchester. A gap that Charles had now filled in. A gap where her friend had been manipulated and abused by her landlord, made pregnant, and had her child taken from her and adopted without her consent.

FIFTEEN

'Well, what has the Magpie been up to now?' Artie asked. 'Hubby doesn't think she's seeing another fella, does he?'

'No. It would be a much easier case if it was that.' Ena dropped her shoulder bag next to her chair at the table and carried on into the kitchen. 'Coffee?'

'Yes, if you're—' Artie got up from the table and followed Ena. 'You're wearing your serious face. Has something happened to the Magpie? Is she in trouble?'

'Not in the way you think. Get the milk out of the fridge, will you?' Artie did as he was asked and when Ena had added milk to both coffees he put the milk back.

'Here,' Ena said, handing him a mug. 'Charles has asked us to investigate a delicate matter,' she said, leading the way from the kitchen across the office to the conference table.

'What is it?' Artie asked once he was back in his seat.

Ena told Artie everything that Charles had told her about Priscilla's illegitimate daughter. They both agreed that it was best that Ena find out whether the girl in Liverpool was Priscilla's daughter before telling Priscilla, to save the heartbreak of the year before. 'Our next job is to investigate the young woman. She wrote to Charles last week and her address is on the letter.'

Artie sat enthralled, his eyes becoming wider as Ena relayed what Charles had told her. When she'd finished, he wiped a tear from the corner of his eye.

'In here,' Ena said, taking the large envelope from her shoulder bag and passing it to Artie, 'is everything Charles knows about the girl.'

Ena gathered up the letters and photographs from Highsmith's investigation and Artie emptied the envelope Charles had given her onto the table. He picked out a small blue envelope containing the letter the girl had sent to Charles. 'Twenty-seven Meridian Street. I wonder if this is her real address?' Turning the envelope over he pulled out a sheet of paper the same colour blue. 'Mary Hornsby, nineteen years of age. Born in Manchester.' Artie examined the rest of the letter. 'She hasn't said which hospital she was born in.'

'There isn't a hospital listed because Priscilla gave birth to her child at home.'

'Poor old Magpie.'

'I wish you'd stop calling Priscilla a magpie. She had a really tough life as a child. She was brought up in the poorest area of Salford. She didn't say the house where she lived was a slum, but the slums were where she played. Her parents were kind and loving, but they didn't have much until her father got a job in Manchester and moved the family there.'

'So that's the reason she steals now?'

'I'm not saying that. She stole when she was a child because she was poor. For a short period in Manchester, Priscilla's life changed; her dad had a good job and her mum took in sewing. They weren't well off, but they weren't on the breadline either. Then her mother died, her father became ill and lost his job. I suspect his illness was the beginning of tuberculosis, which put him in a sanatorium for several years. I admit that, from what she told me, she got a buzz when she got away with stealing a lipstick from Woolworths or picking someone's pocket at the fair for enough money to pay for a ride for her and her friend.'

'She's been stealing for donkey's years,' Artie said. 'Only recently she tried to nick a brooch from the art gallery when you were with her.'

'Yes, and that was the last time she stole anything. She admitted to me that she had a problem. She didn't actually say the word, but she knew she had kleptomania.'

Artie rolled his eyes.

'It's a serious disorder. Anyway,' Ena said, defending Priscilla in her friend's absence, 'she's seeing someone about it.'

'A psychiatrist?'

'Yes, I think so. She didn't say who, but she's determined to stop stealing for Charles' sake. She loves him very much. Anyway,' Ena said, slapping the palm of her hand on the polished tabletop, 'whether it's serious or not, it's unfair of you to keep calling her a magpie.'

'It's meant as a term of endearment,' Artie pouted. 'But, as the Galbraith's are now officially clients, I suppose it should be Mr and Mrs— Oh!' he exclaimed, 'I almost forgot. Matthew Crosier telephoned. He said his mother will see you this afternoon.'

'Did he specify a time?'

'No. He said she'd be in for the rest of the day.'

Ena let out an exhausted groan. 'Well, there's no time like the present,' she said, getting up. 'Read the file while I'm out. Everything Charles knows about Priscilla's prospective daughter. Her name's Mary.'

Artie pulled out several pages of typed script. 'Neat.'

'Charles' secretary typed it up. She's fond of Priscilla and has promised not to say anything to her. Right! I'm off to see Audrey Crosier. If I go now,' Ena said, consulting her wrist-watch, 'I might miss the rush hour traffic.'

'You'll be in the thick of it driving back.'

'Can't be helped.' Ena picked up her bag. 'Shouldn't think I'll be too long. We'll discuss the Galbraith case later,' she said, nodding at the several pages Artie had already started to read.

* * *

From Mercer Street in Covent Garden, the corner of Telford Avenue and Tolgarth Avenue where Audrey Crosier lived was a straight run of forty to forty-five minutes over Lambeth Bridge.

Ena turned off the South Circular to Telford Avenue and drove down the wide tree lined road until she was almost at the end. With the common in sight, she turned left onto Tolgarth Avenue. She parked opposite number one, a traditional late Victorian maisonette on two levels. From the outside it looked considerably bigger than the modern two-storey flats that were currently springing up all over South London. Michael Crosier would have bought it when he was an architect, Ena thought. MI5 didn't pay enough to furnish a place the size of this, let alone buy it. There was no front garden to speak of, just an empty flower border around a small, square, dried-up lawn. Shiny black wrought-iron railings ran the length of the terrace of six buildings, twelve maisonettes, with gates interspersed between them at equal intervals.

Ena crossed Tolgarth Avenue and opened the gate. A short, wide, red-tiled path led to two front doors. Number one, the ground floor maisonette was on the left. She pressed the bell.

The door was opened by an ordinary looking, middle-aged woman wearing a brown skirt and cream blouse. Shorter than Ena by a couple of inches, Audrey Crosier had dark greying hair and brown eyes. 'Mrs Green?'

'Yes. Thank you for agreeing to see me, Mrs Crosier.'

'Call me Audrey, please.'

'Ena.' The two women shook hands.

'Come in.' Ena shut the door behind her and followed Audrey Crosier down a wide passage that ran the length of the maisonette. There were several doors on the left – all closed – and an open door at the end. Out of habit, Ena made a mental note of what she could see on her approach; a writing desk. On it, pushed to the back, an Imperial 'War Finish' typewriter. She wasn't able to see what was on the left of the desk as the door was blocking the view, but on the right was a telephone and a jar containing a number of pens and pencils, and in the foreground several unopened letters. Above the desk, hanging on a nail in the wall, was a calendar. The room on the left, immediately before what was obviously Audrey Crosier's writing room, was the kitchen. Audrey opened the door and when Ena entered, pulled the office door to.

'Take a seat.' Audrey gestured to an oak gate-legged table and two chairs. 'Would you like something to drink? Tea or coffee?'

'A cup of tea would be lovely, as long as you have the time.'

'Time is all I have, Ena.'

There was a hard edge to Audrey Crosier's voice. It was deep, as if she was a smoker. Ena glanced around the room. There were no ashtrays, but then it was a kitchen. Maybe she was angry as well as upset? Ena watched her make the tea and place a teapot, cups and saucer, milk and sugar on a tray. 'Would you like a biscuit?' she asked, reaching up, opening the cupboard and taking down a packet of Rich Tea.

'Not for me, thank you,' Ena replied.

Leaving the biscuits on the worktop, Audrey picked up the tray and crossed to the table. 'Are you comfortable sitting in here? We can go through to the living room if you'd prefer.'

'No, I'm quite comfortable in here, thank you. The kitchen is the place my mum always entertains friends and family. The kitchen is less formal. I can't entertain in my kitchen, I'm sorry to say. It's long and narrow. Nowhere to put a table and chairs. This table is the size of my dining table, but then this is a big kitchen. It's a big flat,' Ena commented. 'It's bright and cheery in here with the sun coming through the windows,' she observed. *Cheery?* She could have bitten her tongue. When Audrey put down the tray, Ena could see her eyes were glossy with tears.

Audrey put a little milk into both cups and poured the tea. Taking Ena's cup from the tray she set it down on a small placemat in front of her.

Ena took a sip. She was about to comment on how refreshing it was, but Audrey had turned away and was gazing wistfully out of the window.

Seeing that the woman was near to tears, Ena said, 'If you would rather I came back tomorrow... Or another day?'

As if she suddenly remembered Ena was there, Audrey turned and looked at her. 'How rude of me. I'm so sorry, I was miles away. No, today is fine. I have had some... news in the post that has unsettled me. But no, really, today is fine,' she said again. With shaking hands she picked up her tea, the cup rattled in the saucer, the tea spilt and Audrey burst into tears.

Ena reached out and took the cup from her and set it down on the tray. 'Would you like me to telephone Matthew and ask him to come over?'

'No!' Audrey replied angrily. 'Matthew must not know.'

'Not know?'

Audrey looked searchingly at Ena's face, her eyes settling on Ena's eyes. 'Mrs Green, Ena, Matthew told me that you are a private investigator.' Ena nodded. 'He said you are working for someone who was in Berlin when my husband died in 1936?'

'That's right.'

'What your client told you about that time was in confidence, yes?'

'Yes, of course. And, what you tell me today will also be in confidence,' Ena assured.

Audrey Crosier, keeping eye contact with Ena said, 'What do you want from me? 1936 was a long time ago.'

'I believe the death of your husband is in some way connected to a case I'm working on. I don't know how, yet, but my associate, who is the primary investigator on the case, and I, intend to find out.' Ena wondered how much she could tell Audrey Crosier without breaking the confidentiality agreement she had with Rupert Highsmith. She decided nothing, yet.

'Audrey, I would like to know what kind of work your husband did before he joined MI5.' Audrey looked at Ena, but said nothing. 'You said that you only know what the intelligence service he worked for told you after his death,' Ena added. 'Do you remember what Michael's superiors said?' Ena didn't want to push Audrey too hard, but as Michael Crosier's wife she had to know something. 'Anything, however insignificant you think it might be, could be of help. If there is a connection between my client and your husband's death, I need to know.'

Audrey bit her lip in thought but didn't speak.

'If you don't want to tell me, or if you feel you can't tell me, I'll respect your decision.' Again Ena wondered how much she dare legally, or morally, tell Audrey about the Highsmith investigation. Probably no more than she had already told her son, Matthew. Ena needed to know what Audrey knew about her husband's death in Berlin in '36 – and decided to give it one last try before calling it a day.

'Audrey, my client is being maliciously targeted in a way that will not only ruin his career, but will destroy his good name and reputation. If I can't prove his innocence in a certain matter, he will lose his job and probably his liberty. I believe what is happening to my client now is in some way connected to the death of your husband.' Ena paused. Had she said too much? She hoped not. She hoped she'd said just enough to make Audrey Crosier realise how important it was for her to tell Ena what she knew about her husband's life before MI5 and his work before going to Berlin. The work he did for Five could have something to do with his death – on the other hand, Audrey might blame Highsmith for her husband's death. If she did, it may even be her sending Highsmith anonymous letters.

Audrey nodded that she understood and stood up. 'Excuse me,' she said and left the room. Ena picked up her cup and took a sip of her tea. It was almost cold. She put the cup back on its saucer.

It was not much more than a couple of minutes before Audrey returned. She put two large brown envelopes on the table. 'The one on top arrived last week, the one underneath, yesterday.'

'May I?'

'Please,' Audrey whispered before picking up the tray and crossing to the sink. She put the used cups and saucers in the washing up bowl, took clean ones from the cupboard, and switched on the kettle. While she refreshed the teapot, Ena opened the envelopes. The first contained a letter that she was sure had been typed on the same typewriter as the letters Rupert had received. Looking closer, the bar on top of the capital T appeared to be slightly smudged as did the tail of the y. It was shorter, as if the curl at the end of it was missing. *The man who murdered your husband is living the High-life.* High-life? Was whoever sent this anonymous letter to Audrey Crosier alluding to Highsmith by saying Highlife? She opened the other envelope and pulled out a photograph of two men. The taller of the two wore a belted mackintosh and a trilby – and, Ena thought, looked like Rupert Highsmith.

'Is the man in the photograph, without a hat, your husband, Audrey?'

'Yes, that's Michael.'

The two men were standing on a bridge, one was looking

over the railings at the river below, the other man was sideways on to the camera with his right elbow on the railings.

Suddenly aware that Audrey was speaking, Ena looked up from the photograph.

'Is this the man who murdered Michael?' she asked, throwing a photograph of Rupert Highsmith on top of the photograph of the two men on the bridge. 'He looks like the man who was with my husband in Berlin.'

Ena inhaled sharply. 'He does, a little, but I don't believe this is the man who killed your husband.' Ena picked up the recent photograph of Highsmith and placed it at the side of the photograph of the men on the bridge. 'Nor is he the man in the photograph on the bridge. Someone wants you to think it's the same man, and whoever that is may be the person who killed your husband. And...'

Ena got up and took the photograph to the window. 'This photograph on the bridge was not taken in Berlin, Audrey. It was taken in London. The river isn't the River Dahme, it's the River Thames.'

'How can you tell?'

'Because the barge you can see moored in the distance is a River Thames barge.'

'They would have had barges in Berlin in 1936.'

'I'm sure they would, but not with Harwich written on the hull.' Ena took the photograph back to Audrey and pointed out the letters that made up the name. 'It's faint because it hasn't been developed properly. Look closely and you'll see the letters.'

'I can see H A R W I and, oh yes, C H,' Audrey said. 'It's very faint, hardly visible at all, but it does say, Harwich, you're right. So, you don't think the man in the photograph with Michael killed him in Berlin.'

'No, I don't. As I said, I think whoever sent the photograph wants you to think he did, but...' Ena shook her head. 'Audrey, could I take the letter and the photograph to show my colleague.'

Audrey looked at the image of her husband with the Rupert Highsmith look-alike again. 'You will let me have it back? Only I don't have many photographs of Michael. He was never keen on having his photograph taken and this one, even though there's another man in it, is a good likeness of him.'

'I'll look after it and bring it back when I've shown it to my colleague.' Ena put both envelopes in her shoulder bag and got to her feet.

Audrey pushed herself out of her chair at the same time. 'I don't go out often, or very far these days,' she said, leading Ena out of the kitchen and along the passage.

At the front door, Ena assured Audrey that she would take care of the photograph and return it when her colleague had seen it. The truth was, she wanted Highsmith to look at the photograph too. Hopefully he would be able to tell her when it was taken and where – and if the man in the trilby was him. If it was him, was there anyone else with him and Crosier that night? If Highsmith knew who had taken the photograph, it could be a step towards solving the case. Ena thanked Audrey and said she'd see her soon.

After putting her bag on the passenger seat of the Sunbeam, Ena jumped in and gunned the engine. With a quick wave, she pulled into the afternoon traffic and was soon on her way back to the office.

SIXTEEN

Ena was about to push on the main door to the office when it opened and an old acquaintance stepped out with Artie hard on his heels.

'Inspector Richardson from Special Branch,' Artie said, his face pinched with displeasure.

'I know who he is.' Ena beamed the inspector a smile. 'Inspector Alan Richardson and I are old friends,' she said, shaking the hand of her old rival. 'Hello, Alan, what are you doing in this neck of the woods?'

'I was on my way to see Dan Powell at Bow Street and I thought I'd drop in and tell you personally that you are both still bound by the Official Secrets Act. I got the impression it wasn't the answer you'd hoped for.' Alan smiled at Artie who shrugged. 'I'm afraid you're still bound by the Act if your investigation has anything to do with the intelligence services.'

'I thought so. I hoped not, but...' Ena looked at Artie and nodded. 'I'm sorry I wasn't here when you arrived. Do you have time for a coffee?'

'I'm afraid not, but it would be good to meet up with you

sometime,' he said taking in both Ena and Artie. 'How about we drag Dan out for a drink one evening after work?'

'To catch up with life in the Metropolitan Police, or in the criminal world?'

'Neither. It would be far more interesting to catch up with life in the world of private sleuthing.'

Ena burst into laughter. 'You've just told us that we're still bound by the Official Secrets Act, so sorry, *DI Richardson*, we are not at liberty to tell you anything.'

Alan Richardson laughed with her. 'Just a drink then. I'll find out when Dan's free.'

'We'd like that,' Ena said, speaking for herself and Artie who had opened his mouth to say something that Ena thought might be controversial.

Artie didn't like Special Branch. He had only met Alan Richardson briefly earlier in the year. Ena had got to know him while working on a cold case investigation when she exposed the mole at MI5. The woman had killed herself in Ena's office, and with the help of a German spy had then framed Henry for her murder. A lot had happened in the short time she had worked to prove her husband innocent of murder. Inspectors Alan Richardson and Dan Powell had been a great help to her.

Ena said goodbye and watched Artie see Alan out of the front door. When she heard the door close, Ena shouted, 'Scotch?'

'That was short and *not* sweet,' Artie said on his return to the office.

'Alan's alright when you get to know him,' Ena said in defence of the man she had thought stiff and uncompromising when she had first met him.

'"No room for discussion! You signed the Official Secrets Act when you worked at the Home Office. I know you're no longer employed by the HO, or by any other government department, but if your work impinges on any of the intelligence agencies, military or otherwise – including government departments – the Act still stands. It cannot be revoked." Being bullied by the branch sticks in my craw!'

'There's nothing we can do unless we abandon Highsmith's investigation, and we're not going to do that,' Ena said, pouring two glasses of Scotch and sliding one across the table to Artie as he took his seat opposite her at the conference table. 'Signing the Act is like backing a horse that's tethered to the starting block,' Ena said, taking a swig of her whisky.

'Looking into the murder of Michael Crosier appears to be a larger part of Rupert's investigation than we first suspected,' Artie said.

Deep in thought, Ena put her hand up to her mouth.

'What is it, Ena? What are you thinking?'

'I'm wondering whether the visit from Alan Richardson means we'll have to inform him – i.e. Special Branch – if we find out who killed Michael Crosier?'

'His death may have no bearing on Rupert's case.'

'What? Both men in Berlin in 1936. It's too much of a coincidence not to be connected.'

'We could keep what we find out to ourselves. Who'd know?'

'We could keep it to ourselves for a while, until we know who's sending this disgusting rubbish to Highsmith.' Ena picked up a couple of photographs. 'Audrey Crosier asked me to find out who killed her husband.'

'Isn't that a conflict of interest?'

'If I found out who killed her husband and I told her, it would be. Or would it? She isn't a client, but anyway, I said I'd do my best, I didn't promise anything. I can't put my finger on it, but I've got an odd feeling about the late Michael Crosier's wife,' Ena said thoughtfully. Opening her shoulder bag, she took out the envelopes containing the photographs of the two men on the bridge that Audrey Crosier had given her and placed them on the table in front of Artie. 'I don't believe in coincidences, I'm sure Crosier's death is linked in some way to these photographs.'

'Is that Rupert?' Artie said, pointing to the taller of the two men.

'Look again. The man looks like Rupert – almost his double – but it isn't him,' Ena said. 'The other man is Michael Crosier. I'd like Rupert to look at these. He may know who this chap is,' Ena stabbed her finger at Highsmith's look-alike.

'It's London and if that's Crosier, the photograph would have been taken before the summer of 1936.'

'It would. And look closely at the typeface on Audrey Crosier's envelope. The same typewriter has been used to write the anonymous letters that Rupert's been getting.'

Ena yawned. 'Drinking at lunchtime always makes me dozy in the afternoons. Oh,' she said, suddenly perking up, 'did the spook from MI5's Scottish office telephone?'

'Yes. He said someone would contact me before the end of the day.' Artie pushed up his shirt sleeve and looked at his watch. 'It's almost five o'clock and I'm bloody starving.'

'Didn't you have time to eat anything at lunchtime?'

'I daren't leave the office in case MI5 Glasgow telephoned.'

'Go and put the kettle on. I'll pop upstairs and make you a sandwich.'

Pushing open the door to number 8a, Ena picked up a couple of letters from the hall mat before going upstairs. Both envelopes were addressed to Henry. She dropped them on the telephone table at the top of the stairs and went into the kitchen to make Artie a cheese and pickle doorstep.

The telephone was ringing when she returned to the office with Artie's sandwich. He was heading over to his desk.

Ena picked up the receiver and handed it to him. 'Dudley Green Associates, Artie Mallory speaking.'

Ena listened to Artie's side of the conversation. 'Hello, Mr

Fraser. Yes, I believe you know Archibald Hollander who was in Berlin in 1936.' There was a pause and then Artie said, 'Oh, there's need to worry, Mr Fraser. The office was swept for bugs only a few days ago. I can assure you—'

Mr Fraser is being cautious, Ena thought. He was right to be. She was sure there were no bugs in the office now, but she wouldn't put it past Special Branch or MI5 to have tapped the telephone line and be listening in to Dudley Green's calls.

'Of course, Mr Fraser. Protocol!' He looked across the room at Ena and pulled a bored face. 'Do you know where the *person of interest* is now? Of course!' Artie put his hand over the mouthpiece. 'He won't tell me over the telephone.' He looked up and exhaled, forcing a lungful of air through his pouting lips. 'Yes, I'm still here. Well, as I said, the offices of Dudley Green Associates are very secure and anything you tell me will be in the strictest confidence.'

Artie looked at Ena again and threw up his free hand. 'I quite understand. If you'd rather we met in a public place.' There was a longer pause and then Artie said, 'Oh? Well, er... yes, I could come up to Glasgow.' Without any enthusiasm in his voice, he continued. 'I'll hear from you later, then.' He put down the receiver. 'He's keeping me waiting again. I bet you a quid this Fraser bloke is stalling because he's having me checked out.'

'It's standard procedure. He won't find anything, unless you've recently taken up robbing banks,' Ena joked.

'And if I check out clean, which I will, I'll be going up to Glasgow.' Artie screwed up his face.

Patience was not one of Artie's strong suits, but patience was what he'd need while he waited for Mr Fraser to contact him again. He got up and joined Ena at the conference table. 'This looks good,' he said, taking a bite out of his sandwich.

'Is the kettle on?'

'Sorry,' he replied, his mouth full of food, 'I forgot.'

Ena tutted, got up and went into the kitchen. Artie was deep in thought when she returned with two mugs of coffee. She placed his mug next to him. 'What's bothering you?'

'It's a bummer having to go up to Scotland.'

'He wants to meet you on his turf that's all. It could mean Crosier or Hollander, or both, were important agents to someone.'

'I suppose I shall find out, eventually.'

'Eat your sandwich. There's nothing you can do until he rings back,' Ena said, absent-mindedly.

The two colleagues sat at the table without speaking, Ena thoughtfully sipping her coffee and Artie eating his sandwich and looking at the photographs that had been given to Ena by Audrey Crosier.

SEVENTEEN

'Hello, you,' Ena said, leaping out of her seat and joining her husband in the middle of the room. 'You're home early.'

Henry laughed. 'I can go back to the office if you want.'

'Not likely.' Ena reached up, put her arms around her husband's neck and kissed him. 'So, why are you home at this time of day?'

'The meeting finished early.' Henry looked across the room at Artie. 'Highsmith was Chair.'

Artie laughed. 'If Rupert was chairing the meeting it's no wonder it finished early.'

'He said the two of you were going to the Lamb and Flag for a drink later.'

'We are, if I ever get out of the office,' Artie complained. 'Why don't you and Ena join us?'

'We could,' Henry said. 'What do you think, darling? We haven't been out for a while.'

'You mean, I haven't,' Ena said, one arm still around her husband's neck.

'We'll have something to eat. Save the wife cooking,' Henry said, winking at Artie.

Ena hated it when men said, *the wife*. Normally she would have reacted with a sarcastic quip, but she let it go. 'What a good idea. Lead the way, *husband*,' Ena countered. Letting go of Henry she grabbed her shoulder bag.

'Ah, but what about Fraser? He hasn't phoned yet.'

Ena looked at the clock. 'It's gone six. He wouldn't expect you to be in the office now, would he?'

'He sounded like the type of man who would expect me to be here at midnight. You go, Ena, I'll hang on for another half hour. I'll see you at the Lamb.'

* * *

'Just in time,' Highsmith said when Artie entered the Lamb and Flag.

'For what?'

'To get the drinks in. Mine's a gin and tonic,' he said with a twinkle in his eye.

'Mild for me, Artie,' Henry said.

'I'll help you carry them.' Ena jumped up and walked with Artie to the bar.

'A gin and tonic and a pint of mild,' he said when the barman approached. 'And?' Artie looked at Ena.

'A Teachers' whisky with a splash of soda water.'

'And a pint of shandy,' Artie added, completing the round of drinks by ordering his own.

'Did you hear from Fraser?' Ena asked, while they waited at the bar.

'The *bloody man* rang back just after you left.'

'Oh dear. Why bloody man?'

Artie put his right hand on his hip and leant his left elbow on the bar. 'I suggested again that he came to the office, but he refused. I even tried bribing him with lunch, but he wouldn't have it, so I said, "Okay, we can meet anywhere you like, you choose." He repeated that he will only meet with me in Glasgow.'

'It could be that Hollander is in Glasgow,' Ena suggested.

'That's what I thought. Anyway, he said that I was to let him know what time my train was getting into Glasgow Central and he'd meet me.' Artie looked miserable and said again, 'Glasgow Central? And he wants me there tomorrow.'

'Tomorrow? That doesn't give you much time to decide what you're going to ask him.'

'I've made notes. They're on my desk. I'll call into the office in the morning on the way to the station and pick them up. I'll run through what we need to know while I'm on the train. It's a long enough journey.'

The barman brought Highsmith's gin and tonic and Ena's whisky. He stood them down on the counter, went back to the pumps and returned with Henry's pint of mild and pint of shandy for Artie.

'Now the shandy makes sense.'

Artie lifted the glass, took a sip and pulled a face. 'At least I'll have a clear head when I meet Fraser and Hollander tomorrow.'

'A couple of beers wouldn't have hurt. Just stay off the spirits.'

Artie shrugged his shoulders, paid for the drinks and with Ena carried them across the room to the table where Henry and Rupert were sitting.

The Lamb and Flag rarely closed on time and tonight was no exception. When the porch light had been extinguished and the thick curtains at the windows drawn, the Lamb looked for all the world to be in darkness.

'Same again?' Henry asked, to which the other three in the party shouted, 'Yes!'

With replenished glasses they chatted about anything and everything, putting the world to rights as four friends rather than intelligence agents and private investigators.

Ena lifted her glass of whisky. 'We should do this more often. Cheers!'

'Cheers!' came a rousing reply.

Having finished her drink, she laid her head on Henry's shoulder and stifled a yawn. 'Sorry, I'm a bit squiffy. You,' she said, lifting her head and looking into Henry face, 'only having two pints, and you, Artie Mallory, drinking shandy, are a pair of lightweights. Not like Rupert and me, eh, Rupert?'

'Someone has to stay sober to drive us home,' Artie said, teasing Rupert. 'And, talking about driving, it will soon be bewitching hour. Time we were making a move.'

'Us too. Though we only have to walk up the road and we're home.'

Henry got up first. Helping Ena out of her chair, she stumbled. He caught her before she flopped down in the chair.

'Ooops!' she said, giggling. Henry took her by the arm. 'See you in the morning, Artie, before you go to Scotland,' she said, blowing Artie and then Highsmith a kiss.

Henry opened the door of the Lamb for Ena to leave first. Turning round, he put up his hand and waved goodbye, before exiting onto Rose Street, where he caught up with Ena.

EIGHTEEN

It was the early hours of the morning when Ena was woken by the muffled sound of the telephone ringing. At first she thought she was dreaming. She half opened her eyes and listened. It *was* a telephone, their telephone. She turned and tapped Henry on the shoulder. He didn't stir. She reached over him, felt for the lamp on the bedside table and switched it on. The alarm clock said twenty minutes to four. The telephone ringing at this hour meant there was trouble of some kind. Hoping it wasn't one of her sisters or her mother, she rolled back onto her side of the bed, sat up and swung her legs over the side. Henry gave a stilted snore and turned away from the light. Wasting no time, Ena ran barefoot into the hall and seized the telephone handset.

'Hello?'

'Ena?' Artie cried.

'Artie? What's the matter? Where are you?'

'St Thomas' Hospital.'

'What? Artie, what's happened?'

'Rupert was hit by a car. He's unconscious,' Artie said,

sobbing. 'The police are here and... Oh, Ena, I don't know what I'd do if I lost him.'

'You won't. Rupert's fit and strong. I'll come down to the hospital.'

'Would you?'

'I'll be with you as soon as I can. Twenty minutes at the most.' Ena ran back to the bedroom and began to get dressed.

'What's going on?' Henry asked, his voice thick with sleep.

'Rupert's been in an accident and Artie's in a state. I'm going down to Tommy's.'

'You've had too much to drink. I'll drive you,' Henry said, throwing back the bedclothes and stumbling to his feet. Yawning, he left the bedroom. Ena heard the pull-switch of the bathroom light click on. She grabbed a clean pair of stockings and a set of clean underclothes from the chest of drawers, quickly put them on followed by a skirt and blouse. As Henry returned to the bedroom, Ena slipped her feet into her shoes and went into the bathroom. After splashing water on her face she cleaned her teeth.

'Are you ready, Henry?'

'Yes. Just switching off the lights.'

Ena flew out of the bathroom, into the hall and put on her coat. When Henry joined her she was holding his coat for him. He slipped his arms down the sleeves, snatched the car keys from the hall table and fled down the stairs to open the front door. Ena followed him out into the chilly early morning air of late September. Pulling the door shut behind her, she ran across the road. Henry was already in the car with the engine turning over. As soon as she jumped into the passenger seat and shut the door, he pulled out of the car park onto a deserted Mercer Street. Other than Covent Garden's market traders, the streets were virtually empty. Soon they were on the Strand heading towards Westminster Bridge and from there, Lambeth Palace Road and St Thomas' Hospital.

. . .

'Henry? Ena?'

Hearing their names being called, Ena and Henry stopped running and turned to see Detective Sergeant Jarvis from Bow Street with a police constable in uniform jogging towards them.

'Do you know what happened, Sergeant Jarvis?'

'Mr Highsmith was hit by a car. I don't know how badly he's been hurt. There was an eyewitness who telephoned 999 who's been taken to Bow Street. We'll know more when he's given his statement. We haven't spoken at length to Mr Mallory, but as you can imagine he's very upset. We said we'd come back tomorrow or, if he'd rather, he could come into the station.'

'Where did the accident happen? Were they crossing a road? Didn't they see the car? Was the driver speeding and didn't see them?'

'The eyewitness said the car attracted his attention because it was going too fast along Floral Street. He said it appeared out of the blue, mounted the pavement and hit Mr Highsmith.'

'Could he describe the car?'

'He wasn't sure. He said it was dark blue or green, and could have been a Ford. Mr Mallory told us that he and Mr Highsmith were just walking along Floral Street to their car. Off the record,' said DS Jarvis looking at the uniformed policeman who lowered his gaze in agreement, 'we think it could have been a hit-and-run. We didn't say anything to Mr Mallory, but the eyewitness said the first he saw of the two men walking along the street was in the car's headlights seconds before the car mounted the pavement.'

'There isn't a corner, or even a bend in Floral Street,' Henry added.

Jarvis shook her head. 'After examining the scene, PC Roberts and I have come to the conclusion that the driver of the car had to have seen Mr Highsmith and Mr Mallory. There will be a full investigation.'

'And forensics?' Ena asked.

'We left the forensic team at the scene of the accident.'

'*Accident?* But you said you didn't think it was an accident?' Henry questioned.

'That it was a hit-and-run is only my opinion. As I said, there will be a full investigation. If what the eyewitness said is true, there was no need for the car to hit either men. Unless the driver meant to cause one or both of them serious injury,' DS Jarvis clarified.

Ena's imagination went into overdrive. 'My God. If the driver of the car was a queer basher, the kind of thug who goes around beating up young men if they think they're homosexual, that would be a reason. But then, how would the driver know Artie and Rupert were homosexual? Were they walking arm in arm, or holding hands?'

DS Jarvis shook her head. 'According to the eyewitness, they were simply walking along the street.'

Then another thought came into Ena's mind and anger rose from the pit of her stomach and lodged in her throat. Could the driver of the car be the same person who sent Highsmith the photographs of him and the boy in Berlin? Could he or she be the author of the anonymous letters?

'From what Mr Mallory has told us, Mr Highsmith must have heard the car approaching because he half turned before pushing Mr Mallory into a shop doorway. The car hit Mr Highsmith because he wasn't able to get out of its way.'

'Which confirms what the eyewitness told you?'

'Yes, and our suspicions that it wasn't an accident.' DS Jarvis looked again at the constable who nodded.

'It sounds very much like a hit-and-run to me too, Sergeant Jarvis,' Henry said.

'Thank you, both of you.' Ena looked from Jarvis to the constable. 'We'd better go and see Artie.'

DS Jarvis reached out and touched Ena's arm. She stopped and turned, as did Henry behind her. 'Prepare yourselves,' she said, her eyes glistening with unspent tears. 'Mr Highsmith has been badly injured. The sister we spoke to said his condition was serious.'

'And does Artie know how badly injured Highsmith is?'

'That I couldn't tell you. I just thought, forewarned...'

'Thank you,' Ena said, again.

'Thank you, Sergeant,' Henry said as together he and Ena entered the hospital's main entrance.

'Can I help you?' a stout middle-aged woman in a navy-blue uniform asked, as Ena and Henry passed through swing doors into a corridor where a sign pointed to Accident and Emergency. Ward 7.

Ena could see as the woman drew near that she had a narrow silver badge that said Night Sister pinned to her uniform on the opposite side of her chest to her fob watch. 'We were told Rupert Highsmith has been brought into the accident ward.'

'Are you relatives?'

'I work with Mr Highsmith.' Henry took his GCHQ ID card from the inside pocket of his jacket and showed the sister.

Clearly unimpressed by Henry's place of work, she turned to Ena. 'And you are?'

'Ena Highsmith, Rupert's sister,' she lied.

'In that case, if you'll follow me?'

At the end of the corridor was a square area with wooden high-back chairs lined up against two walls. On the wall opposite, a sign saying Waiting Area hung next to a clock. Above the clock was a narrow window and beyond that a dark blue sky tinged with the orange of dawn.

Artie, his face pale and tear-stained jumped up as the night sister entered the waiting area. His eyes questioned her, hoping for news, but she passed him quickly and went through the only door beyond the waiting area.

Artie then saw Ena and Henry. 'Ena! Thank God you're here.' He flew across the sterile waiting area and threw his arms around her, before turning to Henry and pumping his hand. 'Thank you for coming. He's in there,' Artie said, pointing to the room that the night sister had disappeared into. 'He's only in there, but they won't let me see him because I'm not a relative.'

'That's ridiculous,' Ena said. 'You live with the man. You don't get much closer than—' At that moment the night sister came out of Highsmith's room. 'I'll have a word,' she said, moving away from Henry and Artie.

'Excuse me?' The night sister didn't acknowledge Ena, nor did she stop walking. She had either not heard her, or she was ignoring her. Ena ran after her and caught up with her. 'Sister?' she said, stepping in front of the woman and stopping her in her tracks. 'Mr Mallory shares a home with my brother. He's as close as family, or closer. Won't you make an exception and let him see Rupert?'

The night sister didn't speak, but Ena could tell by her pinched face, the way she inhaled slowly, lowering and opening her heavy eyelids that she disapproved of two men sharing a home.

'Won't you consider it? My brother would want Mr Mallory with him.'

'Mr Highsmith is unconscious. Perhaps when—'

'As I understand it, if a person is unconscious, having someone they love at their bedside – speaking softly to them helps them to recover. It's now widely thought that an unconscious person is able to hear. Whether or not my brother can hear, I don't know. What I do know is, he would want his *friend* there.'

'Very well. As you are his sister, Mr Mallory may go in to

see Mr Highsmith with you. But you will both have to leave when the doctor arrives.'

'Of course. We'll leave as soon as... Thank you,' Ena called after the night sister as she resumed marching along the corridor.

'Come on, we've only got a few minutes,' Ena said, beckoning Artie to follow her.

Ena pressed her lips together tightly to stifle a gasp when she saw Highsmith lying in the narrow hospital bed wired up to several machines, a tube going into him from a drip on a tall stainless-steel stand and a plastic tube feeding him plasma. His head was bandaged but she could see a large swelling on his left temple. His cheeks and jaw were black, his right eye and his nose were so swollen that he was unrecognisable as there were no contours to his face. She took Artie's hand and gave it a squeeze as he came into the room behind her and then stood inside the door while Artie walked around the bed to Highsmith's left. Taking the only chair in the room from the other side of the door she placed it behind Artie. He sat down and gently slipped his fingers under Rupert's cupped left hand. 'He feels very warm,' he whispered to Ena, sounding concerned.

'It'll be because it's so warm in here. Hospitals are always too warm,' Ena explained.

'I suppose so.'

Ena watched as Artie lightly rubbed the back of Rupert's hand with his thumb. After a few minutes, Artie gasped.

'What is it?'

'He moved his fingers. I felt his fingers move, Ena.' Artie's face broke into a broad smile and tears filled his eyes. 'Rupert knows I'm here.' Then, speaking softly, he said, 'And, I'm staying here. I won't leave you until you wake up.'

'I'm afraid you will, Mr...?'

'Mallory,' Ena said.

'Mr Mallory! Good morning, I'm Doctor Freeman and this

is Nurse Neil. We'll be taking a look at...' Nurse Neil passed Dr Freeman the clipboard from the bottom of the bed. 'Rupert.' After consulting it further for several minutes, Dr Freeman gave it back to the nurse and, as he moved to the top of Rupert's bed, she moved to the foot of it.

'Now, Rupert, let's see if you can squeeze my hand.' The doctor lifted Rupert's right hand. 'If you can hear me, Rupert, would you squeeze my hand?' The nurse, pen poised ready to write down any reaction from the patient, or not as the case maybe, stood rigid.

'Let's try again, shall we, Rupert? Would you squeeze my hand?'

Ena could only see the doctor's back as he leaned over Highsmith, but from the smile on the nurse's face she knew he had shown some sign of recognition. Hopefully he had squeezed the doctor's hand. 'Good,' he said. 'Very good.' Turning to Artie he said, 'I should like to examine my patient, so if you and...' Dr Freeman looked over his shoulder at Ena.

'Ena. Rupert's sister.'

The doctor gave Ena a wry smile and turning back to Artie continued. 'If you would like to take Rupert's sister back to the waiting area, I shall come and speak to you when I know more about what is going on here.'

As Artie and Ena left Highsmith's room, Ena heard the doctor say, 'Now, old chap, let's have a proper look at you. See what damage has been done.'

It felt like they had been sitting in the waiting area for hours. Ena glanced at the clock – they had. She looked across the room to the door of Highsmith's room for what must have been the tenth time. Suddenly it opened and Dr Freeman came striding out.

'The good news is Rupert has only one broken arm. His

shoulder has taken a severe knock. It's dislocated and badly bruised – and he's in considerable pain. Nurse Neil is giving him something that will help with that.'

'He's in pain. Does that mean he's awake?' Artie asked.

'He was awake, but the medication to stop the pain will make him drowsy. Sleep is the best thing for him at present. He should be awake tomorrow and more up to having visitors.'

Ena could see the disappointment in Artie's eyes. 'That's the bad news, is it? A broken arm?'

'The bad news is a little more serious, I'm afraid. Rupert has lost his peripheral vision.'

Artie's hand flew up to his mouth.

'But in most cases, when a person has had a blow on the head, blurred or loss of vision is temporary. I expect Rupert's sight to return to normal once the swelling has gone down.'

Ena had noticed bruising and swelling on Highsmith's face. She'd seen an egg-shaped lump on his temple. She feared Dr Freeman meant swelling inside his head, not on the outside. It would be pressing on the optic nerve if it's affecting his sight. She was grateful the doctor hadn't elaborated. Artie was upset enough.

'So, when the swelling goes down, he'll be able to see alright?'

Artie wanted assurance and the doctor gave it to him. Patting Artie's arm he replied, 'I don't see why not, Mr Mallory. Now, if you'll excuse me, I'm going to get my patient down to X-ray so I can take a good look at the extent of the damage.'

'One of his legs was at an odd angle. It was sticking out,' Artie said, 'when he was lying in the road.'

'That's what we're going to look at now. If you'll excuse me?'

'He will be alright, won't he, Doctor?' Artie asked.

'I can't give you a definitive answer, yet. I shall know more when he has had an X-ray and the neurosurgeon has seen him.

But, apart from looking at the moment as if he has been hit by a car...' Dr Freeman chuckled at his own joke until, looking at Artie and then Ena and seeing that neither were amused, he said, 'I know this is distressing for you, Mr Mallory, but don't worry. Your friend is very fit for his age. I am optimistic that if there is nothing untoward going on beneath the swelling on his head, he will make a full recovery. Now,' he said to Artie, taking Ena and Henry in at the same time, 'if you'll excuse me, I need to get him down to X-ray.' Henry nodded, Ena said thank you and Artie's words spilled out in a jumble of inaudible and tearful whispers.

NINETEEN

The waiting area was suddenly a hive of activity. Two porters in brown coats, the pinched- faced night sister and a young doctor in a white coat with a stethoscope around his neck – a junior doctor Ena thought – disappeared one after the other into Highsmith's room.

Minutes later, Dr Freeman led the porters who, one at the head of a bed on wheels, guiding it, the other porter at the foot of the bed, pushing it, whipped Rupert along the corridor. Nurse Neil walking on the nearside of the bed was talking to the young doctor on the far side. Ena caught the words *car* and *didn't stop.* She was describing how Highsmith had been injured. Her patient, his eyes closed, was barely visible beneath a pyramid of white sheets held away from his body by a full-length basket frame.

Artie jumped up to follow the entourage but Ena caught his arm. 'Artie, let the doctors and nurses do their jobs. Rupert's in the best hands possible.' Still restraining him, she and Henry on either side of their friend watched as Highsmith was whisked through a door at the end of the corridor.

Artie slumped down into the nearest chair. Ena sat next to

him. 'Artie, come home with Henry and me. There's nothing you can do here.' She looked up. The soft mellow light of early dawn poured through the only window in the waiting area. She looked back at her wristwatch. It was five o'clock.

'I think we should go,' Henry added. 'You need to get some rest, old chap, we all do. We'll drop Ena off at the flat and I'll run you over to your place to pick up some clean clothes and your toiletries.'

'And I'll have cooked you both breakfast by the time you get back.'

'Come on, Artie. You'll be no good to Rupert when he wakes up if you're ill.' Henry turned to Ena.

'Henry's right. Come on, love.'

Ena stood up and eventually, with a heavy sigh, Artie joined her. Ena put her arm through his and guided him out of the hospital to Westminster Bridge Road and the car. She opened the back door of Henry's Humber but instead of getting in, Artie pulled his arm from Ena's grip. 'I'll get a cab home. I'll pick up Rupert's shaving stuff, a pair of pyjamas and a clean set of clothes. His are... ripped and stained.'

'Good idea,' Henry said. Ena shot him an annoyed look and frowned. 'We'll get Rupert some clean clothes when we get yours.'

At that moment a black cab came into view from Westminster Bridge. Ena hailed it and the cab pulled up behind Henry's car. 'You two go and I'll take the cab. See you at home in an hour or so?'

'But—' Artie began.

'No buts, Artie. You're not staying on your own while Rupert's in hospital. Get him a clean set of clothes by all means and then come back to Mercer Street with Henry. We have no idea who it was driving the car that hit him. Until we know who it was and why, you could be in danger, so you're staying with us. The spare room will be ready for you by the time you get to our place.' She turned to Henry. 'Make sure he brings enough clothes for several days.'

As Henry steered the Humber into the early morning traffic Ena jumped into the cab. 'Number eight Mercer Street,' she said, closing the door.

The spare bed was already made up with clean sheets. Ena liked to keep the spare bedroom ready in case they had visitors. She'd hoped her sisters would visit her now that she and Henry had a bigger flat. One day, she thought, opening the door of the single wardrobe. Her and Henry's winter coats were the only items of clothing in there. She pushed them to the left making space for Artie's clothes. Before she left she pulled down the sheet on the bed to show white pillowcases. At the door she looked back and surveyed the room. It was a nice bedroom she thought as she went into the kitchen to start breakfast.

She had no idea how long Henry and Artie would be, so put on the oven. While she fried bacon and sausages she let her mind wander. Highsmith, hit by a car? Did Artie still think it was an accident. She didn't think so, and neither did DS Jarvis. Ena put the cooked bacon and sausages on a plate in the oven to keep warm, filled the kettle and put it on to make herself a cup of tea. While the kettle boiled she took a loaf of bread from the cupboard in readiness to make toast, and five eggs from the ceramic hen which she put in a dish at the side of the hob to fry when Henry and Artie got there. No good cooking them now she thought, they'd taste like rubber if they were kept warm in the oven.

When the kettle had boiled Ena made herself a much needed cup of tea, rinsed out the teapot and heaped three spoons of tea leaves into it so it was ready when the men arrived for breakfast. Finally, she took three plates from the cupboard and placed them on the bottom shelf of the oven to warm. That was it, for now. She looked around the kitchen. There was nothing more she could do.

Ena heard the door to the flat open. Leaving the kitchen, she met Henry and Artie on the landing at the top of the stairs. 'Breakfast won't be long,' she said, pushing open the door to the spare bedroom. Artie looked pale and his eyes were red rimmed. 'You'll be quite comfortable in here,' she said. 'Drop your things in here and come through to sitting room. Breakfast will be five minutes.'

'I don't think I could eat anything.'

'You may not feel like eating, but you need to keep your strength up if you're going to be any good to Rupert when he comes out of hospital. Come on.' As if in a dream Artie followed Ena out of the bedroom. 'I'll see what Henry's up to.'

'I've made the tea and put bread under the grill.' Henry put the teapot, cups and saucers on a tray with a jug of milk and the sugar bowl and placed it on the serving hatch between the kitchen and sitting room.

'Thanks, darling. Go through to Artie, will you, while I fry the eggs?' Ena turned the bread over, and put some lard in a big frying pan. When it had melted she added four eggs. Henry would eat two, Artie, who would normally devour two eggs as well as bacon and sausage, would probably struggle to eat one egg today. Slicing tomatoes in half, she took out the toast, replaced it with the tomatoes and turned up the grill. She then put the toast in the toast-rack and took the butter from the refrigerator. 'Henry,' she called through the hatch, 'put the toast and butter on the table, will you?' Turning the tomatoes, Ena took the plates from the oven, dished up the bacon and sausages, and then splashed fat over the egg. Lifting them out of the pan with the spatula she added them to the breakfast plates. She did the same with the grilled tomatoes and passed them through the serving hatch to Henry.

Turning off the oven and the gas jets she filled the kettle in case anyone wanted a second cup of tea, switching it on before joining Henry and Artie at the dining table in the sitting room.

They ate in silence. When Henry and Ena had finished, Artie put down his knife and fork. He'd left half his food, but Ena wasn't going to badger him to eat any more. He'd done well, considering. Henry took the dirty dishes into the kitchen. 'Another cup of tea, Ena?'

'Yes please, darling.'

'Artie?'

'Please.'

Sitting around the table drinking tea, Artie let out a cry of anguish. He looked at Ena, his eyes wide his mouth open. 'Oh God!'

'Are you alright, old chap?'

'What is it, Artie?' Ena asked.

'Fraser. Glasgow. Today!'

TWENTY

Ena put down her cup. 'I'll go to Glasgow in your place, Artie.'

'You can't. Fraser would never agree to it,' Artie replied. 'He'll have done all the background checks on me. He won't talk to you, not without knowing anything about you. We'll have to postpone. I'll telephone the Scottish office and rearrange to meet Fraser next week. Rupert's responding to treatment, I'll be able to leave him for a day.'

MI5 is answerable to the Home Office and the Home Secretary. And, if MI6 is involved, the Foreign Secretary. Ena's friend, Colonel Smith at GCHQ, who she had first met at Bletchley Park was as influential – and was probably able to pull more strings than any of the aforementioned. She scrunched up her shoulders and smiled sweetly at Henry, 'Would you telephone the colonel, darling?'

He glanced at the clock on the mantel. 'He won't be in yet. I'll ring as soon as I think he's at his desk.'

'There!' she said to Artie. 'It's as good as done.' She rubbed her hands together. 'I'm going to Glasgow and you're going to visit Rupert and that's the end of it!'

'What if Fraser won't see you? If he does, he might not take you to meet Hollander?'

'Why shouldn't he?' Ena leaned her head on one side. 'Henry, when you speak to the colonel, will you ask him to square it with this Fraser character that he takes me to meet Archibald Hollander?' She winked at Artie. 'My friend, the colonel, is a powerful man.'

Artie shuddered. 'I know, I worked at GCHQ.'

Ena knew Colonel Smith not only from Bletchley, but through her sister Claire who had known him when she was in the Special Operations Executive during the war. He had also helped Ena when Henry was framed for murdering the mole at MI5 earlier in the year. 'Fraser would have been vetted as thoroughly as you.'

'That's settled then. As you'll be staying here when you return from seeing Rupert, will you call into the office and check the post before coming upstairs? If for any reason I have to stay in Glasgow tonight, you can check the post in the morning before you leave for St Thomas.' Artie looked worried. 'It'll be fine, you'll see. Between the pair of you, I'm sure you can hold the fort here. Anything that can't wait until I return, I expect *you* to deal with,' she said to Henry.

'Will you be alright meeting an agent you don't know, in a city you don't know, on your own?'

'If he's one of Five's lot, of course I will.'

'I'm sorry you have to go to Scotland.'

'Don't be. If it was the other way around, him needing information from us, I'd expect him to come to London. It'll be fine. Stop worrying.' Ena yawned. 'And, I'll be able to sleep on the train. It shouldn't take this Fraser chap long to tell me what MI5 has got on the late Michael Crosier and if Archibald Hollander is with him, all the better, I can catch the night train back to London. If Hollander isn't with Fraser and I can't see him until tomorrow, I'll book into a hotel. There's always a half-decent hotel within walking distance of a large station like Glasgow Central.'

'It'll be interesting to know what the German authorities said about Crosier's murder at the time,' Henry said. 'There isn't much on him in the files at GCHQ.'

'The authorities didn't admit he was murdered. According to Rupert, they rubber stamped Crosier's death as an accidental drowning.'

'Which isn't surprising. A member of British Intelligence murdered in Hitler's flagship city, the city that Hitler and the Nazi Party had hoped would show Germany to be a sophisticated world power?' Henry laughed. 'The murder of any foreign agent would have been a political disaster for the Nazi Party. If Hollander was an experienced negotiator, you can bet your bottom dollar that he'll have made up his own mind about what happened.'

'Let's hope he shares that intel with me!'

'Right! I've got everything I need in my overnight bag in case I have to stay in Glasgow tonight. So, you, my friend,' Ena said, turning to Artie, 'get yourself washed and dressed and down to Tommy's to see that man of yours. Take the Sunbeam, the keys are on the hall table.'

'Are you sure? Won't you need the car to get to Euston station?'

Ena grinned at Henry. 'My husband will drive me to the station, won't you, darling?'

Henry got up, kissed Ena on the top of her head and said, 'Taking her to the station is the only way I can be sure she's actually going to Glasgow. We'll have a few beers tonight, Artie.'

Ena laughed. 'I'm sure you will. While the cat's away...' Artie turned to leave the room for the bathroom, smiling. It was the first time Ena had seen him smile since Rupert's accident, if indeed it had been an accident. 'Give Rupert my love,' she called after him.

A muffled, 'I will,' came back in reply.

'He'll be alright, won't he?' Ena asked Henry.

'Who, Rupert?'

'Well, of course I hope Rupert will be alright. But I was actually thinking about Artie getting upset while driving. But ignore me, I'm sure he'll be fine. Oh, another thing, whoever was driving the car that hit Rupert might know where he lives. Promise me you won't let Artie go back to the flat in Knightsbridge?'

'He won't.' Henry held Ena's hands, pulled her towards him and kissed her. 'Now, go and check your bag. Make sure you have everything you need for the journey.'

'I will,' Ena said, returning Henry's kiss. Leaning away from him she yawned. 'I think I'll sleep all the way to Glasgow.'

'Did you remember Artie's notes?'

Ena tapped her shoulder bag. 'Got them when I went to the office for my notebook and pen.'

'You will be careful?' Henry said.

'Aren't I always?'

'No.'

'Stop it. I can see the only way I'm going to stop you from whittling is to...' Ena stood on tiptoe, lifted her head up and kissed Henry full on the lips. He responded by wrapping his arms around her tightly and kissing her again.

The train began to hiss. Steam belched from it and it jolted forwards making a clonking sound. A whistle blew from somewhere along the platform. 'That's me then,' Ena said, easing herself from Henry's embrace.

He opened the carriage door and Ena climbed the two

narrow steps. He passed in her overnight bag and she stepped back as he closed the door.

'I was being serious when I said be careful.'

'I know, and I will, I promise. Oh, and darling, when you get hold of the colonel, would you ask him to give this Fraser chap a description of me. Tell him I'm wearing a camel coloured coat. And would you telephone Charles at his office? Tell him I've been unexpectedly called away and I'll be in touch with him as soon as I'm back in London. Don't forget, darling. *Don't* telephone him at home. It has to be at the office.'

'Anything else, ma-am?' Henry touched his forelock.

'No, that's it! Oh, yes,' Ena said, 'there is something. Telephone Dan Powell at Bow Street and ask him if he could put someone outside Rupert's door at St Thomas' in case whoever tried to run him down comes back to finish the job. And, could you find out what Highsmith's been working on. As he's been working out of Cheltenham, you'll be able to access his work. Go back six months if you can. Something during that time could be related to the hit-and-run.' It probably is Ena thought. 'I'm sorry to ask you to do all these things, darling. I am grateful,' she said, as the train lurched forwards.

'I'll make the telephone calls from your office when I check the post,' Henry shouted.

'Don't forget to go to Cheltenham for Rupert's files,' Ena reminded, but a whistle that sounded like a foghorn drowned out her words.

The train set off on its way north with a steadily increasing chugging. Ena hung out of the window and blew Henry a kiss. He reciprocated before making his way back along the platform to the exit.

TWENTY-ONE

Ena looked at her watch. Henry would have telephoned Charles by now. There was nothing she could do for Charles until she got back to London. She wondered if Rupert was fully conscious yet. She hoped he was, although she knew that being unconscious was one way of giving someone with a head injury time for the swelling to go down – which it would have to do before the doctors could operate. She would telephone Henry when she got to Scotland, check that he had made the calls on her behalf – and if Artie was back from the hospital, find out how Rupert was doing.

Ena closed her eyes and enjoyed the gentle rhythm of the train chugging through the countryside on its way north. She must have dozed off because when she opened her eyes there was another woman in the carriage. She glanced at her watch. She had slept for a couple of hours. It wasn't long but she felt better for it. She smiled at the woman sitting by the door. She was about Ena's age and was reading an Agatha Christie novel, *Ordeal By Innocence*. She eagerly turned the page, devouring the make-believe world of Miss Marple, Christie's fictional female detective. Ena leaned her head against the backrest and closed her eyes. Miss Marple would have solved the murder of Michael Crosier in no time, she thought, smiling. She had read several Agatha Christie novels and had enjoyed them. She had meant to ask Henry to get her *Ordeal By Innocence* a couple of years ago as a Christmas present. Christmas 1958 if memory served, the year it was published. She had forgotten to ask him then, and now she rarely had time to read. A loud clunk followed by a judder sent the carriage rocking from side to side. Ena opened her eyes and sat upright with a jolt.

The woman smiled at her. 'The clonking noise is the wheels going over the points,' she explained. 'I do this journey every month.' She slipped a bookmark between the pages of her book and put it on the seat next to her.

'I've dropped off twice,' Ena said. 'I shall bring a book the next time I travel by train, then I won't worry about sleeping through my stop.'

'I used to fall asleep, but I was always woken by the clonking sound when the train changed from one track to another, as it did just then. It's like an alarm clock. I leave the train at Crewe. Thanks to the points, I have never slept through my stop.'

'I change trains at Crewe,' Ena said. 'Do you know how long it is until we get there?'

'Quite a while yet. An hour at least. If you want to sleep, I'll give you a nudge before we arrive.'

'Thank you.' Ena wished she'd brought a book. On the other hand... She yawned. Her eyes grew heavy. She had hardly slept the previous night and gave in to sleep.

Having successfully changed trains at Crewe, Ena relaxed. The next stop was Glasgow Central. She read though Artie's notes, jotting down salient points in her own notebook to remind herself of the most important things she needed to ask Archibald Hollander about his time in Berlin, in 1936. She wrote: *Hollander. MI5. Clean up after Crosier was killed.*

Ena needed to ask Hollander how much, if anything, did he think MI5 know about Michael Crosier? Had Hollander met Michael Crosier when Crosier worked for MI5, London? If he had, how well did he know him? Did Crosier have any enemies that Hollander knew of? What, if anything, did he know about Crosier's death before he left England for Berlin? And, what did the German authorities say about an English architect, a tourist, being killed in Berlin? For that's what Crosier's cover was. Or, did they know he was a military intelligence agent that had been killed?

Deep in thought Ena looked out of the window. Why was MI5 at Hitler's Olympics in '36? Surely it should have been MI6 in Berlin in the thirties. But then Highsmith had worked for Six, he also worked for the Prime Minister, Stanley Baldwin, which was probably why he, as MI5 counter-intelligence was there. Ena had a long list of questions. Some she would ask Hollander and some she needed to ask Highsmith, when he recovered. If he recovered. She shuddered at the thought of him not surviving his injuries and how it would affect Artie. She pushed that thought out of her mind. It didn't bear thinking about.

Ena had told Artie it didn't matter if she had to stay in Glasgow overnight. If it wasn't that she'd promised her friend Charles she would investigate the *potential* daughter of his wife Priscilla, it wouldn't have mattered. But what if the girl turned up at Charles' office in London while she was in Scotland, before she'd had time to check her out. It would be worse still if she turned up at the Galbraith's home. If the girl had found out where Charles worked, she might also have found out where he and Priscilla live. The phony daughter, Linda, had known where the Galbraiths lived. What if... Ena sighed. There were too many 'what ifs'. She needed to put Priscilla's illegitimate daughter out of her mind and concentrate on the job in hand. When she returned to London she would be able to give

Charles' case her full attention! Even so, she sent up a quick prayer that the girl didn't come to London unannounced while she was in Scotland.

Ena turned away from the window and the sun, which was now on her face, and put all thought of Charles Galbraith's investigation out of her mind. As the train chugged northwards, she dipped in and out of sleep. The sun or the train, she wasn't sure which, had changed direction again and she felt uncomfortably hot.

The night sky was dense. A thick shadowy pitch-dark night without stars or moon. It was full of bats. They were flying towards her. She ducked so they would miss her head, but she wasn't quick enough. They wheeled, and they squealed and squawked, and their webbed wings became tangled in her hair. Someone shouted, "Ena?" She turned to see a dark coloured saloon car bearing down on her. A voice called to her from out of the darkness, "You have a choice, Ena. Fall from the summit of Ben Nevis into Loch Linnhe, or jump from the train into the River Clyde." Gripped by a terrifying fear that she would not survive falling from the mountaintop to the loch below, she opened the door of the train. The icy cold wind took her voice. The dark night was closing in on her. She was unable to cry for help as she slipped from the train. Just as she was about to hit the fast-flowing river she felt someone grab her by the shoulder and she woke with a start.

'Ticket, miss?'

Ena looked up at a man wearing a black uniform. 'Of course,' she said. She rummaged through her shoulder bag, found her wallet, took the ticket from it and offered it to the ticket collector. He nodded and then turned to a man and woman sitting opposite.

Disorientated and still half asleep, Ena looked about her.

She was on a train. The woman who had been reading the
Agatha Christie novel had been replaced by a man and woman.
Of course, she thought, the woman had left the train at Crewe.
Then, for the longest moment Ena felt intense panic. Had she
slept so deeply that she'd missed her connection. She inhaled
deeply and the process of changing trains came back to her. She
breathed a sigh of relief and closed her eyes.

Shaken awake by two jolts – one immediately after the other –
as the train crossed the main track from Crew to Glasgow, to an
internal track that would take the train into Glasgow's Central
Station. The train rocked and clunked. As it slowed Ena heard
the puffing sound as steam was blown through the stack and the
hissing of the air-pump as it produced pressure for the brakes.
The train shunted and then slowed to a standstill, stopping a
few feet short of the buffers on Platform thirteen.

To the sound of other locomotives arriving and departing,
hissing steam, train doors slamming and children running and
shouting along the platform, Ena reached up for her small case,
lugged it down from the overhead rack and with her shoulder
bag in place, she made for the door.

Turning sideways to make herself as narrow as possible, Ena
lifted her case as high as she could in order not to decapitate
three rowdy children all under the age of manners and sense, as
they ran past her. Their mother – at least that's who Ena
assumed the tired, dishevelled looking woman laden with children's coats and bags was – ran after them. She smiled apologetically at Ena, but didn't stop.

Leaving the platform behind her, Ena scanned the people
on Glasgow Central's busy concourse. Somewhere among them
was MI5 Glasgow's Mr Fraser.

TWENTY-TWO

'Mrs Green?'

'Yes.' Ena turned to see a man who stood well over six feet tall, with a full red beard and wild red and grey hair that curled over the collar of a woven dark grey coat. 'Mr Fraser?' she said, offering him her hand.

'Just, Fraser.'

'Fraser! Right!' Ena said, withdrawing her hand when Fraser didn't respond by shaking it.

Fraser looked her up and down. Ena smiled. He didn't.

'*Colonel Smith,*' he whispered, 'telephoned me to say there had been a change of plan. That the man who should have come here today has been in a car accident.'

'That's right.' Ena decided not to complicate matters by telling Fraser that it was Highsmith who had been in an accident, not Artie. He didn't need to know the details, especially as it was Highsmith who she was working for. Until she knew Fraser better she'd keep him on a *need to know* basis. That Ena had come in Artie's place was all he needed to know.

''Tis you then! Colonel Smith said he'd known you since the war.'

Ena nodded. 'I er...'

Fraser took Ena's overnight bag in one hand and raised the other. 'No need for explanations. If the colonel trusts you, 'tis good enough for me.'

Ena didn't reply to Fraser's comment. Neither he nor the comment required an answer. She followed him the short distance from the platform where she had alighted the London train to the main concourse. 'Do you have a return ticket to London?'

'Yes. It's an open ticket. I wasn't sure whether I'd be going back to London tonight or I'd have to stay over. Depends on Archibald Hollander.'

'You'll not be going back tonight.' He pointed to the cafeteria. 'You need to eat. 'Twill be a while before you'll be able to eat anything once we've left Glasgow.'

'I don't understand. Aren't we meeting Mr Hollander in Glasgow?'

'No.' Fraser led Ena into the station cafeteria. 'Best you get some food. I'll get the tickets,' he said, turning on his heels to leave.

'What tickets?' Ena called after him. 'Where are we going?'

'Aberdeen.'

'Aberdeen?' Ena said under her breath. That must be where Hollander is, she thought as she joined the long queue at the food counter where two women in white caterers' coats and hats were frantically dishing up eggs, bacon and sausage. Further along there were Cornish pasties, sausage rolls and Scotch eggs. Ena was hungry but didn't fancy fried food. It looked too greasy for her palate, and the pastry, which Ena considered to be buffet food, looked dry. When it was her turn to be served, she asked for a ham sandwich. She hadn't thought to ask her companion if he wanted anything to eat or drink. In case he did, she changed her order to two sandwiches and two cups of tea. By the time she'd paid for the refreshments, Fraser had returned and was sitting at a table just inside the door.

'I didn't know what you liked, so I got you a ham sandwich. Hope that's okay?' She put the sandwich down in front of him. 'And, a cup of tea.'

He looked at the food and nodded. He then gave Ena her ticket to Aberdeen. She turned it over in her hand. It was an open return to Glasgow.

She bit into her sandwich eagerly. The bread was dry and there was not enough butter, but the ham was tasty.

'So it's in Aberdeen that I'll get to meet Mr Hollander?'

'No.'

'No?' Ena looked up from her food. 'Where then?'

'Archie Hollander stays in Mainland.'

Ena hadn't heard of a town called Mainland in Scotland. Before she had time to ask where Mainland was, Fraser said, 'Shetland.'

Ena's mouth fell open. 'We're going to the Shetland Islands?'

Obviously the strong silent type, Fraser nodded once, but didn't volunteer any more information about the journey that lay ahead of them. All he said was, 'Archie Hollander is there.'

'Right! We'll be going over to Shetland on a boat I presume?'

'Aye.'

Which means I won't be catching the late train back to London tonight, Ena thought.

Ena, first to board the Aberdeen train, found the compartment. It was empty. Once inside she plumped to sit on the right of the window, dropping her shoulder bag on the seat next to her. She liked to face forwards. As the sun was on the other side of the train, she hoped it would take longer than three hours, which was how long she estimated a journey of around one hundred and twenty miles to be, before it crept round to their side of the train.

Fraser followed her in, lifted her overnight bag onto the luggage rack head and sat in the window seat opposite her. Ena turned her body a little to the left, so she was sitting at an angle and could stretch out her legs. Fraser, noticing there was a newspaper on the seat next to the door, got up. The paper, the Aberdeen Evening Express, must have been left by someone travelling from Aberdeen to Glasgow. Fraser picked up the paper and, returning with it, lowered his large frame onto the middle seat.

Ena looked out of the window, pretending she hadn't noticed her travelling companion's thoughtfulness. If it had been anyone else, she'd have thanked him and started a conversation, but in the short time she had known the burly Scotsman, it was clear to her that he was a man of few words. Thanking may even embarrass him.

Leaving the city of Glasgow behind, they travelled though rich green countryside, and with hills and forests in the distance, Ena began to relax. She closed her eyes and in a half-awake, half-asleep state she recalled what she knew of the top-secret facilities on the Shetland Isles. Several RAF airfields and sites were established on the Isles, and there was also a Norwegian naval unit that the islanders called the "Shetland Bus" established by the Special Operations Executive as early as 1940. The Shetland Bus had made over two hundred conducted covert operations, carrying intelligence agents, refugees, instructors for the resistance, and military supplies across the sea. If Fraser knew Colonel Smith, maybe he was in the SOE. He may even have worked in covert operations.

'What time does the ship sail for Mainland?'

'As soon as we get to the docks.'

'And that will be...?'

'Don't know. We'll take a taxi from the station. There'll be a fishing vessel waiting for us.'

'I see,' Ena said. The question she'd asked Fraser he hadn't answered, but she left it. If the fishing boat was waiting for them the captain was probably intelligence, or had been. She was hungry. She wished she'd had eggs and bacon in Glasgow Central instead of a sandwich. By Ena's reckoning they would be aboard the fishing boat most of the night. She lifted her feet one at a time. Her legs felt stiff.

'I'm going to the ladies,' she said. Standing up, she staggered to the left as the train rocked. She soon regained her balance. 'I need to stretch my legs.' Fraser gave a short nod.

When she had used the toilet and washed her hands, Ena combed her hair. Looking in the small mirror above the sink she saw dark rings under her eyes. She was tired. Maybe there'll be somewhere to have a sleep on the boat. Or, maybe not. 'It's a fishing boat,' she said to herself, and opening the toilet door made her way back along the corridor. Entering the compartment she rolled her shoulders. She also had a stiff neck.

TWENTY-THREE

Gusting wind took Ena's breath away and whipped her hair about her face. She turned her back on the bitter onslaught and pulled the thick Shetland wool blanket that Fraser had given her – courtesy of Captain Gregor Blair, the skipper of the *Maighdeann-mhara* – tightly around her shoulders. Her cheeks were frozen and tears formed like icicles at the corners of her eyes, but after being cooped up in trains for so long, she felt exhilarated.

The boat's captain, a jovial Scotsman, was just as Ena imagined a Scottish fisherman would be. Tall, almost as tall as Fraser, but older. If he had worked for the Intelligence Services, he'd be retired now, she thought. He had a full beard, mostly white with strands of red in it, showing beneath his cap, greying red hair. She looked at Captain Blair and then at Fraser. Both had wild red hair, both were six feet tall – give or take an inch – and both were heavy set. They could have been brothers.

She was miles away thinking about the possible relationship between the two men when the boat rocked and a high wave slapped its side. It happened again and Ena clung onto the rail and planted her feet firmly on the deck.

'We caught a high-un,' Captain Blair said. Ena nodded. 'Soon be calmer.'

There were several more high waves before the sea became calmer and the boat began to level.

'Why don't you go below, Mrs Green? Get your head down in my cabin. You'll not be disturbed.'

Ena nodded. 'I should like to be on deck before we sail into Lerwick harbour. Would you wake me in time?'

'Aye. I'll wake ya before we dock.'

Ena slept, eventually. It had taken a while for her to get off, as the wind had howled and the boat had rocked and rolled in it. She woke the following morning to a couple of sharp raps on the cabin door. 'We'll be docking shortly, Mrs Green,' called a familiar voice that she recognised as Fraser's.

Ena splashed cold water on her face, cleaned her teeth and was up on deck as the rugged coastlines of Shetland's main island, Mainland and a smaller island came into view.

'It's a beautiful morning,' Ena remarked. She inhaled deeply. 'Now that's what I call fresh air.'

'Aye, it is that.'

'What's that island called?' she asked, pointing to her left.

'The Isle of Bressay,' the captain said. 'The water between the two islands is called the Bressay Sound. Hold on to your hat,' he shouted. 'We're heading down the Sound and it can be windy.' Ena laughed. She wasn't wearing a hat, instead she covered her ears with cupped hands.

When she was able to speak again she tried to pronounce the name of the fishing boat. 'What does, Maigdeen am mean.'

'Maighdeann-mhara,' the captain said, 'is Scottish Gaelic for mermaid. It can also mean handmaiden and seamaid.'

Ena copied the way Captain Blair had pronounced

maighdeann-mhara phonetically and the captain clapped his large hands.

'We'll soon be dropping anchor in Lerwick harbour.'

Fraser, during one of his rare bouts of conversation, had told her that when they docked in Lerwick there would be a blue sky and sunshine. 'But,' he'd grinned, 'that doesn't mean it'll be warm. Not with the Norwegian Sea to the west and the North Sea on the east.'

Ena thanked Captain Blair saying she looked forward to seeing him again on the return journey to Scotland. He saluted her and she reached up and kissed him on his cold, bearded cheek.

'Take care of Mrs Green, Fraser,' the captain said, as Fraser drew near. 'De ya hear me, man?'

'If he doesn't take care of me, I'll let you know, Captain,' Ena said, laughing.

'Aye, you do that.' Captain Blair shook Fraser's hand and said, 'Until tomorrow at dawn, then?'

'Aye,' was all Fraser said, before turning to Ena and taking her overnight case out of her hand.

Ena grinned at the captain and pretended she had to run after her companion.

She'd had a couple of hours sleep on the boat going over to Mainland, but still felt tired. It was the kind of tired that would disappear after a hot bath and a decent breakfast. 'Were you able to book me into a hotel?' she asked, catching up with Fraser and falling into step at his side.

'The Ship Ahoy Hotel. 'Tis in front of you.'

'It's modern.'

'Aye. What did you expect?'

'I don't know. Perhaps something older looking. Will I be able to see the harbour and the sea from my room?'

'Aye.'

Ena was excited by the prospect of a sea view, and tiredness forgotten she almost skipped into the hotel. When she had signed the visitors' register at reception – and had been given the key to her room – number seven on the first floor, she relieved Fraser of her overnight bag. 'I'm in need of a bath and something to eat. What are you doing?'

He didn't answer her question, but said, 'What time would you like me to come back for you?'

'In an hour and we'll have lunch together. We could eat here? That is if you don't already have plans.'

'I have to see someone, but that should'nay take long.' Fraser's brow furrowed. He looked worried.

'What is it?' Ena asked. 'If you'd rather not join me, I understand. It just seems a bit silly for us to eat on our own – you in one place and me here in the hotel. I have questions to ask you before I meet Mr Hollander. You could brief me, so to speak, over lunch. So, what's it to be, pub lunch or hotel restaurant?'

Fraser flushed scarlet. Ena suspected he was not used to being invited to lunch by a woman.

'Well, aye, then. If you're not averse to eating with a man who enjoys a pint of ale with his food, the pub along by the harbour. The Boatman Inn, then.' Fraser pointed in the direction they had come from when they left the *Maighdeann-mhara*. 'We passed it just now.'

'I remember seeing the Boatman. I'll see you there in an hour and you can tell me all about Archibald Hollander, what he's like and how I should approach him.'

* * *

The first thing Ena needed to do was telephone Artie. He'd be worried sick by now. He'd thought, as she had, that she was meeting Hollander in Glasgow last night, not the next day in the Shetland Isles. She took her overnight case up to her room. Noticing that there was no telephone she headed back downstairs to reception and asked if there was one she could use.

'Telephones are over there,' the receptionist said, pointing to three old fashioned wooden cubicles on the far side of the lobby.

'Thank you. Can I dial London direct from here?'

'No, there's no direct line to England. You have to go through the hotel's main switchboard,' the receptionist replied, going over to a black switchboard with plugs and wires waiting to be brought to life.

Ena hightailed it over to the first available cubicle, went in and picked up the receiver.

'Number please?' the receptionist asked.

'Covent Garden, London, 7771.' A couple of seconds later she was connected.

'Dudley Green Associates, Artie Mallory speaking.'

'Hello, Artie, it's Ena.'

'Ena! I've been going frantic. Where are you?'

'Tell me how Rupert is first, then I'll fill you in with what's happening here.'

'He's much the same. In and out of consciousness. His doctor says that's to be expected and that he's doing well.'

'Hang on to that, Artie, after all his doctor should know. Give him my best when you next see him.'

'Will do.'

'Has there been any post that I need to know about?'

'No! Now for goodness' sake, Ena, where are you?'

'On Mainland. It's the largest of the Shetland Isles.'

'What the hell are you doing up there?'

'Meeting Mr H.'

'Ah!' There was a pause in the conversation. 'It's like that, is it?'

'I don't know. It could be.' Ena was sure the public telephones in the hotel wouldn't be tapped, but Highsmith, like her husband Henry, worked in a world of spies and espionage at GCHQ where anything was possible. A world that Ena thought she had left behind when she resigned from the Home Office, but it seems there's no escaping your past – not working on Highsmith's investigation. However, in case anyone was listening in to the call, she didn't elaborate. 'Anyway, don't worry, I'm fine. I'll have my meeting and then I'll be taken back to Aberdeen.'

'When?'

'Tomorrow. Crack of dawn, I think.'

'Is the man who met you in Glasgow alright? I mean, is he safe? Do you feel safe?'

'As houses. He looks a bit rough around the edges and he sounds gruff, but he's a big softy. Look, I'm going to have to go. I'm meeting him in a pub for lunch and, after spending the night on a fishing boat, I'm in need of a bath. I'll telephone again when I can. If you don't hear from me, I should be home tomorrow evening. Don't sit and wait for me in the office after you get back from the hospital, go up to the flat. I'll fill you in with what I've found out about H when I see you.'

'Ena, be careful.'

'I'll be safe enough with my escort. He's built like the proverbial brick out-house.'

'I meant be careful of him.'

'I will. Oh, and Artie? Tell Henry that everything's going to plan and I'll see him tomorrow night.'

'Bye.'

'Bye.'

TWENTY-FOUR

Ena got to the Boatman Inn early. She looked in both the public bar and the smokeroom, but Fraser wasn't in either of them. She was thirsty and bought herself a pint of shandy. When the froth settled and she was in no danger of spilling it, she took it outside, found a vacant table on the edge of the pub's garden – away from the nearest group of people – and sat down with her beer to admire the view of the boats in the harbour.

By the time Fraser arrived, Ena's stomach felt hollow. She was hungry, or was she nervous? She lifted her glass to show him that she had a drink and ran through what she wanted to ask him about Hollander and, more importantly, what she had planned to ask Hollander when she met him. She had gone over it so many times in her head that she was in danger of thinking she'd asked questions that she hadn't asked, and forgotten to ask questions that she needed to ask.

'I took the liberty of ordering you cod and chips.'

Fraser put his pint of dark beer on the table, swung his long legs over the bench and sitting down, chuckled. It was the first time Ena had heard him laugh.

When their food arrived, Ena gasped at the size of the cod. 'This looks... Big!'

'Cod, caught locally,' Fraser informed her.

Not by the lovely Captain Blair, Ena thought, but didn't say.

They ate in silence. When they had finished, Ena remarked on how tasty the fish was. 'I'm full now,' she said, taking a swig of her shandy. 'When do I get to meet Archibald Hollander?'

'Soon as you've finished your drink, I'll take you to him.' Fraser knocked back the few ounces of beer left in his glass and Ena did the same. 'He's not far,' Fraser said, lifting his legs over the bench – this time with some effort – and standing up.

Ena picked up her shoulder bag. 'We need to pay the bill.'

''Tis paid. The train must have cost you a pretty penny, so...'

The train did cost – and a lot more than a pretty penny – but Fraser had also forked out for train fares. If it hadn't cost anything to sail to Mainland from Aberdeen on his pal's fishing boat, he had paid for the train from Aberdeen to Glasgow out of his own pocket. Because he was helping Ena in a private investigation, there would be no expenses from MI5 for him.

Ena didn't want Fraser to pay for her food. She rarely allowed anyone to pay for her, except Henry. Husbands were different.

She looked up at Fraser. She didn't want to offend him. Old fashioned men didn't approve of women paying. Many thought women were the fairer sex – or the weaker. Fraser was certainly old fashioned. Ena was not. Nor did she subscribe to being the weaker sex.

'Thank you, Fraser,' she said, as she followed him back into the pub, through the bar and out into the fresh salty air of Lerwick harbour.

Fraser had a long stride, but once they had left the harbour and were walking towards the town centre, he slowed his pace. He was a strange man, Ena thought. When he spoke, he sounded bad-tempered. He looked like the type of man you wouldn't want to meet on a dark night, but for all that he was kind and considerate. A gentle giant, she decided, and smiled up at him. 'Lerwick's buzzing with people. Is it always this busy?' Ena asked, as Fraser led her through Harrison Square and into Burns Walk.

'It's market day. Fish and wool day.'

Ena stopped to read a handwritten notice in the window of a wool shop. *Men and Women's knitwear – Jumpers, pullovers and cardigans – hand made in Shetland and Scotland to suit the changing seasons. Our popular Fair Isle knitwear, designed at our home in the North of Scotland, is made from Shetland wool.* Fraser had kept walking. Ena had to run to catch him up. 'It isn't important, of course,' she said, 'but will we have time to look around the market after we've seen Archie Hollander?'

'We're here,' Fraser said. And without replying to Ena, he turned into Saint Olaf Street.

Ena looked about her. 'This is where I'll be meeting Hollander?' she asked, following Fraser along a path to a church. She had no idea whether the ancient old stone church was Catholic or the Scottish equivalent of the Church of England. 'Has Archie Hollander become a man of the cloth?'

'No, he is buried here.'

'What?'

Fraser pointed to a headstone. The simple inscription read, "Archibald Hollander, 1901 to 1950. RIP."

Ena, hardly able to believe her eyes, read the inscription again. 'Dead? Why didn't you just tell me Hollander was dead? It would have saved us both a lot of time and...' She was about to say money, but thought better of it.

'Colonel Smith said you wouldn't take the word of someone you didn't know and that it was best for you to see for yourself.'

The colonel was right, Ena thought, but wouldn't admit it to Fraser. 'Hollander dead!' she said again. 'Which is why we weren't able to find a record of him working for any of the intelligence services after 1950.'

'Fraser?' someone shouted.

Ena looked round to see a priest in his late forties striding down the narrow church-walk towards them, his black buttoned-to-the-neck cassock flapping in time with the jaunty speed of his gait. He greeted Fraser with outstretched arms. 'How are you?'

'Well, Father, thank you.' Fraser turned to Ena. 'This is Father O'Broin. He is the priest here at the Sacred Heart Church. Mrs Green has come in place of the man I told you about, Father. She is investigating the death of a colleague of Archie Hollander.'

Father O'Broin glanced at Hollander's grave. 'Dear Archie,' he said, before turning his attention to Ena. 'Good afternoon, Mrs Green.'

'Good afternoon, Father. I er...' Ena was totally thrown by meeting Archibald Hollander's priest. She cleared her throat. 'As Fraser said, I'm investigating the death of a colleague of Mr Hollander; a death that is shrouded in misgivings.'

'Go on,' the priest urged.

'Well, a friend of mine feels he is to blame for a man's death because the man had no experience in the field of work in which my friend employed him. My friend was nowhere near the man when he was killed, but the man's wife asked me to look into her husband's death because she believes he was murdered.'

'I see.' Father O'Broin rubbed his chin thoughtfully.

Too thoughtfully for Ena's suspicious mind. And did he really see? Ena doubted he did. Twenty-four years ago, Father O'Broin would have been training for the priesthood. The basic training before ordination was six to eight years. However clever a theologian, he could only have been in his early twenties at that time.

'How can I be of help?'

'Sorry?' Ena had been so deep in thought that Father O'Broin had caught her off guard. 'Mr Hollander was a parishioner of yours?' The priest nodded slowly. 'I was wondering, as he is dead, if you could tell me whether he confessed to knowing anything about a man who died in suspicious circumstances in Berlin, 1936?'

Giving the question serious thought, Father O'Broin shook his head. 'No.'

Ena looked from the priest to Fraser and back. 'No, he didn't tell you anything, or no you can't tell me?'

'The latter. I'm sorry, Mrs Green, I cannot reveal what is told to me in the confessional.'

'But Mr Hollander is dead. He's been dead for ten years. Surely it can't matter now. You see it is possible that the man's widow, or his son, is accusing an innocent man of his murder.'

'And the person being accused is your client?'

'Yes, he is my client, but I also wish to help Mrs Crosier, the woman whose husband was killed. She is still very distraught. After twenty-four years she hasn't been able to come to terms with the loss of her husband. I was hoping to give her closure.'

'I understand your predicament, and I feel for the widow of the man who was killed, but I'm sorry, Mrs Green, I cannot break the seal of the confessional.' Father O'Broin looked at Fraser. 'Perhaps you could tell Mrs Green what Archie told you, Fraser?'

Ena shot Fraser an angry look. 'Hollander told you about Crosier's death?'

Fraser nodded half-heartedly. 'In confidence.'

'It has been ten years. I don't think you would be breaking a confidence if you told Mrs Green what Archie told you,' the priest said.

'Me'be, Father.'

'It is your decision of course. You must do what you think

best.' The priest turned back to Ena, 'Forgive me, Mrs Green. but I have a house call to make. An elderly parishioner.' He looked at his wristwatch. 'I'm late.'

'I'm sorry if I've delayed you, Father?'

'Dinna fash, the old lady I'm about to visit would say. Don't worry.' He laughed. 'There's nothing wrong with her that a cup of tea and a chat won't fix. Goodbye, Mrs Green.'

'Goodbye, Father, and thank you.'

'I hope your investigation reveals something that will help your client, as well as the grieving widow. Fraser,' he said, turning to the burly Scotsman and putting his hand on his forearm, 'don't be a stranger. Come and see me next time you're on Mainland. My door is always open.'

It was clear by the way the two men spoke to each other that Father O'Broin and Fraser knew each other well.

The priest walked off down the path at a pace, his black cassock billowing behind him. Ena and Fraser followed at a slower pace. As they turned into Saint Olaf Street, the priest walked on.

TWENTY-FIVE

Disappointed that she hadn't learnt anything from Father O'Broin, Ena lost interest in the market. She led the way to the seafront with Fraser following. 'I love the sea. It's vast and remarkable.' Looking out to where the sea met the sky, she continued. 'It's no wonder Columbus had a hard time convincing the men who sailed with him that the world was not flat,' she said. 'From here it looks as if the world might end on the horizon. If we didn't know better, we might think if we sailed beyond it, we'd drop off the planet.'

Ena looked up at her companion. 'I'm sorry to rattle on about the sea. I find it mesmerising; mysterious and frightening at the same time. I suppose it's being brought up in the middle of England. My home town is as far away from the sea as you can get. Skegness is the nearest seaside resort and that's a three-hour drive.' Ena knew she was waffling, but she needed to buy some time.

She let the momentum of the slope take her as she ran down to the promenade railings, took hold of the handrail on top and looked out to sea. Great luminous clouds floated above the ocean one way, and in the other direction the harbour and all the colourful fishing boats. 'Oh!' she exclaimed, seeing an elderly man and woman gather their belongings, get up and begin walking towards the harbour. 'A bench.' She pushed herself off the railings. 'I'll grab it before anyone else does.'

Moving quickly she claimed the seat. She patted the wooden slats next to her and Fraser ambled over and sat down. For some time they sat in silence admiring the view, watching boats of all sizes sailing in and out of the harbour. 'Will the *Mermaid* still be in port?'

'Yes. She'll be putting out to sea at first light.'

'And I'll be going back to Aberdeen on her?'

'Aye!'

'Fraser?' Ena ventured after ten minutes silence.

'Uh-huh.'

'You brought me all the way to Mainland letting me believe that I was going to meet Archibald Hollander, when all the time you knew he was dead. It would have been a lot less trouble for you, and for me if you'd simply told my associate that he had died in 1950.'

'It would, but Colonel Smith said—'

'I know what the colonel said.' How well the colonel knew her, Ena thought. She considered for a moment and then said, 'I want you to know that if we had spoken sooner, I think I would have believed you.'

'Me'be. No matter. You do now?'

Ena laughed. 'Well, priests don't lie. Not that I think you would lie either, so yes, I believe you.' She sensed Fraser relax and decided that now would be a good time to ask him what Hollander had told him. 'Father O'Broin said that after ten years you wouldn't be breaking a confidence if you told me what you knew about Hollander in Berlin.' Ena turned her gaze from the sea to Fraser. 'I've signed the Official Secrets Act, so anything you say to me won't go any further.'

Fraser nodded that he understood, but said nothing.

'There are things about the investigation that aren't bound by the Official Secrets Act, but I cannot tell you because of client confidentiality. What I can tell you is my client, not the wife of the late Michael Crosier, but a British intelligence officer who was held in high esteem, not only by the intelligence services at the time but by many government officials, was also in Berlin when Crosier was killed. It's him who my colleague and I are working for. He is receiving anonymous letters – the most recent accusing him of killing Michael Crosier. He told me he didn't kill Crosier.'

'And you believe him?'

'I do. That's why I wanted to speak to Archibald Hollander. I had hoped he would be able to tell me about Crosier. Hollander was supposed to have taken over from my client, been Crosier's handler in Berlin. Instead, he became the cleaner; sent to *clean up* after Crosier's death. I had hoped he'd be able to tell me whether Crosier had been murdered, and if he had, by whom?'

Ena sighed. Although it's a moral sin for a priest to break the seal of the confessional, Father O'Broin had told Fraser that he could tell her what Hollander had told him. Ena turned and looked up at the big man. She smiled. His face remained immobile as he continued to look out to sea. Ena needed to tell Fraser about her investigation, without giving him Highsmith's name.

'So,' she ventured after some minutes, 'was it what happened in Berlin that Hollander confessed to Father O'Broin? All I've been told is that Hollander was brought to Berlin to deal with the German authorities after Crosier's death, but from where? As I understand it, Crosier was a pen-pusher at MI5 who befriended my client because he was desperate to get out of the office and work in the field. From what Hollander told you, is that your understanding of the situation?' Fraser remained tight-lipped.

'Fraser, someone set my client up. Someone pretending to

be Crosier sent my client a message asking him to meet him at a café in Berlin. Crosier must also have been set-up, because he was sent a message to meet my client at a completely different location. The following morning my client learned that Crosier had been found dead in a river running through a small town where he had no business to be.'

Fraser hauled himself from the bench and lumbered over to the railings.

Ena remained seated. It was clear to her that she wasn't going to get anything out of him and decided to go back to the hotel. 'I'd never tire of this view if I lived here,' she said joining Fraser, 'but I don't, so I shall drag myself away. I'm going back to the hotel. I'll have something to eat and get an early night. You said Captain Blair sets sail at dawn? I'll get reception to wake me. I don't want to miss the boat,' she said, attempting a joke. Turning from her surly companion, Ena walked away.

'His orders were to kill Rupert Highsmith.'

Ena stopped dead. She turned and faced Fraser. So shocked was she by the revelation that she was unable to speak. When she found her voice she said, 'Hollander?'

Fraser shook his head, 'Crosier?'

'Crosier?' Ena was hardly able to take in what Fraser had said. 'But he worked with Highsmith in London. If Crosier had wanted to kill Highsmith he could have done it any number of times. Why wait until they were in Berlin?'

'As you said, Highsmith was highly thought of. A hit on him in London would mean questions would be asked at Number ten. There'd have been an investigation if he'd been killed on home ground.'

'I see. Or do I? But Crosier was in Berlin at Highsmith's request.'

'That's right. It couldn't have worked out better for Crosier. You told me yourself, he was a pen-pusher who was desperate to work in the field. It was a good cover.'

'Rupert thought that by getting Crosier a placement in Berlin he would be doing him a favour and, although Berlin was a dangerous place, the job of observer was relatively safe.'

'Someone has been planning Highsmith's death for a long time!'

'Tell me,' Ena said, 'Highsmith was in Berlin for two weeks and apart from going to the Games his brief was to mix with Berliners, find out if they'd been taken in by Joseph Goebbel's propaganda machine. Highsmith could have been killed at any time. Why wait until after the Games?'

'Nothing was to sully Hitler's Olympics. The Games happened for one reason only, to give Adolf Hitler the opportunity to show the rest of the world how efficient Nazi Germany was – and through the media prove to people from forty-nine different countries that there could be a master race. Berlin was packed with people from all over the world. Not only the British but the rest of the world had to see the splendour of Hitler's perfect city, perfect stadium, airport; the Nazi dream. The Nazi Party had to be seen to be squeaky clean – and the people who wanted Highsmith out of the picture knew that.

'When the Games finished and Nazis who had been brought in from other parts of Germany returned home, the law enforcement agency were left to police thousands of tourists. They were stretched to the limits, which is why they would sweep the murder of a British intelligence officer under the metaphorical carpet and call it an accident.'

'Which was exactly what they called Crosier's murder.' Ena turned around and, leaning her back against the railings, looked up into Fraser's face. 'Who was it that wanted Highsmith out of the picture? Which government? The Germans or the Russians?'

'The British.'

TWENTY-SIX

Six members of the British government wanted Rupert Highsmith dead.

Fraser's words reverberated in Ena's ears. She knew that while working for MI5, Highsmith had also worked for Stanley Baldwin from 1935 to 1937 – the Prime Minister's third term in office. She also knew from reading her late colleague Stanley Parfitt's diary that Baldwin – like many other world leaders, had initially wanted to placate Hitler.

'Was it because Stanley Baldwin wanted to appease Hitler; he was doing his best to accede to Hitler's demands? I mean, Baldwin had once publicly acknowledged Hitler's achievements, calling him a remarkable man?'

'No. Quite the opposite. It was because of Highsmith that Baldwin had begun to change his mind about Hitler. Baldwin was quoted as saying, "Hitler is a ticking time bomb." Until then the PM had advocated international disarmament, but the intelligence Highsmith sent him from Berlin during the Games was so damning of the Nazi Party that Baldwin changed his mind. Baldwin had enemies within his own party. Far right members of Parliament, Hitler supporters who wanted a new order. It was them who planned the assassination of Highsmith because they thought he had too much influence over Baldwin.'

'Which he did, thank God.'

'Let's walk,' Fraser said, as a young couple who Ena had noticed earlier, claimed the bench that she and Fraser had vacated.

When they had put enough distance between them that they would not be overheard, Ena said, 'So who killed Michael Crosier?'

'Archie Hollander.'

'Hold on. Are you saying that the man who was sent to handle the German authorities after Crosier had been killed was also his killer? Did he return to England after killing Crosier and go back to Berlin to deal with the authorities?'

'Aye.'

'Good Lord, wasn't flying in and out of Berlin *twice* in such a short space of time risky?'

Fraser shook his head vigorously. 'Hollander travelled under an alias. He was a professional. No one except himself, Colonel Smith and Prime Minister Baldwin knew Crosier's cover had been blown.' Ena was about to ask Fraser to explain, when he said, 'Crosier was a 'sleeper agent'. East German, trained by the KGB under deep cover. He got married in London, bought a home in London, even had a child. Then, after working as an architect he got a job at MI5. He appeared to all who knew him as a quiet unassuming chap who pushed paper around all day. The least likely person at Five, or anywhere else for that matter, you'd think was an assassin.'

'What about the members of Parliament who tried to oust Stanley Baldwin?'

'They were told Crosier had been drinking, an argument ensued between him and a couple of local men which ended up in a fight and Crosier falling into the River Dahme and drowning.'

'Surely they wouldn't believe that?'

'What they believed was immaterial. They were in no position to dispute it. They dropped off the radar one by one after Crosier was killed. Of the traitors we knew about, one was killed in a skiing accident in Austria. One guy was elderly and retired, one became seriously ill and was on long-term sick leave – not expected to return to the House or stand at the next election, and the one we knew as Lord X was thrown from his horse while out riding and died in the ambulance on the way to hospital.'

'Is that true?'

'No. A deal was made with Lord X. For the information he gave us, he got a one-way ticket to Moscow and enough money to live out his days in comfort in a villa overlooking Lake Baikal. He was not only the whistle-blower, he was a sleeper. Probably recruited by the KGB in East Berlin around the same time as Crosier, though he said he'd never met Crosier. But no matter. He had been a Member of Parliament for two decades but the KGB didn't activate him until 1936 when Stanley Baldwin, thanks to Highsmith, began to realise that Adolf Hitler was a warmonger. It was then that Lord X received orders to disrupt Parliament, divide the Conservative party – right and far right – cause as much dissension as possible and find someone to take out Rupert Highsmith.

'Hollander told me that only Lord X knew that Crosier had been sent to Berlin to kill Highsmith and that Crosier had been killed instead. No one else knew the truth. It was too dangerous. They were all aware that knowledge of that kind could get you killed. Before he left England, Lord X told Hollander that after killing Highsmith, the plan was to assassinate Prime Minister Baldwin.' Fraser let out a gruff laugh. 'It was a monumental cock-up on their part.' Fraser's neck and face turned the colour of beetroot. He cleared his throat. 'Excuse my language. Baldwin's would be assassins jumped like rats from a sinking ship after Crosier's death. Apart from Lord X no one except Hollander and later, Baldwin – knew there was a plot to assassinate the Prime Minister, except,' he leaned towards Ena, 'your guardian angel at GCHQ, Colonel Smith.'

Ena smiled at the title Fraser gave the colonel. 'If the information in the last drop that Highsmith sent to Stanley Baldwin hadn't got to him... Well, it doesn't bear thinking about. Archie Hollander did a lot more than save Rupert's life.' Turning her back on the wind blowing into the harbour from the sea, Ena said, 'I'm sorry Hollander's dead. I would have liked to have met him. He sounds like an amazing man.'

Fraser shrugged. 'He did his job, no more.'

Ena didn't agree, but Fraser had known Hollander and she hadn't. She looked up at the sky. Grey clouds hid the sun and a strong wind whipped the tops of the waves, white. She shuddered as if someone had walked over her grave.

TWENTY-SEVEN

The smell of smoke and oil filled Ena's nostrils as she once again entered Glasgow's Central Railway Station. She wrinkled her nose. 'Scotland's mainland is a bit different to Mainland Shetland.'

Fraser chuckled. 'It is that.'

She stopped to check the timetable. 'The train leaves in five minutes,' she said over her shoulder. When there was no reply she turned round. Fraser had gone. She circled a group of school children listening to their teacher give a potted history of steam trains. 'Fraser?' she shouted. Ena could see the big man exiting the station cafeteria. 'Fraser,' she shouted, running towards him, 'I thought you'd left without saying goodbye.'

He held up a white paper bag. 'I've got you a couple of sandwiches for the journey and a bottle of lemonade.' He looked up at the station clock. 'You'll need to put a spurt on if you're to catch the train. Platform five,' he said, leading the way. 'Come on or you'll miss it.'

The ticket collector was closing the train's doors as Ena and Fraser ran down the ramp and onto the platform. Fraser opened the first door they came to, took her overnight bag from her and threw it in. Ena leapt in after it. He passed the sandwiches and the lemonade to her and when the platform attendant blew his whistle, pushed on the door until it was securely closed.

Ena pulled down the window. 'I should like to tell Highsmith that Archie Hollander saved his life in Berlin. You see, he blames himself for Crosier's death. Highsmith believes Crosier was killed to stop them from meeting up. I think Rupert deserves to know the truth?' Fraser made no comment. 'He has been carrying the guilt of Crosier's death around with him for twenty-four years. If I tell him the truth, it won't go any further.' Fraser's brow furrowed. 'I also feel he should know that because of him, those who would have brought the government down and seen Hitler in power were stopped.'

Fraser nodded. 'And Crosier's widow?'

'I won't tell her. I may not tell her anything at all. We still don't know who's sending Highsmith anonymous letters. Until I can rule her out, she's a suspect,' Ena said. 'If she's innocent I'll say that there was an altercation between her husband and another man resulting in her husband being killed. I won't tell her the real reason he was in Berlin. There's no point in taking away the love she had, and still has for him. I'll tell her that the man who killed her husband is dead. I won't tell her about you or Father O'Broin.'

Fraser smiled. It suited him, Ena thought. 'I'm sorry Archie Hollander is dead. I think I would have liked him.'

'You? Like a man who killed in cold blood?'

Ena laughed. 'You shouldn't believe everything Colonel Smith tells you. But yes,' Ena said, 'by killing one man, a traitor, Archie Hollander saved the lives of thousands of men and women. If it hadn't been for him and Highsmith, men like them, and the intelligence they supplied the British government in the war, Operation Sea Lion may have come to fruition and Adolf Hitler would have moved his mistress, Eve Bron, into Blenheim Palace, the family home of his old Nemesis Winston Churchill and we'd be slaves now. Instead, the people of Great Britain are free.'

Ena felt emotion form a lump in her throat. 'I can't imagine how hard it must have been for Archie Hollander to live with what he'd done, but I'm sure your friend, Father O'Broin, helped him to come to terms with it.'

The whistle blew again, the train lurched and then began to slowly chug forwards.

'Thank you, Fraser,' Ena said to the bear of a man standing before her.

The big Scotsman gave Ena one of his rare smiles, turned and walked away.

Ena watched Fraser until he was consumed by smoke and steam. She then wiped tears from her eyes and pushed up the window.

Ena found her compartment. It was empty. She sat next to the window, facing forward, as she always did if she had a choice. The train chugged its way south through Glasgow's central and southern suburbs. She was tired. She needed sleep, but there was so much information to evaluate. The most important being that Michael Crosier had asked to go to Berlin, in August 1936, to kill Rupert Highsmith. When Highsmith recovers, Ena decided she would tell him that Hollander had saved his life. She smiled, wondering how much of what Fraser had told her about Hollander was really himself. Her gut instinct told her that Fraser *was* Archibald Hollander. That information, she would keep to herself.

The rhythmic chuffing of the steam locomotive soon left the high-rise apartment blocks and the back-to-back tenement houses of Glasgow behind and sped through Scotland's scenic landscapes; its lochs and mountains, and its dense woodlands.

Ena closed her eyes and allowed the warm sun to bathe her eyelids.

A clunking sound as the train switched tracks woke Ena with a start. The landscape, still beautiful, was probably Northumberland. She took the sandwich Fraser had bought her on Glasgow station from its paper bag and began to eat. The edges had started to curl, but it tasted good. She hadn't realised how hungry she was and devoured it in no time.

TWENTY-EIGHT

Artie opened the door to the sitting room of Rupert's Knightsbridge flat. *His* and Rupert's home, he reminded himself. Rupert had lived there for a decade before Artie moved in, but insisted that it was his and Artie's flat. There was a stillness, an eerie silence about the room. Even the traffic on the Brompton Road couldn't be heard. Artie looked around. The warm brown colour of the leather chesterfield and winged armchair appeared cold. A brass standard lamp stood in the corner. Brass ornaments brought home from a trip to Turkey when Rupert had worked out there took pride of place on the top of his bureau. Everything about the room said Rupert, was Rupert. Even the champagne cooler – a recent purchase that Rupert had said was *the latest thing* – sat empty on top of the drinks cabinet, its four sculptured holes unfilled. A neighbour had taken delivery of a box containing six bottles of Moet & Chandon Brut Imperial. Artie had thanked the neighbour and brought the box in, stowing it in a cupboard in the kitchen out of the way. Later he would take a couple of bottles from the box and put them in the refrigerator so they would be chilled and ready when Rupert came out of hospital. That would be the first thing he'd do. Pop the cork on a bottle of Moet and pour two glasses to toast Rupert's homecoming. Artie burst into tears.

When he had recovered, he began in earnest to look for the telephone number of Rupert's twin sister. Rupert had told Artie how close they'd been as children, but they had drifted apart when they grew up. 'Agh!' Her name was on the tip of his tongue. Her name will come he told himself, as he recalled what he knew about her. She was a veterinarian and she had met her husband, also a vet, while they were both studying at college. They had married, moved to Kent and set up a veterinary practice there. Artie wracked his brains – gone through the alphabet in an attempt to recall Rupert's sister's name – but to no avail.

He pulled down the top of the writing bureau, took out Rupert's personal telephone book and opened it. A small black and white photograph fell out of one of the compartments. He lifted it up to see a skinny boy with fair hair in dark swimming trunks that were too big for him. He could tell by the boy's eyes that it was Rupert when he was a child. Standing next to him was a girl in a bathing costume, wearing a straw sunhat. He turned the photograph over and read the inscription on the back – Me and Sis. Bournemouth.

Artie returned the photograph to the cubby hole it had slipped out of. He felt like a thief going thought Rupert's private things. The bureau was never locked. It was understood that, like the drawers in Artie's writing desk, the contents were private. Artie stared at the telephone book and then flicked through it until he got to S. He hoped there would be an entry that said, Sister's number. There wasn't.

Now there was nothing for it but to look through the entire book and hope his sister's name jumped out at him. He began with A and worked his way through. The last entry was in W. Wallace. Laura and Ted. Market Downton, Kent. Tel: 78788.

Artie inhaled with relief and dialled the number. The telephone rang for what seemed like an eternity. He was about to put down the receiver when a clipped voice came on the line.

Market Downton, 78788.

'Hello? Mrs Wallace?'

'Yes.'

My name is Artie Mallory. I am... I'm...' *Oh, God, who am I to this woman. Has Rupert told her about me? If he has, what has he said? There is no second guessing what he may or may not have told his sister. Keep it professional. Artie thought.* 'I'm calling on behalf of Rupert...' Artie heard the woman gasp.

'What is it, Mr Mallory? Is my brother in trouble?'

'No, not in trouble. I'm afraid he's been in an accident and is in hospital. I thought you'd like to know.' Artie bit down on his bottom lip. Like to know? You fool, he chided.

'Is he badly injured, Mr Mallory?'

'Yes, I'm afraid he is, but the doctors are hopeful—'

'I'll be there in two hours,' she said and hung up, leaving Artie listening to the sound of a disconnected line.

He replaced the receiver on its base, returned the telephone book to its compartment and closed the bureau.

Rupert's doctor at St Thomas' had insisted after Artie had been at Rupert's bedside all night that he go home and get some sleep. Artie had no intention of sleeping in case the hospital telephoned, but he would lie down and rest. His eyes felt gritty. He blinked rapidly to moisten them and left the sitting room yawning. Wandering along the passage, past the kitchen on one side and bathroom on the other, he entered the bedroom he shared with Rupert. The room, decorated in light cream wall-paper with small bunches of blue field flowers, light modern furniture, and cream bedding was neat and tidy. Artie kicked off his shoes and dropped onto his side of the bed, exhausted. Hot tears forced their way out of the corners of his eyes; a warm steady flow to his temples, his hair and onto the pillow. He turned from lying on his back to his side and pulled on Rupert's pillow until he could tuck it under his chin.

He buried his face in the pillow and inhaled the scent of the man he loved. He imagined he could smell Rupert's cologne and for a while he felt almost content. Bringing his knees up he wrapped his arms around Rupert's pillow and drifted off to sleep.

Laughter and chatter filtered into the room. Friends calling good night to each other and see you tomorrow. He put his arm through Rupert's arm and they walked jauntily from the Lamb and Flag to where the car was parked. It was suddenly very dark, a heavy mist, as heavy as lead swirled around Artie's legs. Artie couldn't move. No sooner had it become dark than it was light again. A harsh bright light shone behind them, making gangly elongated shadows of their bodies along the road.

A second later Rupert pushed Artie away from him with such force that he fell into a doorway. Before he could ask what was going on he heard the roar of a car's engine followed by a sickening thud as the car powered into Rupert, the bonnet of the car lifting him off his feet and tossing him in the air. Artie watched as Rupert, like a rag doll, fell to the ground.

'No! no, no, no,' Artie cried. He pushed himself up from his place of safety and ran to Rupert's broken body. There was blood coming from Rupert's head, one arm was at a right angle, it looked as if he was reaching out to Artie and his legs stuck out of the lower part of his torso at odd angles. Artie fell to his knees, lifted Rupert's head and shoulders and kissed his bloody forehead. Cradling him in his arms, he begged him not to die. 'No!' he shouted, as two huge men in white coats took Rupert from him.

'Out of the way!' they shouted and lifted Rupert onto a stretcher.

'Stop!' Artie cried. 'His arm is hanging down.' Artie gently

lifted Rupert's arm, the arm he had reached out to him with, and laid it on the stretcher at Rupert's side.

'What's your friend's name?' one of the men asked.

'Rupert,' Artie cried. 'His name is Rupert.'

Somewhere in the distance a bell was ringing. Short bursts of two rings, then silence, then two more bursts. 'Rupert?' Artie shouted so loudly he woke himself. He tried to sit up, but was tangled in the sheets. Frantic to rid himself of his restraints, he struggled until he was free and pushed himself up into a sitting position. Breathing heavily and covered in sweat he looked down at his clenched fists. He opened his hands and stared in disbelief. There was no blood. He looked around the room. There was no Rupert and no car. He had been dreaming.

Artie took several deep calming breaths to recover. He looked to his right, to the side of the bed where Rupert slept, and traced the ruffled counterpane and crumpled eiderdown up to Rupert's pillow. There was an indent where his head had laid. He would wash the sheets and pillowcases before Rupert came home. There wasn't time now. He would just straighten them. He slid off the bed, pulled back the eiderdown and counterpane and pulled the sheets on his side of the bed level. He went round to Rupert's side of the bed and did the same. After plumping up the pillows he made the bed, turning the top sheet over like a cuff to show the pillows. He then pulled up the counterpane to cover the pillows and gave the eiderdown a shake. He walked around the bed to check the eiderdown was level. At the bedroom door, Artie looked back and prayed that Rupert would soon be back in his own bed.

Artie heard the bell again. Ding-dong, and immediately afterwards another ding-dong. This time the bell wasn't in his dream. Someone was at the door.

TWENTY-NINE

Artie closed the bedroom door and ran along the hall. He was about to open the front door when he heard a key turn in the lock. A second later the door opened and a middle-aged woman, a female version of Rupert, stood in front of him.

'I'm sorry,' she said. 'How rude of me to use my key. It's just that when the door wasn't answered...'

'I'm sorry about that. I hadn't realised how tired I was. I only intended to close my eyes for a minute, but I fell asleep. Come in... Laura?' Artie stood to one side to allow Laura to enter.

After shaking Artie's hand, Laura dropped the house key that Rupert had given her into a silver dish on the hall table. 'I was in such a flux, I forgot to ask you where you were calling from and when the door wasn't answered when I rang the bell, I thought you had telephoned from somewhere other than Rupert's flat. Sorry,' she said, 'there I go again. I meant, yours and Rupert's flat.'

'There's no need to apologise,' Artie replied. 'Rupert lived here on his own for some years before I moved in.' Artie took Laura's case out of her hand. 'I'll put it in the guest bedroom.'

'There's no need. I won't be staying. I also realised after I'd hung up that I hadn't asked you which hospital Rupert was in. I came here on the off chance you were here.'

'He's in St Thomas.'

Laura nodded several times, slowly. 'Tommy's is a very good hospital.'

Artie detected a sadness in her voice. 'I'll use the bathroom, freshen up,' she didn't wait for Artie's reply, 'and then I'll get going—'

'Laura?' She turned and faced Artie. Her eyes were wide and glistening with tears. 'Rupert would want you to stay here.'

'I left my husband telephoning the Grosvenor Hotel. He'll have booked me a room by now. Besides, at a time like this, you don't want me under your feet.'

'You won't be under my feet. Since the accident I've been staying with my colleague, Ena and her husband, Henry, in Covent Garden. Not that I've spent much time there. I've been at the hospital. Laura, if you wish to be on your own, stay here and I'll go back to their flat, which they are expecting me to do anyway.'

'I thought it would be less trouble for you if I stayed at the Grosvenor.' Rupert's sister now spoke without the air of authority she had demonstrated when she first arrived.

'I shall put your case in the guest room in case you change your mind about staying here and we'll go down to St Thomas' together. But first, I'm going to make you a cup of tea.'

'Thank you,' Laura said over her shoulder before turning into the bathroom.

By the time Laura had finished freshening up, Artie had made the tea and spread the condiments out on a low mahogany table in the sitting room. He looked up as the door opened. Laura, her hair combed and her make-up refreshed, lowered herself onto the chesterfield. Artie poured her tea and pushed the tray holding the milk jug and sugar bowl towards her for her to help herself. 'I'm sorry we don't have any food in. We have biscuits, if you'd like?' he said, getting to his feet.

Laura shook her head. 'I couldn't eat anything.' She took a sip of her tea. 'This is very welcome.'

'When we've finished, we'll go down to St Thomas'.'

Laura swallowed the last of her tea and put the cup down on the saucer. Standing up she placed the used crockery on the tray.

'I'll take that.' Artie took the tray out of her hands. 'It will take me one minute to wash these up,' he said, heading for the kitchen. When he returned, Laura was tying a silk scarf around her neck.

'Ready?'

'As I'll ever be.'

Artie picked up the spare key that Laura had left in the dish and gave it back to her.

Her brow furrowed. 'Are you sure?'

'Of course I'm sure. Rupert would be angry with us both if he thought you were staying in a hotel when you could be staying here. I shall go back to Ena and Henry after I've been to the hospital.'

'You don't have to stay with your friends tonight, not if you'd rather be here. I'll be in the guest room, so I won't disturb you.'

Artie nodded. It would make sense. 'Thank you.'

The nurse gave Artie a warm smile. 'Hello,' she said. 'The doctor is in with Rupert. Would you mind taking a seat? He won't be long.' She smiled at Laura. 'Are you a friend of Rupert's?'

'I'm his sister.'

'Another sister? How many sisters does Rupert have?'

'Mrs Wallace is Rupert's twin sister,' Artie said, quickly.

The nurse squinted at Laura and said, 'Because you have the same colour hair you look more like Rupert than your sister does.'

Before Laura could ask who Rupert's other sister was, Dr Freeman came out of Rupert's room. Seeing him, the nurse excused herself from Laura and Artie, and said something to the doctor that neither Artie nor Laura could hear. When she had finished speaking, with a broad smile Dr Freeman walked over to Artie and shook his hand. 'Mr Mallory.' He then smiled at Laura. 'You're Rupert's twin, I'm told?'

'Yes. How is my brother, Doctor?' Laura asked in an authoritative tone.

'He isn't out of the woods by a long chalk, but he is improving. We're keeping him heavily sedated as he has multiple injuries.'

'What are they, the injuries?' Laura asked.

'His external injuries are a broken right hip and several small fractures to his right leg. His left leg is broken in several places. He sustained a head injury which we don't want to investigate until the swelling has gone down.'

Laura put her hands up to her mouth and gasped in horror.

'Mrs?'

'Wallace,' Artie offered.

'Mrs Wallace,' the doctor said softly. 'Your brother has a long way to go but,' he looked at Artie, 'as I have told Mr Mallory, Rupert is extremely fit for his age. His heart is strong and my colleagues and I think, while he probably won't play rugby again,' the doctor chucked at his own joke, 'we are confident that if there are no underlying problems that haven't shown up on the X-rays – and he has had several now – he should, in time, recover.'

Laura exhaled with relief. 'Can I see him?'

'Yes, of course. But, Mrs Wallace,' the doctor said, restraining Laura gently by loosely holding her arm, 'as I explained to Mr Mallory and your sister when Rupert was first brought to us, prepare yourself to see a very sick man.'

Laura nodded. 'I am prepared.' She turned to Artie. 'Shall we?'

THIRTY

Having slept most of the way from Glasgow Central to Euston, Ena, although a little grubby, felt remarkably refreshed. Leaving the train she headed for the bank of telephone boxes on the far side of the concourse.

Fishing in her handbag for her purse, she opened it and took out two shillings. She picked up the telephone handset, dialled the number of Dudley Green Associates and when the phone was answered, pushed in one of the shillings. Giving Artie no time to announce the agency, she said, 'Artie, it's Ena. I've just arrived at Euston. How's Rupert?'

'It isn't Artie, darling. It's me.'

'Henry? What are you doing in the office? Is something wrong? Where's Artie?'

'Nothing's wrong, Artie's fine. He's popped over to the flat to look for the telephone number of Rupert's sister. He thinks she should be told her brother is in hospital.'

'I agree. She should be told.' There was a long pause. It was Ena who spoke first. 'Does that mean his condition has worsened?'

'No, Artie isn't telephoning her because he's worse,

although he isn't any better. Artie thought, and I agreed, that she should be told in case he takes a turn for the worse.'

'Perhaps I should go straight down to Tommy's?'

'Darling, come home and I'll fill you in with what's been happening here.'

'That sounds ominous.'

'Just come home. I've missed you.'

'I've missed you too.' Ena heard the pips signalling her to put more money in the coin box or her call would end. 'Bye. Oh, take the post...' was all she had time to say before she was cut off. She replaced the telephone handset on its cradle and left the booth.

Ena looked from the office door to the door of the flat and wavered between the two. She was sure Henry would have heard her say take the post up. If he hadn't heard her, it didn't matter. The first thing she wanted after sleeping for so long on the train was a cup of tea. She rolled her shoulders – and then a bath and clean clothes. By the sound of her rumbling tummy she needed food too, but it was the thought of a cup of tea that persuaded her to give the office a miss. She put her key in the lock of number 8a, opened the door and called, 'Hello?'

'The traveller returns,' Henry said from the top of the stairs. He ran down to her, wrapped his arms around her and kissed her. 'Welcome home, darling. Let me take your bag.' Ena kicked off her shoes, picked them up by their heels and followed Henry upstairs.

After a cup of tea, Ena took a long leisurely bath and washed her hair. She put on her bath robe, and with a towel wrapped around her head like a turban she joined Henry in the sitting room. Sitting on the rug between Henry's legs she towel dried her hair.

'I shall need to brief Artie, but tomorrow will do.'

'He telephoned from St Thomas' just after you phoned to say you were at Euston. Rupert's sister had come up from Kent and she and Artie were at the hospital visiting him.'

'Will he be coming back here tonight? I take it he has been staying here.'

'He has, yes, but I think he'll stay at the flat tonight so Rupert's sister isn't on her own.'

'That's a turn up for the books, Rupert having a sister.'

'She's his twin.'

'Good Lord! The man really is a mystery. Did the hospital tell Artie to get in touch with Rupert's relatives?'

'No, Artie knew Rupert had a sister, which is why he went over to the flat earlier. He found her telephone number and rang her. He said he thought she should know her brother was in hospital.'

'Has she got a husband?'

'I presume so. He can't have come with her or Artie wouldn't need to stay at the flat.'

'Poor woman. It must have been a shock for her.'

Henry agreed. 'Artie said she's a female Rupert. At first she seemed a bit haughty, but apparently she's taken to Artie.'

'Does she know Artie's her brother's lover?'

'I'm sure she does.'

'Artie isn't effeminate. Nor is Rupert come to think of it.'

'She's his twin, she'll know her brother is homosexual. She's probably pleased that at his age, he has at last found someone he can be himself with.'

Ena laughed. 'I don't think Rupert's ever found it difficult to be himself, but I'm pleased she likes Artie. There's nothing to dislike about him. He's a love. Did he say when he'll be back in the office?'

'No, but he has been in every day. He pops in before going

to the hospital and again at night when he gets back. I expect he'll be in tomorrow.'

'Did you know any of the intelligence agents in the Glasgow office when you were at MI5?'

'No. I worked mostly with agents from London, the south and the southwest. Why?'

'I just wondered if you'd ever come across either of the agents I went up to Glasgow to meet, 'Fraser and Hollander? They both worked out of MI5 Glasgow? Fraser still does.'

'If they were in Berlin in '36 at the time Rupert Highsmith was there, they were before my time. Why?'

'I just wondered if you'd ever come across either of them that's all.'

'As I said, before my time.' Henry laughed. 'I was at Oxford University in '36, Bletchley until 1945.'

'And then Fraser's life and his career becomes sketchy.'

'But you got the information you needed to help Highsmith, didn't you?'

'Not really. Hollander had been dead for a decade, and Fraser,' Ena couldn't help but smile remembering the big bear of a Scotsman, 'Fraser was a strange character. He took me all the way to Mainland, Shetland, to show me Archie Hollander's grave.' Ena shook her head.

'What is it?'

'I don't think Archibald Hollander was in the grave. I don't think anyone was.'

'Then what was the point of taking you to see it.'

'Fraser said Colonel Smith had told him that I wouldn't believe Hollander was dead unless I saw the grave for myself.' Ena leaned on her elbow and looked at Henry. 'Did the colonel say anything to you about Fraser or Hollander when you telephoned him for me?'

'No. He said he'd square it with Fraser that it was you going to Glasgow to meet him and not Artie. He didn't mention Hollander.'

'Hollander was a cleaner-caretaker. He was sent out to deal with the authorities after Crosier's death. And, for the sake of peace, he reported back the German authorities' version of events; Crosier was drunk and fell into the river and drowned. Verdict, accidental drowning.

'But Crosier was a sleeper. An assassin, trained by the KGP. Highsmith had been sending Baldwin intel that made Baldwin change his mind about Hitler. The PM started to meet with the military chiefs of staff and instead of disarming he ordered them to prepare for war. Highsmith was blamed for Baldwin's U-turn and Crosier was sent to Berlin to kill him.'

'Who ordered the hit on Highsmith, the East Germans or the Russians?'

'A right-wing splinter group of Stanley Baldwin's MPs.'

'Henry's mouth dropped open with shock. 'So, was it High-smith who threw Crosier into the river?'

'No, Hollander. The agent sent to clean up after Crosier had been killed, was his killer.'

'And you learned all this from Fraser?'

'Yes. There was a plot to kill Highsmith planned by the right wing of Stanley Baldwin's cabinet. The plot was leaked to Colonel Smith, who sent Hollander over to Berlin to take Crosier out before he could take Highsmith out.'

'How did Fraser know all this?'

'He said Hollander had told him before he died. I met the priest who heard Hollander's last confession too. And while he didn't disclose anything, he gave plenty away without realising. He said, while he couldn't divulge what had been said to him in the confessional, Fraser could tell me. He said Fraser and Hollander were close – and that Fraser knew as much about Hollander as he did.'

'And were they close?'

'Oh, yes! They were close alright.'

'Come on, then. What did you deduce, Holmes?'

'Don't take the mickey. Getting to the truth of a situation is as much about getting the measure of the person you're talking to, reading between the lines and picking up on a slip of the tongue as a deduction. If you really want to know what I think...?' Ena didn't wait for Henry to say he did or he didn't, but carried on, 'I don't think there was a grave beneath Hollander's headstone in the church yard. Not one with a coffin interred in it anyway. I think the gravestone in its simplicity said it all. *Archibald Hollander. Rest In Peace.*'

Henry's eyebrows met in a questioning frown. 'I'm confused.'

'I think Archibald Hollander worked for MI6. I think his life at Six ended ten years ago, but I don't think he's buried in the grave I saw, because I don't think the man is dead.'

Henry laughed. Having worked at MI5 since the end of the war and now at GCHQ – both intelligence services work closely with MI6 – he knew how all Secret Intelligence Services worked. 'Go on.'

'The SIS went to a great deal of trouble and wasted a lot of my time to keep me from finding out the truth about Crosier's death in Berlin. I was taken on a wild goose chase all the way to the Shetland Isles and shown the grave of a man who I don't believe has ever existed, except as a pseudonym. I believe the late Archibald Hollander is really Fraser.'

'It's possible?'

'It's more than possible, Henry, it's the only explanation. You know it's done all the time. I think Fraser had had enough of being a caretaker; the clean-up man for the Secret Intelligence Services and that ten years ago he killed Hollander off – metaphorically speaking – and Fraser was reborn. I expect, if Fraser's file wasn't classified "top secret – eyes only" and the early years of his career weren't blacked-out it would read,

"Fraser, alias, Archibald Hollander..." So,' Ena continued, 'that is why there's a headstone. And that is what I shall tell Artie and Rupert, when Rupert recovers.'

'And what about Michael Crosier's wife?'

'I shall tell her what the SIS expects me to tell her; that her husband was killed by a person or persons unknown.'

'Maybe knowing that her husband's killer has been dead for ten years will help her to move on.'

'Maybe,' Ena said, deep in thought.

'What is it, Ena? What's bothering you?'

'Two things just don't gel. One, why is Audrey Crosier still unaccepting of her husband's death being an accident, and the other is, after all the bloody running around the security services made me do, I am still no closer to finding out who sent Highsmith the anonymous letters and photographs.'

'Photographs taken in Berlin?'

'Yes. In which case the sender has to be someone connected to Berlin in '36.'

'Or someone connected to the failed assassination of High-smith, someone who was in the right-wing splinter group during Stanley Baldwin's last term in office as PM.'

'Or someone connected to Michael Crosier? *Or someone connected to Michael Crosier*,' Ena repeated. As Artie's at the hospital, would you help me with this?'

'If I can,' Henry said.

'Would you find out how many of Stanley Baldwin's cabinet who served from 1935 to 1937 are still alive? And I'll find out as much as I can about Audrey Crosier and her son, Matthew.' Ena jumped up and moving to the door said, 'I'm going to tele-phone Inspector Powell, check that he was able to put a policeman outside Rupert's door. Whoever it was that tried to kill him in the hit-and-run is still out there.'

THIRTY-ONE

Ena woke, squinted at the alarm clock on the bedside cabinet, ignored it and turned over. Another five minutes, she thought, and reached out to put her arm around Henry. The bedclothes were pulled back, which told her that her husband was already up. She lay and listened for sounds, and heard him humming. He was in the bathroom, shaving. He always hummed while he shaved. Ena got up, put on her dressing gown and left the bedroom.

'Good morning?' she called, opening the bathroom door. Standing behind her husband Ena put her arms around his waist and snuggled into him, her head resting against his back.

Henry leaned forwards, wiped the steam from the mirror above the sink, making a porthole through which he could see and turned his head sideways to shave by his ears.

'I was hoping we could have a lie-in and...' Ena giggled at the unsaid words.

'Mmm...' For a moment they locked eyes through their steamy reflections in the mirror.

'There's nothing I'd like more, but I have to go to Cheltenham today. I spent the time you were away in the London office, but I need to get back to my own desk. Since the Soviets shot down the U-2 aircraft in May, Harold Macmillan has been having regular meetings with the military.'

'I thought it was an American problem. Wasn't the U-2 their surveillance aircraft?'

'Yes, but we've been involved from the start of the programme. We still have pilots in the United States.' Henry leaned over the basin and splashed water on his face, removing the last of the shaving foam. 'It's kicked up a major international storm,' he said, dabbing his face dry with a towel. 'The PM is launching a review of Britain's efforts to gather signals intelligence from our aircraft and submarines. And,' Henry said, turning around and kissing Ena on her forehead, 'if you want me to find out how many members of Stanley Baldwin's cabinet from 1936 are still alive, it would be quicker and easier at Cheltenham.'

Ena stood on tiptoe, lifted her head and planted a kiss on Henry's lips. 'I know... And I'd better go down to the office and look at the post. See if there's anything that needs attending to today. I have to telephone Charles Galbraith and Artie. I'll ring Artie first, before he leaves for the hospital and Charles when I think he'll have arrived at his office.'

Artie and Henry had opened the post when she was away and, by the look of the handwriting, Artie had made notes on Ena's pad. 'Bills,' she groaned. She took the letters from their already opened envelopes and read them, putting them in order of importance. The post that arrived that morning looked far more interesting. Two letters in identical blue envelopes. One was addressed to Mr and Mrs Green, the other to Mr Mallory. Ena ran the letter opener along the top of the envelope addressed to her and Henry and took out an invitation card from Jeanie McKinlay. As she read the card her face lit up. It was an invitation to the engagement of Jeanie and her physiotherapist boyfriend, Gerry Cooper. Jeanie had written a PS on the back. *It's a small gathering, just a few friends. I hope you and Henry can come.* Ena put the invitation back in the envelope. 'Lovely,' she said aloud, 'a happy occasion. Something to look forward to.' The post that had arrived earlier in the week, the dreaded bills, could wait. Dropping Artie's envelopes on his desk, she made a mental note to buy an acceptance card. She then picked up the telephone and dialled Artie at the flat he shared with Highsmith in Knightsbridge.

'Artie, it's me. How are you and Rupert's sister faring?'

'Not so badly now Rupert's conscious.'

Ena exhaled with relief. 'I'm so pleased.'

'He still has a long way to go, his doctor said, but he has opened his eyes several times. The doctors were worried that he might have lost his memory, but he knew me yesterday. He knew his sister too. Everyone involved in looking after him are delighted with his progress. He still has swelling on the brain, and needs an operation on his legs, but they don't want to give him anaesthetic until he's stronger. He's on morphine for the pain. The main thing is he's on the mend. It's going to take time, but he will get better, thank God.'

'His sister must be relieved.'

'She is. And, now Rupert's improving, she'll be able to go home for a couple of days during the week. She and her husband have a veterinary practice. It isn't only domestic animals, you see, they're veterinarians for farm animals too. As Rupert progresses she'll go home for longer and eventually work on weekdays and come up to London to see him at weekends.'

'I can't tell you how pleased I am to hear Rupert's improving.'

'His doctor said he isn't out of the woods yet, but if he carries on improving at the rate he has been doing, he'll be able to come home in about six weeks. Of course it depends on when he can have his legs set, but they are optimistic. So, Ena, tell me about Fraser? Did you find out anything while you were up in Scotland?'

'Yes. But I'm still not sure our telephones aren't being tapped, so I'll tell you when I see you. Unfortunately, I didn't learn anything that will help us with *the case we're currently investigating*. If you know what I mean?'

'Yes. That's a shame. I could call in tonight? I'm sure Laura won't mind going back to the flat on her own. I'll bring the Sunbeam back too.'

'Look, it won't take long to get you up to speed with the case, so why don't you both stop off here on your way home from the hospital and I'll make something to eat.'

'No need to make food for us. As Rupert's so much better, Laura and I are going out for lunch. Coffee will be fine.'

'If you're sure? The less I have to do tonight the better. I'm going up to Liverpool tomorrow. Driving up there will be great. I've had enough of long train journeys.'

When Ena had finished speaking to Artie she telephoned Bow Street police station and asked for DI Powell. The desk sergeant put her straight through.

'Hello, Ena.'

'Inspector, would you have ten minutes if I called into the station?'

'Of course. Is something wrong?'

'Not wrong exactly, but I'd like to know how the investigation into the hit and run's going. I'd also like to fill you in with what I learned while I was away. I have a phone call to make, but could be with you in twenty minutes.'

'I'll be here.'

When Ena had said goodbye to Inspector Powell, she dialled Charles Galbraith's office number. His secretary took her name before putting her through.

'Ena! I wondered if you were back from Scotland yet. Henry said you were up there on business.'

'I got back yesterday. How are things? Have you heard from the young woman claiming to be Priscilla's daughter again?'

'No, not a word. I should like to know one way or another, but until she telephones, or writes...' Charles sounded despondent.

'I thought, if you agreed, I'd go up to Liverpool tomorrow. Go to the address she gave you. I'll try and see her. I might even get the chance to speak to her, if that's alright with you?'

'Yes, of course it is. If only you could speak to her, find out whether she is my Priscilla's child...' Ena could hear emotion in Charles' voice. He cleared his throat. 'Thank you, Ena, thank you.'

'You're welcome, Charles. I'll go to the address you gave me, and take it from there.'

THIRTY-TWO

Ena told Inspector Powell as much as he needed to know about her trip to Shetland without going into detail or giving him names. It wasn't that she didn't trust the inspector, she did, probably more than anyone outside her husband, Artie and Colonel Smith at GCHQ, but the details were complicated and on a need-to-know basis.

'I'm worried that because we still don't know who was behind the hit-and-run, there could be another attempt on Highsmith's life. Were you able to put a policeman outside his door?'

'Yes.'

'Thank you.' Ena let out a sigh. 'Has there been any developments? Has anyone come forward?'

'A man walking towards Artie and Highsmith saw the car. But Detective Jarvis has already told you, I think?' Ena nodded. The problem was the headlights of the car were on full beam and shining in his eyes, so he didn't get a look at the driver.'

'Registration number?' Ena asked.

'No, he was more concerned that someone had been injured. And a good thing he was. He saved Mr Highsmith's life. When he saw what had happened, he instinctively ran to see if he could help. He was a first aider on the ambulances in the war and said that he took one look at Mr Highsmith and knew there was nothing he could do for him because he was too badly injured. He ran to the Lamb and Flag and hammered on the door until the landlord came down and opened up. As the man knew where Mr Highsmith was, the landlord let him use the telephone for an ambulance.'

'Can he remember anything at all about the car?' Ena asked.

'Only that it was a saloon car, it wasn't a new model, and it could have been dark green. He said he couldn't swear to it because he was more interested in getting to the man the car had hit to help him.' The inspector took a pack of cigarettes from the drawer in his desk, opened it and offered a cigarette to Ena. She took one and the inspector struck a match and lit it, before taking a cigarette for himself and lighting it.

Exhaling a stream of smoke, DI Powell continued. 'I've had uniform going door to door in the area but no one saw anything. A couple of people said they heard a commotion, but again they didn't see anything. I've also got a team going around the garages. There was glass at the scene. I'm hopeful that someone somewhere has taken a dark coloured car in for a new bumper and headlight.'

Ena knew from her time at the Home Office that enough time had passed for the car to have disappeared. 'I wish I could tell you about the investigation that Artie and I are currently working on but because of Highsmith's job...' DI Powell nodded that he understood. 'And, because he's a client and the work is confidential... Damn it!' Ena said, stubbing out her cigarette. 'You're aware that Highsmith does sensitive work at GCHQ?' Covert operations, Ena thought, but sensitive work fitted the purpose. 'I don't think it's breaking too many rules to tell you that this is not the first time someone has tried to kill Rupert Highsmith.'

'Do you think the hit and run was carried out by the same person?'

'No. An assassin tried to kill Highsmith in Berlin in '36. He bungled the job and was killed.'

'A professional?'

'Apparently.'

'He is going to be hard to find. Harder than a rejected lover, or a narrow-minded bigot who hates homosexuals. Can you think of anything that will help this investigation?' DI Powell asked.

Ena shook her head. 'The assassin had a wife and son who both live in London.'

'Could one of them be taking revenge? The wife, maybe?'

'I did wonder about a revenge killing, but I don't think so. I've met both of them and neither struck me as the type to harbour a grievance for such a long time. And yet,' Ena said, 'there was something that didn't sit right with me when I met Audrey Crosier, the wife of the would be assassin who was killed in Berlin. She was still very upset about her husband's death. It was as if she was still in mourning. After twenty-four years, it seemed a bit odd to be still that affected.' Ena stood up to leave. 'I need to do some food shopping, Artie's bringing Rupert's sister round to meet us later, and with me having been away for a couple of days the refrigerator's empty. Goodness knows what Henry lives on when I'm not at home.'

'He probably eats out,' DI Powell said, laughing.

'I expect he does,' she agreed. At the door, the two friends shook hands. The DI returned to his office and Ena headed down Bow Street to Old Compton Street, to the corner of Old Compton and Wardour Street and the Italian Grocery Store and Delicatessen where she bought rosemary focaccia, ricotta cheese, water biscuits and fresh crusty bread.

.   .   .

That night, when Artie and Laura had left, Henry told Ena he had found out all there was to know about the six members of Stanley Baldwin's cabinet who had plotted to have the PM killed. They were Nazi sympathisers who fled their posts in British politics after Michael Crosier failed to assassinate Rupert Highsmith.

'All but one of the men who plotted to have Highsmith killed and Baldwin ousted as PM are dead. The Russian sleeper who gave up his co-conspirators, if he is still alive, will be in his late eighties now, too old to take on a clandestine operation like a hit-and-run on a London street.'

'But not too old to order a contract killing,' Ena said. 'What about Highsmith? Did you find out what he had been working on?'

Henry poured two glasses of Teachers' whisky and lit a cigarette. Ena didn't want one.

'I did,' he said, handing Ena her whisky. After taking a sip, Henry put his cigarette in the glass ashtray on the coffee table and took a buff A4 envelope from his briefcase. He tucked the nail of his forefinger under the sealed flap, ran it along the top of the envelope until it was open and pulled out several sheets of A4 paper. He had never taken documents out of the office before and rarely spoke to Ena about his work. Not because most of the communiqués that came across his desk were classified top secret, which Ena was fully aware of, as she herself had been in the same situation when she worked at the Home Office – but because working for MI5 and GCHQ since leaving Bletchley Park at the end of the war, he preferred to leave work in the office.

Bending the paper over and running the palm of his hand along the fold to make a crease so Ena could see immediately what he wanted her to read, he passed it to her.

'Pamela Beha, CIA? So, Highsmith has been working with

the CIA since the Russians shot down the U-2 glider earlier in the year. If it was the Russians?' Ena questioned.

'Agent Beha couldn't actually prove it was the Russians, but she knows, as Highsmith does, that it was.'

'This is bad,' Ena exclaimed, still reading.

'And, according to Beha, it's going to get a whole lot worse for US intelligence,' Henry said.

THIRTY-THREE

As Ena began to read the paragraph at the top of the next page her eyes widened in disbelief. 'Is this a transcript of a press release?'

'Yep! And it's going out soon.'

Ena read on. '"*These men are going to reveal the Western SIGINT activities concerning the interception of the communications traffic of Western allies.*" That'll mean our allies, our military and our crime agencies will be exposed, as well as the intelligence agencies of God knows how many other countries.'

'SIGINT collects foreign intelligence from forty or more countries and NSA routinely reads the communications. And, speculation that there were sexual deviants involved has already generated intense press coverage.'

'Good Lord! Senior civilian and military officials of America's National Security Agencies must be pulling their hair out.' Ena looked up from the condemning document and met Henry's eyes. 'Do you know the cryptologists who are defecting to the Soviet Union?'

'Know of them, but I haven't met either of them.' Henry looked away from her before casting his eyes down.

'What is it? Do you know someone who's involved in this? Henry?' Ena persisted. Henry took the paper from Ena and turned it over.

'Read the paragraph that's underlined.'

Ena read as Henry directed. When she had finished the paragraph, she said, 'Someone at GCHQ is involved with the cryptologists? Someone is helping them to defect? But who?' Ena took a sharp involuntary breath. 'No, no, no. Not Rupert Highsmith. He would never... Would he?'

'I don't know.' Ena shot Henry a look filled with rage. She was about to jump to Highsmith's defence when he said, 'No! I don't think so, but I need proof. Let me play devil's advocate. There are two possible scenarios here. One, that Highsmith is involved.'

'But you don't believe he is.'

'Ena, let me finish. We had intelligence some time ago that hinted that defections were brewing. And, because Highsmith *volunteered* to go undercover some of CIAs agents thought it suspicious.'

'I wouldn't have thought it suspicious. Highsmith was a cryptologist in the war. It made sense for him to go undercover.'

'He was, yes, and it did make sense.' Ena began to speak, but Henry put up his hand. 'The problem was, Highsmith wasn't a team player, he never has been, and, it wasn't personal, but at first he didn't want to work with agent Beha.'

'Who wants to work with the CIA?'

'*So*, to clarify,' Henry said, ignoring Ena's comment, 'Highsmith volunteered to work undercover. He flew solo at first, working on a small codebreaking job. Then he was moved into the same building as the American cryptologists and, because of his background, he got to know them and eventually they began to trust him.'

'What are you thinking, Henry?'

'Highsmith was cagey about the work he was doing with Six

and according to Agent Beha he kept her out of the loop a couple of times; kept what he was working on close to his chest. I'm afraid that if he had become involved with these men – in any way—'

Ena shook her head vehemently, picked up her glass and knocked back her drink, banging the glass down on the coffee table. She took a cigarette from Henry's packet and lit it.

'Ena, if you listen to what I have to say for two minutes without going off the deep end, you'll understand what I mean.'

'Sorry,' she whispered.

'I don't think Highsmith is working for the Russians. I think, because he's a loner, never informed GCHQ or MI6 – and hasn't shared information with CIA, the two cryptologists have used that to make it look as if Highsmith is working with them.' Henry drank down his drink. 'He takes unnecessary risks, makes up the rules as he goes along, you know he does. He has played a double agent before to get in with enemy agents and get information from them.'

'Yes he has. It's what he does best. It's part of his job. It was part of your job once, remember?'

'All I'm saying is he's a clever bugger. He's capable of anything,' Ena began to interrupt Henry again, and again he cut her off. 'Hear me out!' he said sharply. Ena leaned back on the sofa and folded her arms in a gesture of defiance. 'If the American cryptologists found out Highsmith wasn't one of them, that he was working with Beha and the CIA, it would have been reason enough for them, or their Russian paymasters, to order Highsmith's death.'

While Ena again read the text that would incriminate Rupert Highsmith, Henry poured them each another drink. He gave Ena hers and when she had finished reading she took a drink and said, 'Highsmith is all the things you say he is, he plays a lone game and he takes risks, but he is not a double agent. He is not a traitor.'

'But if the Russians thought he was, and then found out he was gathering intel on the American cryptologists it would kill the press release stone dead. Then there would be no time to tell the world why they were defecting. What better reason to take Highsmith out?'

'None.' Thoughts flooded Ena's mind. 'To order a hit on Highsmith is one thing, but the Russians wouldn't bother about discrediting him by sending him anonymous letters and suggestive photographs, would they...?' Ena let the question hang.

Henry exhaled loudly. 'No, they wouldn't do that. Unless...'

'Unless what?'

Henry's brow creased in thought. 'Unless by discrediting him it made the intelligence services doubt the information that he'd already given them. Make them believe he was being blackmailed, so they would doubt the intel and his loyalty. There has been gossip and innuendo hanging over Highsmith for years.'

'And what about facts! There were Soviet spies in top jobs at MI5 and the Home Office for years,' Ena said, 'but Rupert Highsmith? No! Rupert is not a spy.'

THIRTY-FOUR

Ena sat in the car on the opposite side of the road from number twenty-seven Meridian Street, Liverpool, going over the conversation she'd had with Henry the night before, and wondering if the Russians were behind the hit-and-run that had almost killed Highsmith. If Highsmith had got too close to exposing the American cryptologists and their proposed defections – and worse still, divulging secrets that would topple some governments – it would be reason enough to kill him. But, however she tried, Ena could not see the KGB, or any other intelligence agency, sending photographs and anonymous letters.

Ena stretched out her arms, rolled her shoulders, and at the same time consulted her wristwatch. It was just after eight o'clock in the morning. A good time she'd thought to see someone leaving home for work. She assumed at the age of nineteen, Mary Hornsby did work. The time ticked by slowly and at nine o'clock with no sign of Mary, Ena turned the key in the ignition. She was about to drive off when the front door of the house opened and two girls came out giggling. Closing the door behind her, a girl with titian coloured hair skipped down the steps behind a girl with blonde hair. They had reached the pavement when the door opened again and a slender middle-aged woman with light brown hair, peppered with grey, called out to them. Both girls turned, but only the girl with red hair ran back up the steps. The middle-aged woman handed the girl a brown paper bag and she threw her arms around the woman and kissed her on the cheek.

After putting the package in a satchel that hung from the girl's shoulder, she turned to the woman in the doorway and said something before running down the steps and joining her friend on the pavement. Arm in arm the two young women walked along the street in the direction of the town.

Ena had had a clear view of the girl with red hair. Her round pretty face was framed by titian curls and her eyes sparkled when she laughed. Ena smiled to herself. She looked exactly like Ena imagined Priscilla to have looked when she was the same age. Ena blew out her cheeks. There was little doubt in her mind that the girl she had seen coming out of number twenty-seven Meridian Street was the child that her friend was made to give up for adoption.

Ena gunned the Sunbeam's engine. She waited until the girls had turned the corner before pulling out into the traffic. Indicating, she turned right where the girls had turned. The traffic was heavy, but she spotted them on the opposite side of the road, talking and laughing at a bus stop. Waiting behind several vehicles, Ena took her camera out of her satchel and snapped two photographs of the girl in quick succession before driving on.

Ena listened to the telephone ringing out. She was about to put the receiver down when it was answered.

'Dudley Green Associates?'

'Artie, it's Ena. I've just seen a girl come out of number twenty-seven Meridian Street, the address that's on the top of the letter Charles received, and she's the image of Priscilla. Same hair colour, same shaped face, smile... A woman came out of the house behind her which I assume was the girl's adoptive mother. She looks nothing like her daughter. Her features are completely different. She's attractive, but her face is narrow, she has angular features – a straight nose and light brown greying hair – and she's taller than the girl by several inches. The girl, as I said, has titian red hair and a round face like Priscilla.'

'Do you think you have enough to report back to Charles?'

'My gut tells me that I have just seen Pricilla's daughter, but I think I need to see her again before I tell Charles.' Ena thought for a moment. 'I wonder what time the girl will be back from... I don't think she was going to work. She was dressed casually, flared trousers and a floppy hat. She looked more like a student. I'll come back this afternoon and have another look at her. Any news your end, letters, telephone calls?'

'No mail today. A couple of telephone calls. One from George Darby-Bloom, she didn't leave a message, she said everything is fine with her and Betsy and she'll give you a call next week.'

'She'll have phoned about the Christmas Show that she and Betsy are putting on at the Prince Albert in December. From what I can gather it's the wartime songs and dances. The cast will be kids from the East End who go to the Drama and Dance academy that George's father left the money for. Margot's involved too, but she doesn't know it yet.'

'A wartime sing-along.'

'Something like that. How's Rupert?'

'Improving at a rate of knots. Last night the doctor said now the swelling's going down, he'll soon be well enough to have surgery on his legs.'

Listening to Artie imparting good news about Highsmith, Ena leaned against the glass panels in the side of the telephone box and glanced along the pavement. 'Oh my God!'

'What is it?'

'The woman I saw with the girl with red hair is walking towards the telephone box. I'll call you back.' Ena put down the telephone, opened the door of the telephone box and, leaving it to swing shut, began to cross the road.

'Excuse me?' the woman called.

Ena stopped in the middle of the road and looked over her shoulder. Seeing the woman waving at her, she walked back to the pavement.

'May I ask why you were watching my house earlier today?'

The question took Ena by surprise. She caught her breath. 'Well...' she said. She needed time to think of a good enough reason to spy on someone. She didn't have one.

The woman tilted her head. 'Well...?'

The woman had seen her so there was little point in lying. 'My name is Ena Green. I'm a friend of Mr and Mrs Galbraith. Charles and Pricilla Galbraith?' Ena paused to see the reaction the woman gave on hearing the name Galbraith.

She didn't react, but said, 'I see.'

She knew who they were, in which case she probably knew her daughter had written to Charles. 'I understand your daughter wrote to Mr Galbraith recently. I was wondering if I could meet her, ask her a few questions, with you present of course.' The woman didn't answer. 'I'm returning to London tomorrow and wondered if this afternoon would be convenient. I'm staying at the Crown Hotel. We could have tea, if you're free of course. If not, tonight, if it would be more convenient for you?'

'My daughter, Mary, gets home from college at around five o'clock. If you'd like to come to the house after we've had our evening meal.'

The last thing Ena expected was an invite to their house. 'Yes, thank you. What time would be best?'

'Shall we say, six o'clock?'

'That'll be fine for me. And again, thank you.'

The two women walked back towards number twenty-seven together. When Mrs Hornsby began to mount the steps to her house, Ena crossed the road to the Sunbeam.

'Some detective you are!' Ena chided. 'If a housewife can spot you when you're on surveillance,' she mumbled to herself as she got in the car, 'you'd better smarten up your act.'

THIRTY-FIVE

So eager was she to meet Mary that Ena miscalculated the time it would take her to drive from the hotel in the centre of Liverpool to the Hornsby house in Meridian Street. She sat in the Sunbeam and waited until ten minutes to six before making her exit and crossing the road to number twenty-seven. Taking a deep breath, she climbed the steps to the front door and rang the bell.

To Ena's surprise the door was opened by Mrs Hornsby's pretty titian-haired daughter. 'Hello, I'm Mary. Come in.'

'I'm early. I hope I'm not disturbing you.'

'No, we've finished eating.'

Ena followed Mary into the sitting room where she was met by Mrs Hornsby. 'Sit down, Mrs Green. I'll make a pot of tea.' Smiling at her daughter, she patted her on the shoulder and left the room.

'Mum said you're here on behalf of Mr Galbraith?'

'Yes, he asked me to come up to Liverpool to meet you.' Ena wasn't sure how much Mary knew about the Galbraiths and decided not to elaborate until Mrs Hornsby returned. 'What are you studying at college, Mary?'

'Art and design. I'm hoping to work in the fashion industry when I finish college. It's a bit of a way off yet. I've only been on the course a year. So far it has been the history of clothes, how fashion has developed and changed through the years. I'm glad I wasn't a teenager during the war,' she said, laughing. 'Serge and itchy cotton.'

'Don't remind me,' Ena said, laughing with Mary. 'I was about your age when the war started.'

'Were you in London in the war?'

'No. I live there now, but from 1939 until the end of the war, I worked in an engineering factory in the Midlands.'

'Must be exciting living in London,' Mary said, her eyes lighting up. 'Liverpool's exciting too. It's a smaller city, of course, but there's always something going on or somewhere to go. There's a lot of clothes shops and the clothes are as mod as they are in London. We have coffee bars with jukeboxes, youth clubs and dances with bands. The latest craze for lads is busking. Buskers are young men who play guitars and sing songs in the street. Almost every boy at college has a guitar. Some of them busk in the city centre. Have you heard of The Beatles, Mrs Green?'

Ena laughed. 'Yes. I've heard of buskers too,' she said. 'I might look like a square—'

Mary blushed. 'I didn't mean you were a square.'

Ena put her hand up to the side of her mouth and, pretending she was sharing a confidence, said, 'To be honest I am a bit square. I confess that my record collection is mostly jazz, but I do like modern music.'

'Records?' Mrs Hornsby said, returning with tea and biscuits. 'We could open a shop with the number of records Mary has, couldn't we, love?'

Mary grinned and said, 'Y-e-s, Mum.'

'Mrs Green, do you have sugar?'

Ena shook her head. 'Just milk, thank you.'

'Help yourself.' Mrs Hornsby handed Ena a cup of tea and put a plate of biscuits within easy reach. 'Mary?' she said, passing her daughter a cup of tea before taking her own from the tray and sitting down. They drank in silence. When they had finished, Mrs Hornsby said, 'How can we help you, Mrs Green?'

Ena liked Mrs Hornsby's forthrightness, but it had caught her off guard. She looked from mother to daughter, both wanted answers and so did she. 'As you know I'm here on behalf of Charles Galbraith.' Mary moved closer to her mother. 'Mr Galbraith would like to be sure that Mary is the daughter of his wife, Priscilla. Could you tell me the name of the adoption agency you used when you and your husband adopted Mary?'

Mrs Hornsby took hold of Mary's hand. 'This is hard for me, Mrs Green, but it's time the truth was told.' She took a deep breath and started to explain. 'Some years after my husband left us, I learned that he hadn't dealt with an adoption agency. She looked into Mary's face and smiled. 'Love, would you pop and refresh the teapot? I don't know about Mrs Green but I should like another cup of tea.'

'Mrs Green?' Mary asked.

'Thank you, yes, I'd love another.'

When Mary had left the room, Mrs Hornsby lowered her voice to little more than a whisper, 'Mary's adoption was not legal. Nor was it consensual.'

'Were you aware that the way Mary was conceived was not consensual either, Mrs Hornsby?'

Tears filled Mrs Hornsby's eyes. Putting her hand up to her mouth she said, 'No, I was not.'

Ena felt for the woman. It seemed that everyone had suffered at the hands of her husband.

'My husband was a cruel man,' she said, dashing her tears away with the back of her hand. She took a calming breath and, as if it had given her courage, said, 'I am ashamed that I didn't look for Mary's real mother, but by the time I found out what my husband had done, I loved her too much to give her up. Mary was the only good thing to come out my marriage to Reg Addison.' She shuddered when she said his name. 'I just hope that one day her real mother will forgive me, but you see I couldn't bear to lose her. I don't want to lose her now, but—'

'I know Mrs Galbraith very well and I know how much she would love to see her daughter, and have her in her life. I also know that she would not blame you for what your husband did, nor will you lose Mary.' Ena heard Mary's footsteps on the tiled floor of the hall.

'Mary doesn't know how she was conceived, Mrs Green. And I'd rather she didn't find out,' Mrs Hornsby said hurriedly. 'Ah, here she is.' When Mary entered the room, her mother jumped up and took the tray with the tea things on it from her. 'Thank you, love.'

Ena watched as Mary refreshed her cup with milk and tea, before doing the same to her mother's.

Ena took a sip of her tea. 'How long have you lived in Liverpool?' she asked.

'Twelve years,' Mary said. 'I went to infant school and the first two years of junior school in Manchester. I don't remember anything about my first school. I can remember one or two of the teachers from my junior school, but not any friends.'

'I'm sorry to say that neither Mary nor I were allowed friends to come to the house in those days, but Mary has made up for it since. The most popular girl at the Grammar School, she was. She still is popular, but she's at college now,' Mrs Hornsby said proudly.

Mary blushed. 'Mum will tell you next that I'm always out with friends. And, I am,' she giggled.

THIRTY-SIX

When she had finished her second cup of tea, Ena stood up and put the cup and saucer on the table. 'I'd better get back to my hotel. Thank you for the refreshment. It's been a pleasure meeting you both,' she said, looking first at Mary and then at her mother.

'It's been the same for us, aye, love?'

Mary nodded.

Mrs Hornsby got to her feet and offered Ena her hand, which Ena shook, before thanking her again for her hospitality.

Mrs Hornsby began to collect the used cups and saucers. 'I'll take the tea things into the kitchen, love,' she said to Mary. 'Will you see Mrs Green out?'

Mary nodded, jumped up and crossed to the door. Opening it she smiled at Ena and said, 'after you, Mrs Green.'

At the front door, Ena suddenly remembered the girl who had said she was Priscilla's daughter the year before. 'Mary, do you know a girl named Linda Bradley? She's twenty-two and lived in Manchester around the same time as you?'

Mary thought for a minute. 'Linda Bradley? The name

doesn't ring a bell, but then I left Manchester a long time ago. Why do you ask?'

'It isn't important,' Ena said, stepping out of the house into the warm September evening air. She wondered how Linda Bradley knew that Priscilla had had a child and turned back to Mary. 'I hope you don't mind me asking, but have you told anyone that you were adopted?'

Mary raised her eyes to the sky in thought. 'No,' she said quite definitely. Then, 'Oh, but last Christmas, a lad – well, he was about twenty I should think, – came to the youth club where my friend and I go. He wasn't a member, he just turned up to the Christmas party. I didn't go out with him or anything but he was really friendly and he came to the youth club a couple of times in the New Year. And,' Mary caught her breath, 'the last time I saw him he told me that he was from Manchester and that his mum had been my real mum's friend when they were teenagers.'

'It must have been a shock for you, finding out you were adopted like that.'

'I was shocked when he said his mum had been a friend of my real mum, but I already knew I was adopted. Mum told me when I left school. When we broke up for the summer, my best friend said that she and her parents were going to the continent for a holiday – France and Italy, mainly. Her parents said she could take a friend and she asked me. I asked Mum if I could go, and she agreed but said I'd need to get a passport. It was then that she told me.'

'And so you contacted your real mother's husband.'

'Yes. I wasn't going to. I thought if my real mother didn't want me when I was born, why would she want me now? But,' Mary looked over her shoulder in the direction of the kitchen, 'Mum said that she wouldn't have wanted to have me adopted. She said in those days, if a young girl had a baby and she wasn't married, her parents made her give the baby up for adoption.'

'Yes, most parents did. She's a very understanding woman, your mum.'

'She's the best. I hope one day to meet my real mother, but Mum will always be my mum. Nothing will ever change that.'

'So, will you contact Charles Galbraith again about meeting your real mother?'

'Yes. I'm not sure when. I don't want to cause any upset.' Mary looked thoughtful and then said, 'Does she have other children?'

'No.' Ena knew Priscilla wasn't able to have children because of what Mary's father had done to her, but that information was not hers to share. 'No,' she said again, 'she has no other children.'

Ena liked the understanding, caring, young woman. 'You're a credit to your mother,' she said and smiled at the girl whose red hair was the colour her friend Priscilla's hair would have been at her age, before it had become peppered with grey. Ena smiled at the young woman standing before her. It wasn't the colour of her hair that persuaded Ena that Mary Hornsby was Priscilla's child, it was her pretty round face, her ready smile – and the mischievous sparkle in her hazel-green eyes.

THIRTY-SEVEN

Ena and Artie bumped into Dan Powell coming out of the hospital's main entrance.

'Is everything alright, Inspector?' Ena asked, unable to hide the panic in her voice. 'Is it Highsmith?'

'Yes,' the DI said, 'I'm here because I have an appointment with his doctor. He's going to tell me whether his patient is up to being interviewed about the hit-and-run yet. And,' the inspector said, nodding in the direction of a uniformed policeman nearing the exit to leave the hospital grounds, 'the constable who has been on duty outside Mr Highsmith's room has just been relieved by the constable on nightshift.'

'Phew! I thought for a moment... Never mind.' Ena turned at the sound of her name being called, to see Artie waving from inside the hospital's foyer. 'I'd better go.'

Ena ran to catch up with Artie. Seeing the expression on his face, she put her arm through his. 'Don't wear that worried face when we go in to see Rupert or he'll start worrying about you and he's got enough on his plate.' Artie nodded and forced a smile.

'That's better.' Ena pushed open the door leading to the

waiting area next to Highsmith's room. The chair the police constable should have been sitting in was empty. A cold feeling washed over her. She let go of Artie's arm and stopped walking.

'What is it?'

'Where's the copper doing the nightshift?'

'Gone to the toilet?'

'Maybe.' As she said it Ena knew it wasn't likely that the policeman would go to the toilet this soon after taking up his position on guard. If he had, surely he'd have asked someone to keep an eye on Highsmith's room; make sure no one went in unless they were authorised to do so, like a doctor or nurse. Ena put her ear to the door. She heard a muffled sound and, thankful Highsmith wasn't on his own, she opened the door a fraction. A stout nurse with blonde hair that curled beneath her cap was on the far side of Highsmith's bed. She put a syringe on the instrument trolly and then checked the drip through which he was being fed. She then leaned over him and began inspecting the wires attached to the machine monitoring his heart, or pulse, or both – Ena didn't know. She hated hospitals. She'd never had a strong stomach. Visiting Highsmith was fine now he was getting better, but the night he was brought in after the hit and run... Ena winced at the memory and opened the door a little further. 'Is it alright if we come in?' she asked in a hushed voice so she didn't wake the sleeping patient.

The nurse responded with a nod. Ena watched her straighten the blanket covering the frame that kept the bedclothes from Highsmith's legs, before moving to the foot of the bed and consulting his notes.

Ena whispered thank you and stood to one side to allow Artie to enter first. She looked up at the small oblong window in the top of the machine that was monitoring Highsmith and watched the spidery spikes, like stalagmites, jabbing upwards in time with his heartbeat. She was about to ask the nurse if there was any improvement in his condition when he opened his eyes.

Seeing Artie, Highsmith smiled. He whispered, 'Hello,' in the frail voice of an old man.

To give Artie and Highsmith a moment alone, Ena turned to the nurse who was replacing the clipboard on the bottom of the bed. She seemed not to notice her patient was awake, and turned towards the door. She then stopped, retraced her steps to the instrument trolley and picked up the syringe. She left without acknowledging her patient or his visitors.

Ena felt uneasy watching the nurse leave. She looked to see what the nurse had written on the clipboard. She scanned the entries and the times. The last entry was four o'clock that afternoon. It was now five o'clock and there was no entry. Something was wrong. She went to the door. There was still no policeman in the chair outside. She looked along the corridor. The doors at the end swung open, catching Ena's eye. A police constable – probably the one who should have been sitting outside Highsmith's room – was leaving with the nurse.

Ena beckoned furiously to a young doctor who came through the doors as the nurse and policeman were leaving. 'Mr Highsmith may have been drugged or poisoned.' The doctor didn't ask for more information, but ran into Highsmith's room.

Ena flew down the corridor and crashed through the doors at the bottom. There was no sign of the blonde nurse or the policeman – if he was a policeman, which Ena doubted. She ran to the next set of doors, pushed them open and shouted, 'Stop!'

The phony PC turned and gave Ena a menacing look before striding away. The nurse didn't turn around. Keeping her head down she ran after the man. Ena chased after them. At the hospital's main entrance, the man and nurse parted company. Ena had a split second to decide which of them to follow and decided on the nurse. As she was slim and the nurse was overweight, she had a better chance of catching the nurse. Also, there was something about the way the nurse walked that was familiar. Ena hadn't seen the woman's face full on. She'd only seen her in profile for a second when she was looking down, but she was sure she had seen the nurse before.

'Inspector?' Ena shouted, surprised to see DI Powell coming out of a door next to the hospital's entrance with Highsmith's doctor.

The doctor nodded. 'Excuse me!' and ran into the hospital.

'Mr Highsmith's doctor got a call from Artie while I was with him. There was someone in his room.'

'Yes, a woman wearing a nurse's uniform. She avoided eye contact with me.'

'Didn't the constable outside Mr Highsmith's door try to stop her?'

'No,' Ena said, pointing in the direction that she had last seen the bogus policeman run. 'I don't know where he is now, but I know he isn't a policeman. The nurse went this way. I'm going after her.'

As DI Powell turned on his heels and ran along the path to the car park, Ena turned left and ran along the outside of the hospital until she came to what looked like an identical entrance to the hospital's main entrance. Above the doors was a sign saying, Day Patients – and beneath that, Staff Canteen. Ena's heart sank. Day patients meant there would be a lot of doors leading to a lot of waiting rooms, consulting rooms, even treatment rooms. She went in and tried the first door along the corridor. It was locked. She tried the second door and then the third, they were all locked. *Day patients* meant exactly that, she tutted. It was after five o'clock, the daytime departments were closed. It's the canteen then, she thought, smiling. She had no idea what time the staff canteen closed and followed the sign.

Walking briskly along the corridor she met two young nurses coming towards her. If they noticed her, they didn't care that she wasn't in uniform. On the wall at the end of the corridor was a sign with a zigzag line saying, Canteen. Ena ran up the stairs. As she neared the top, she could hear muffled sounds of chatter and laughter. She needed to know whether the blonde nurse in Highsmith's room was in the canteen. She backed down two stairs, poked her head around the lower part of the wall and straight away retreated. A nurse in the corridor was bending down, picking her cap up from the floor.

Taking several calming breaths, Ena prepared to look along the corridor again. Holding her breath, she poked her head around the corner of the stairs. The nurse had stepped away from the canteen's swing doors and was looking at her image in the glass of a door on the right. From her position at the top of the stairs Ena could see the back of the woman reflected in the glass panel of the door opposite. She watched as she put her cap back on and secured it with kirby grips that she took from her pocket. She then ran her hands down the side of her uniform to straighten it and turned to the right to look at her profile. Ena's hands shot up to her mouth to stifle a gasp. The nurse who had been meddling with the intravenous drip in Highsmith's room was Audrey Crosier.

THIRTY-EIGHT

Someone tapped Ena on the shoulder and she almost jumped out of her skin. Turning she exhaled with surprise. 'Did you get him?'

'No, we lost him,' the inspector replied in a whisper.

Ena put up her hand to stop him speaking and poked her head around the corner of the wall again. The corridor was empty. She turned back to the inspector. 'How?'

'A couple of orderlies saw me running after him and took chase. They grabbed him as he was getting into his car on the far side of the car park, but he fought them off. Knocked one of them unconscious.'

'Damn. But then it's unlikely that a couple of orderlies would be able to deal with someone like him.' He was probably trained in armed combat by the KGB, Ena thought. 'By the way. It was Audrey Crosier in Highsmith's room.'

The inspector's eyes narrowed. It was his turn to be surprised. 'What?'

'The nurse in Highsmith's room was Audrey Crosier. She's wearing a blonde wig and padding but it was her, I'm positive.'

'Is Mr Highsmith alright, do you know?'

'No idea, but Crosier didn't have a lot of time on her own before we went into his room. What about the police officer who should have been on guard outside his room?'

'A couple of the lads are looking for him. The bogus copper couldn't have taken him far. There wouldn't have been time between the shift change and you going up there.'

The sound of chatter filled the corridor as the door to the canteen opened, turning quickly to a muffled sound as it swung shut. At the top of the stairs, Ena and DI Powell stepped into the corridor as if they had just arrived, as a nurse and a sister passed them and began their descent.

Ena looked through the window in the left door, and DI Powell the window in the right. Except for half a dozen doctors in white coats and sisters in navy blue uniforms, everyone else in the room wore pale blue nurses' uniforms, white pinafores and white caps – and they all looked the same.

'Damn!'

'What is it?' DI Powell asked.

'I can't go into the canteen with you. Audrey Crosier knows me. She mustn't know I'm onto her. She was careful not to let me see her face in Highsmith's room, and I was careful not to let her see I was following her after she and the bogus constable separated. As far as she's concerned, I was following a stout blonde nurse who disappeared.'

'So, the blonde nurse is how tall?'

'Five foot six, or seven. Taller than average for a woman, but not as tall as me by a couple of inches. She's big, overweight. At a guess she'd weigh over thirteen stone, so ignore slim. I didn't get a chance to see her eyes, but Crosier's eyes are brown. And she's older than most of the nurses I've seen around here. She's about fifty-six, fifty-seven,' Ena said, scanning the faces of nurses facing her direction. Ena's heart began to beat quickly. A nurse, taller and bigger than the three nurses she was sitting with, bent down and picked up a tray from the side of her chair.

She stood up and began stacking dirty crockery, knives and forks onto it.

'See the woman who just stood up. Towards the middle of the room, three or four tables in from the counter, collecting dirty crocks?'

'I see her,' DI Powell said.

'She could be Audrey Crosier.' Ena watched as the woman with her back to the door – and Ena – sidestepped to her right past several tables holding the tray aloft. Free of the tables, she made for the counter and put down the tray. Ena bit her bottom lip, waiting for the woman to turn round. When she did, Ena could see she wasn't Crosier. 'Damn!'

'This isn't going to be easy,' the inspector said.

'Maybe not. But—'

'What is it?'

'Straight ahead on the far side of the room. The table furthest away from us next to the window. A dark-haired nurse is leaning forward talking to a man with sandy coloured hair.'

'She has her back to us?'

'And the man she is talking to is in profile.'

'I've got them.'

'There's a woman sitting opposite the man wearing a navy-blue uniform and next to her, facing us, is an older nurse with blonde hair.'

'Is it Audrey Crosier?'

'Looks like her.' Ena stood on tiptoe, pressed her nose against the glass in the door and squinted to focus better on the older nurse. 'It could be Crosier.' Ena watched as she and the sister got up and zigzagged their way to the hot beverages counter. Ena held her breath for what seemed like an age. She then sighed with exasperation. 'It isn't her,' she said, watching the two women return to their table – each carrying a tray of hot drinks and sandwiches.

'We'll never spot her from out here. We'll have to go in.'

'But she knows you.'

'She doesn't know me, sir,' Detective Sergeant Jarvis said from behind the inspector.

Ena exhaled with relief. 'Good to see you, Sergeant. The nurse who was with Highsmith when Artie and I visited him earlier is in there somewhere. She's in her mid to late fifties, stocky but shapely, wearing a blonde wig, and has brown eyes.'

'Fancy a cup of tea, sir,' DS Jarvis asked her boss.

'Yes.' Before they could enter the canteen. two nurses got up and after picking up their bags and pushing their chairs under the table, they made for the door. As they drew near, Ena held one side open and DS Jarvis held the other. When they had passed through it into the corridor, Jarvis went in followed by DI Powell. A couple of nurses on a table near the door looked up at the inspector when he entered. Neither were Audrey Crosier.

'There are so many uniforms, how the hell are we meant to see the woman among this lot?' Shaking his head, the inspector groaned. 'I'll get us some coffee.' He walked the short distance to the counter and stood in the tea and coffee queue as DS Jarvis zigzagged her way through the centre of a couple of dozen tables saying *excuse me* and *thank you* to people as they shuffled on their chairs to tuck them more tightly under their tables, some dragging briefcases and handbags out of her path.

From left to right and back again, while she waited for the inspector to return with coffee, DS Jarvis scrutinised the features of every female facing her. And there she was. She felt a surge of excitement and quickly looked away. There was no doubt in her mind that the middle-aged nurse with blonde hair, a broad face, and a cap that didn't sit right on such thick hair – or in this case, a wig – was Audrey Crosier.

THIRTY-NINE

Detective Sergeant Jarvis glanced again at Crosier, only to see the inspector directly behind her making his way through the tables with a cup of coffee in each hand. Jarvis held her breath as the inspector turned and shuffled sideways through the narrow gap between Crosier's chair and that of a nurse on the table behind.

'Your coffee, Sergeant?' DI Powell set both mugs on the table before pulling out a chair and sitting down.

Not daring to look anywhere but at the inspector, Jarvis picked up her coffee mug. Smiling, she held it in front of her mouth and, pretending to take a sip said, 'She's here.' The DI's eyes sparkled. 'You walked past her with the coffees. You almost touched her.' The inspector glanced to his right, to where he had come from. 'Don't look!' DS Jarvis ordered. 'She's facing this way.'

'Is she close?'

'Unfortunately, not. She's nearer to the door than she is to us.'

'I need a reason to get near the door too then. How's your coffee?'

'Fine. Oh,' she said, falling in to what the inspector meant. She took a drink and grimaced. 'This is awful. You know I don't like black coffee.'

Inspector Powell stood up and seized Jarvis' mug. 'I'll put some milk in it,' he said, this time going to the drinks counter round the outside of the seating area instead of through it.

Jarvis watched the DI put down her coffee mug without stopping and walk towards the exit. She chanced a quick look at Crosier. She was on her feet and moving quickly in the direction of the door. Jarvis got up and started after her. The inspector had also seen Crosier and had quickened his pace. Just then, two ambulance men came into the canteen and Crosier ran to them. 'Fire!' she shouted, before bolting for the door. The two nurses nearest the door must have heard her because they stood up and also began to shout 'fire' before running out of the canteen. Suddenly people on other tables hearing the word got to their feet. Some stopped to pick up their bags from the floor or the backs of chairs, while others pushed chairs over in their panic to get out of the canteen.

Ena groaned. The door had swung back with such force it had knocked the breath out of her. Holding her chest she stumbled along the corridor as a tsunami of people burst through the doors taking her with them as they ran down the corridor.

As the bottleneck at the exit grew to half a dozen people deep, Jarvis threw up her arms. Neither she nor DI Powell stood a chance of getting through the crowd and catching up with Audrey Crosier.

The ambulance men raised their hands.

One shouted, 'Stay calm. Don't run!'

The other, 'Walk slowly! Single file!' he ordered, but no one took notice.

No one could hear the instructions above the noise of people shouting and the scraping of chair legs on the canteen floor as they were being pushed back. A few chivalrous men pulled women to their feet, propelling them towards the exit to escape a fire that DS Jarvis and DI Powell knew was not going to be.

Jarvis joined the inspector. He was shaking his head. 'Calling fire is the oldest trick in the book.'

'It's one that I should have been watching out for too, sir.'

The staff canteen was deserted but for Jarvis, the inspector, and the two ambulance men.

'What just happened?' one of them asked.

Jarvis scrunched up her shoulders. 'I've no idea,' she said. She looked at the inspector. 'I'm going to see how the patient is.'

'And I'll find a telephone box. Good night, lads,' the inspector said to the ambulance men who were still shaking their heads at a loss as to why someone would shout fire when there clearly wasn't one.

Taking Jarvis by the elbow and walking her to the door, the DI said, 'I'd better telephone Alan Richardson at Special Branch and tell him about Audrey Crosier. He won't be happy that we've lost her.' What a bloody mess! Oh, and the constable who should have been on night duty? I almost forgot about him. While I'm phoning the branch, would you find out if he's been found?'

'Yes, sir.'

'I'll see you in the waiting area outside Mr Highsmith's room,' the DI said from the door. 'Oh, my God,' he exclaimed, 'where's Ena?'

The now familiar waiting area was deserted. A doctor swept past at a sprint and entered Rupert's room before Ena could ask him how Highsmith was. She crossed to the chair next to the door, the chair on which the policeman who had been guarding Highsmith had sat, before he was replaced by the imposter in league with Audrey Crosier. She wondered if the real police constable had now been found. She hoped he had – and she hoped he was alive.

She got up and put her ear to the door. A deep voice was speaking slowly, but she couldn't make out what was being said. Then a second person began to speak. It was a man's voice but higher vocally than the first. She pressed her ear hard against the wood, but was unable to hear.

Feeling helpless, she moved away from the door and sat down. The sudden memory of Crosier holding a syringe flashed into Ena's mind. Her heart began to thud with fear. The bitter taste of bile rose from her stomach and lodged in the back of her mouth. She swallowed hard, inhaled and held her breath for fear she was going to be sick.

God only knows what would have happened to Highsmith if she and Artie hadn't gone to see him when they did. What Audrey Crosier could have done if they hadn't walked in on her didn't bear thinking about. Ena closed her eyes and inhaled again, but felt no better.

The door to Rupert's room opened and a female doctor came out. Ena jumped up and ran to her. But, before she could ask about Highsmith, the doctor, giving her a courteous smile said, 'I'm afraid I can't stop. Mr Highsmith's doctor will come out and speak to you shortly.'

Ena nodded that she understood. However, she couldn't shake off the overwhelming feeling that something was terribly wrong. She wanted to go into the room, but instead she sat down again. A second later she was on her feet when Henry, followed by Inspector Powell, arrived.

'Dan has filled me in with what happened in the cafeteria. Are you alright?' Henry asked, wrapping his arms around Ena.

'Yes, I'm fine. It's Rupert I'm worried about.'

'Any news?' DI Powell asked.

'No.'

At that moment, the door to Rupert's room opened and

Artie came out. With his head hung low he entered the waiting area in a daze.

Ena ran to him. 'Artie?' she whispered, taking his hand. 'What is it?'

Artie lifted his head. Tears fell from his eyes. 'He's dead, Ena. Rupert's dead.'

FORTY

Overwhelmed by anger and guilt, the hollow ache in the pit of her stomach told Ena that she should have realised the nurse in Highsmith's room with the syringe was Audrey Crosier. If she had only acted sooner, Highsmith would still be alive.

'Artie, I'm so sorry. I should have recognised Crosier before she had time to use the syringe.' Ena turned to Henry. 'Look after him, darling. I need to tell the doctor that Rupert was poisoned.'

'Ena, no,' Henry whispered. He reached out to stop her, but he wasn't quick enough. Ena, determined, had disappeared into Highsmith's room before he could stop her.

'Rupert?' Someone behind her closed the door. The sharp click of the lock mechanism striking home made her jump. Spinning round she saw Colonel Smith. Then she looked back at Highsmith and the doctor. She caught her breath. 'Colonel Smith? I'm sorry, I— Does Artie know Rupert is alive?'

'Yes, he was going to tell you and Henry as soon as you were away from the hospital.'

'I see. Well, I came in to tell the doctor that I'd seen a woman dressed as a nurse holding a syringe. When I realised the nurse was Audrey Crosier, I knew she was in Rupert's room to kill him.'

'Which she would have done if you hadn't alerted a doctor to the situation.'

Ena nodded. She had at least done that. 'I expect the syringe contained a poison?'

'We think it was ketamine. She would have injected Rupert, but you coming in when you did interrupted her. She discharged the poison into the saline drip. A slower way of killing someone, but just as fatal.'

Ena went over to Highsmith, smiled at him and laid her hand on his forearm. 'You're like a cat, Rupert. You have nine lives. I'm glad you're still with us,' she said.

'But he isn't,' Colonel Smith contradicted with a jovial smile, 'as far as you or anyone else is concerned – for the time being anyway – Rupert Highsmith is dead.'

'Of course. I came in to tell you that Mr Highsmith was poisoned. I've done that, now I shall leave.' She took a handkerchief from her jacket pocket.

Colonel Smith opened the door and Ena left wiping away her tears and looking to anyone who was watching, like a grieving friend. 'Come on,' she said, putting her arms around Henry and Artie, 'let's go home.'

'I should come home with you and Henry,' Artie said, as they walked towards the car.

'Of course. We wouldn't let you go back to an empty flat on your own.'

Henry unlocked the passenger door, but didn't open it. 'Any conversation we have about Highsmith from this moment on, he's dead. There's a strong possibility that both the Dudley Green office and our flat have been bugged.' He looked at Artie. 'Your flat with Rupert too, I shouldn't wonder. So,' he repeated, before pulling open the door for Ena to get in, 'Rupert High-smith is dead!'

Artie took a shuddering breath and nodded.

The three of them were exhausted after the busy and emotional day they'd had. Ena made ham sandwiches and mugs of coffee as it was too late to cook a meal. When they had eaten Henry took a bottle of Teachers out of the cupboard and three glasses.

'I'm going to bed, Henry,' Ena said, yawning, 'I don't want a Scotch. Your bed is made up, Artie. I don't expect you'll sleep much, but the rest will do you good. Your toothbrush is where you left it last time you stayed. Anything you need from your flat you can get tomorrow.' Ena looked at Henry.

'Yes,' Henry said, pouring him and Artie three fingers of whisky. 'I'll run you over to Knightsbridge in the morning to pick up your toiletries and some clean clothes.' He passed Artie his drink.

Ena put her hand on Artie's shoulder, but spoke to Henry. 'Don't stay up drinking too long, darling, Artie needs to rest,' she said, and with a wink, left the sitting room.

The following morning Ena cooked breakfast. Artie said he didn't feel up to eating anything, but she insisted he did and when they had finished eating, Henry and Artie left for the flat Artie shared with Highsmith in Knightsbridge.

After washing the dishes, Ena went down to the office. As always, she felt a tickle of excitement when she unlocked the street door to Dudley Green Associates. She picked up the post and went through to the office. It was spotlessly clean, as always. Mrs Hardy who Ena had known some time – and who was her first client when she started the investigation agency – still came to clean the office every Friday morning. Ena was grateful to her. She was sorry too that because Mrs Hardy's cleaning business had grown, the only time she could fit in the offices of Dudley Green was between six and eight in the morning, which meant she rarely saw her. One of these mornings, she thought, I'll come down early.

Ena closed the door behind her and shivered. It felt cold, which was not surprising what with her having been away for several days to the Shetland Isles and following that to Liverpool, and Artie spending most of his time at St Thomas' visiting Highsmith.

Thinking about Liverpool reminded Ena that she hadn't updated Charles Galbraith about meeting Mary and Mrs Hornsby. She needed to make an appointment to see Charles soon as she didn't want Mary coming down to London until she'd spoken to him.

She went through to the kitchen and picked up the kettle. Empty, which was to be expected since no one had needed to make a hot drink for some time. She took the kettle to the tap and after running off what she thought would be the water that had been standing in the pipe, she filled the kettle and switched it on. While it boiled, she opened the refrigerator. To her surprise there was an unopened bottle of milk. Taking off the foil-top she sniffed. It was fresh. She smiled. Henry had thought of everything.

Having made a mug of coffee, she took it to her desk. She then took her notebook and a pen from her shoulder bag and, after taking a sip of the coffee, picked up the telephone and dialled Charles Galbraith's direct line.

'Charles Galbraith.'

'Good morning, Charles, it's Ena.'

'Hello, my dear. Priscilla and I were only talking about you and Henry last night. She was wondering when we were going to see you next. Would you give her a call when you have the time and arrange something? She'd love to see you, we both would.'

'I will. Thank you, Charles. In the meantime, I've some news for you. When would be convenient for me to pop into the office?'

'I'm free this afternoon and tomorrow morning.'

'In which case, I'll see you later. Would two o'clock suit you?'

'Make it one o'clock and I'll take you to lunch at the Café Rouge.'

'Oh, that sounds very tempting, Charles, but I have to decline your kind offer. I've been away on business for the best part of two consecutive weeks – and what with Artie spending most of his time at St Thomas' visiting his friend who was in a road accident, I've an awful lot of catching up to do.'

'Are they alright?' Ena could hear the concern in Charles' voice.

'Artie is, but...' She hated lying. Even though she was speaking to a friend who had nothing at all to do with the intelligence services, she knew she must in case the office or the telephone was bugged. 'I'm afraid his friend died last night.'

There was silence for a few seconds before Charles said, 'Give Artie my condolences, please, Ena.'

'I will, Charles. Thank you. I'll see you at two o'clock.'

FORTY-ONE

Ena took her coffee over to Artie's desk, dropped into his chair and picked up his notebook. As she drank her coffee she read through his notes. Most referred to the small bundle of letters held together by an elastic band that had come while she was in Liverpool. She took off the band and released the letters. Only two needed her attention. Both were outstanding bills. Taking the envelopes she put them on her desk, and then took her coffee mug into the kitchen and replenished her drink. On her return she took Dudley Green's cheque book and two envelopes from her desk drawer, wrote out two cheques, filled in the remittance slips for each, addressed the envelopes and stuck a second-class stamp on them both. Pushing them to the front of her desk – to post on her way to see Charles – she leaned back in her chair and finished her coffee.

The notes she'd made on Mary Hornsby were comprehensive, but needed typing up. She took the typewriter from the top of the filing cabinet to the conference table, removed the cover and lined up a sheet of carbon copy paper between two sheets of white A4 paper. Taking care to keep the sheets level, she slipped them in the typewriter, turning the roller until the papers gripped.

Ena pulled on the carriage return lever, typed Dudley Green Investigations, the address and date – top right on the first page – and then typed up her findings that proved the young woman, Mary Hornsby, who had recently written to Charles Galbraith, was the daughter of Priscilla Galbraith.

Satisfied that she had included every detail relevant to the inquiry, Ena took the last sheets of paper from the typewriter and separated the top sheet from the carbon copy. Collating both sets of documents – original and carbon copies – she went over to the filing cabinet, took out an empty folder, wrote The Galbraith Investigation on top of it and deposited the office copy in it.

Locking the filing cabinet Ena went back to the table, stacked the original copy neatly and placed it, and the photograph of Mary that she had taken at the bus stop in Liverpool, in an envelope for Charles. She looked at the clock. Almost twelve. Typing up the details of the investigation had taken her longer than she had first thought. If she was going to have something to eat before meeting Charles at two o'clock, she needed to get a move on.

Grabbing her shoulder bag, Ena checked that she had her purse and car keys before putting in the folder. She nipped into the kitchen and looked around. Anything electrical she had already switched off. Crossing the office she took her jacket from the coat rack, put it over her arm and opened the door. She had gone through it and was about to lock it when the telephone began to ring.

With a groan, Ena went back to her desk, dropped her bag and picked up the receiver. 'Dudley Green Investigations, may I help you?'

'Ena, it's Dan Powell. Alan Richardson would like a

meeting with you and Artie this afternoon. Would that be convenient for you both?'

'Not really. Unless it's late this afternoon. I was just on my way out when you phoned. I have to see a client at two and Artie isn't even here. We'll both be here tomorrow, if that's any good?'

'I'll let Alan know. If he can't do tomorrow, what time do you expect to be back in the office today?'

'Three o'clock or just after. Better tell him three thirty to be on the safe side.'

'Thanks, Ena, I'll speak to you later.'

She replaced the receiver, held her hand on it until she was certain that enough time had elapsed for DI Powell's call to disconnect, and picked it up. She was sure Artie would have come straight into the office, if he was back from Knightsbridge. She dialled the telephone number of her flat upstairs and was not surprised when it wasn't answered. After dropping Artie off at his and Highsmith's flat, Henry would have driven to GCHQ. Artie, when he had gathered what belongings he needed, would be coming back to Mercer Street by public transport.

Crossing to Artie's desk, Ena opened his diary and scribbled a short note under today's date, *Gone to see Charles Galbraith at his office. Hang on here until I return. There's a possibility that your favourite Special Branch inspector is coming here at three thirty. I suggested tomorrow would be better for us, but he may not be able to arrange his diary to accommodate.* Staring at the note she added. *It was Dan Powell who phoned. He didn't say why Richardson wants to see us.* 'Why would Alan Richardson want a meeting today?' Ena mused. *Just a thought, but maybe there's been a breakthrough in the Highsmith case.*

Leaving the pen at an angle across the open page of Artie's diary to ensure it didn't close, she picked up her shoulder bag, hooked it over her shoulder and made for the door. Who knows

why Special Branch do anything? she thought. They're a law
unto themselves.

Ena ran up to the café at the top of the street for a sandwich.
She decided on Parma ham and tomato as she didn't want to
breathe spices over Charles Galbraith. She ate in the car, before
setting off for his office.

Having parked in a visitor's bay in the car park at the back
of Charles' office, Ena went round to the front of the building
and rang the bell. The door was answered almost straight away
and she was shown into the cool foyer. A few seconds later
Charles appeared and welcomed her. In his office, he offered
her a seat.

Charles was as always, gracious and charming. He waved
away Ena's apology for being a few minutes late, picked up the
telephone and asked his secretary, Ruth, if she would make
himself and Ena a pot of tea.

While they waited for their refreshment they talked about
the weather, how it was unusually hot for the time of year.
Charles asked after Henry, and Ena asked after Priscilla. When
Ruth brought in the tea, she exchanged pleasantries with Ena.
Continuing in an amiable fashion while she poured the tea,
Ruth commented on how well Ena looked. Checking with
Charles that there was nothing else, she left the office.

'I don't know what I'd do without Ruth,' Charles said, about
his secretary of almost forty years. He took a sip of his tea.
Putting the cup back on its saucer, he leaned his elbows on the
desk, put his hands together and made a steeple of his fingers.
'It's good to see you, Ena,' he said, beaming her a smile.

'Thank you. It's good to see you too, Charles.' Ena took the
envelope containing the report on Mary Hornsby from her
shoulder bag and placed it in front of Charles.

He cast his eyes down, looked at the envelope for a long minute, and then looked back at Ena.

She smiled. 'I think you'll find Mary Hornsby is an interesting and very nice young woman.'

Charles didn't open the envelope, but laid his hands on it palms down. 'Did she say whether she is going to get in touch again, Ena?'

'She said she would, but she didn't say when.'

Charles nodded. 'Well,' he said, 'these things take time. You can't rush something as important as...' He let the end of the sentence fade and opened the envelope. Pulling out the report he began to read.

To give Charles a little privacy, Ena took her cup of tea to the window and looked out. On the other side of the street was a small park where people were taking advantage of the good weather. Office workers sat on benches eating their sandwiches, men in shirt sleeves strolled along casually, other men had taken off their jackets and thrown them over their shoulders, and women were in summer dresses. Ena was miles away watching a woman with two children eating ice creams when she heard Charles clear his throat. Turning, she saw him straightening the pages of her report. With tears in his eyes, he returned them and the photograph of Mary to the envelope.

'I'll read it later. Priscilla is going to be so very happy, Ena. She has always hoped, prayed, that one day she would meet her daughter.'

'And she will, Charles, but as I said, I thought it best not to press her for a specific date. Let her get in touch when she's ready.'

'Quite right, Ena, quite right.' He took the handkerchief from his top pocket and flicked it until it opened into a white square. 'You'll think me an old fool,' he said, wiping his eyes.

'Not at all. It's an emotional time. However, since you

haven't read the report, there is something I need to tell you before you tell Priscilla that we've found Mary?'

Charles looked up at Ena. Lines appeared on his forehead.

'It's nothing to worry about,' she said, hoping what she was about to say would put his mind at rest. 'Mary's mother, Mrs Hornsby – Hornsby is her maiden name – was married to Priscilla's landlord, Reg Addison.' Ena paused to give Charles time to take in what she had said. 'Mrs Hornsby believed for many years that her husband had privately adopted Mary. She didn't learn about Mary's birth until Addison left her for another woman. It wasn't until after she found Mary's birth certificate among papers that her husband had left behind that she knew the truth. By then she had formed a strong and loving bond – a mother's bond – with her child. Some years later when Mary needed a passport, Mrs Hornsby told Mary that she was adopted.'

'The poor child.'

'Actually, Charles, Mary wasn't, and isn't, a poor child at all. Mrs Hornsby is devoted to her. She brought her up to be strong, caring and confident. Mary is happy and bright. She is a well-rounded young woman.'

Ena glanced at her wristwatch. 'I'm sorry, Charles, I have to go. I need to be back in the office at three thirty. So,' she said, standing up, 'will you let me know when you hear from Mary?'

Charles promised he'd let Ena know as soon as Mary got in touch. He also promised he wouldn't tell Priscilla until then.

FORTY-TWO

'I see you've started without me,' Ena said. She hoped her voice conveyed the annoyance she felt. Crossing the room to her desk she dropped her shoulder bag on the seat of her chair and draped her jacket over the back of it. 'I had hoped you'd decided against having the meeting here when I found the front door locked.'

'This is a rather sensitive meeting,' Alan Richardson said. 'We didn't want strangers coming in.'

'This is my place of work, Alan, and the *strangers*, as you call them, would be potential clients.' Out of the corner of her eye Ena saw Henry cringe. 'And what are you doing here, darling?' she asked her husband. 'I thought you were going to work?'

'I'm the colonel's proxy.'

'I see,' Ena said, joining Alan Richardson, Inspector Powell, Henry and Artie at the conference table, and sitting in the only vacant chair. 'Right! What have I missed?'

'Not a lot,' Artie said, 'I've taken notes.' He passed Ena a sheet of paper with Top Secret stamped across the top in red block-capitals. Raising her eyebrows, she glanced around the table. Everyone had identical documents in front of them.

'Look at my notes,' Artie said, nodding to Ena that she should read what he had given her. 'I'll make some drinks.'

While Artie took the tea and coffee order, Ena read the document. *The office at Dudley Green Investigations is bugged* was the first line. Ena looked up at Alan Richardson. He lifted his shoulders and smiled. Ena raised her eyebrows. She didn't return his smile. *Rupert Highsmith is not dead. He has been moved to another hospital.* This time it was Henry she looked at. He winked and she shook her head. She read on. *The nurse in Highsmith's hospital room was NOT, repeat NOT, recognised by Ena Green. In each discussion take the lead from Colonel Smith or Henry Green.* Rereading the last line Ena looked at Henry again. So, her husband really was standing in for the colonel.

By the time Ena had finished reading the instructions, Artie was back. He put a tray of tea and coffee on the table, gave Ena hers and sat down with his own. 'Did they tell you Rupert is alive, Ena?'

'What? No I—'

'Rupert isn't dead.'

'But I went into his room. I saw him.'

'Because the ketamine was injected into the saline drip, not directly into Highsmith's bloodstream, the doctor you told to go into him was able to pull out the drip in his arm before the poison reached his vein.'

'But he wasn't breathing...'

'A muscle relaxant,' Henry said. 'Harmless, but effective.'

'Why say he's dead?' Ena asked, 'I don't understand.'

'To make whoever is trying to kill him think they've done the job. If it was the Russians,' Alan Richardson said, 'they'd be cocky and more likely to make mistakes.'

'And have they?' Ena asked. She looked around the table.

'No, I didn't think so. But we could be doing just that.' No one spoke.

It was Henry who questioned her. 'How, Ena?'

'What we are discussing is classified top secret.' She stabbed a finger at the document she had just read. 'Wouldn't it have been safer to have held this meeting somewhere else?' She looked at Henry. 'A secure room at GCHQ perhaps?'

'Ena's got a point,' Artie said, 'We were broken into a while ago and we found several bugs.' He looked at Alan Richardson.

'These premises are safe,' Richardson said.

Ena leaned back in her chair. When the Special Branch inspector didn't elaborate, she said, 'Alan, how do you know the office is safe?'

'Because I had the room swept for devices while you were away on business.'

Ena looked at him, couldn't help but smile and turned to Artie. 'Did you know about this?'

'No!' Artie replied curtly.

'Next time, have the decency to ask one of us. It would, after all, be the polite thing to do.'

The intended embarrassment worked and everyone in the room fell silent. It was Inspector Powell who broke it. 'Ena, you were the only one that saw the nurse in Mr Highsmith's room at St. Thomas' hospital. Did you recognise her? Had you seen her before?'

'There was something about her that seemed familiar. I was sure I'd seen her somewhere before, but to be honest,' Ena rolled her eyes, 'I didn't get a proper look at her. I'm sorry, I only saw part of her face and that was when I was behind her. I didn't even see her in profile. I thought it odd that she didn't speak to us when we went in to see Highsmith. She didn't look at me when I spoke to her, either. She kept her back to me. When I saw she had a syringe, alarm bells began to ring. Why did she need a syringe when she was checking wires and tubes? By the time I realised something was wrong she had gone – and so had the syringe.'

'As you're the only one here who has met Audrey Crosier, could she have been the nurse?'

Ena didn't answer immediately. She sighed as if she was deep in thought. 'It's possible I suppose, but...' She sighed again, and again feigned thinking. 'No!' she said with certainty. 'Crosier would be around the same height as the nurse, but she has brown hair, the nurse in Highsmith's room was a blonde.'

'She could have dyed her hair,' Inspector Powell suggested.

'Or was wearing a wig,' Henry offered.

'Yes, she could have done either of those things, but the nurse in Highsmith's room was physically wrong to be Crosier. I wouldn't call Crosier slim, but she isn't...' Ena took a few seconds to find the right word, 'big either. Crosier is much slimmer than the nurse and her shape is completely different. Crosier is pear shaped, carries weight on her hips. The nurse was a completely different build.'

'Body padding?' Alan Richardson threw in.

'Possibly. But body padding makes you look bigger all over. The nurse had a narrow waist, but big hips and backside. Bigger breasts than Crosier too. Audrey Crosier is in her mid to late fifties. I got the feeling that the nurse was younger – maybe forty-six or forty-seven.'

'My money's on Audrey Crosier,' Henry said with a crafty smile, rotating his hand as if he was winding up a toy.

'Ena?' the inspector said.

'No. I've met Audrey Crosier, I'm positive it wasn't her. Besides, what motive would she have?'

'Revenge, because Highsmith got her husband the job in Berlin and he was murdered there?'

Ena shook her head. 'No one carries a grudge around for twenty-four years before taking revenge.'

'Stranger things,' Richardson said.

'No, and for two reasons. One, Michael Crosier asked High-smith several times to get him a job in the field. I think he was bored with being a pen-pusher. But, whatever the reason, Audrey must have known about it. And, two, Highsmith didn't kill Crosier. He received a message from Crosier, or someone professing to be Crosier, asking to meet him in a café in Berlin. Crosier was killed in a small town miles away.'

Alan Richardson drained his coffee, put his document and pen in his briefcase and pushed his chair back from the table. 'Thank you, Ena.' Standing up he circled the table and, shaking her hand, pressed a note into her palm.

Inspector Powell got to his feet, did the same with his document as Richardson had done, smiled at Ena and nodded his thanks.

'I'll see you out,' Henry said, getting up and following the two men out of the office. Ena heard muffled words of farewell as the men took their leave. She looked across the room to the door. Henry didn't return.

'Do you know which hospital they've taken Rupert to,' Ena asked Artie.

'No. Richardson said it was best I didn't know.' Artie pulled a grimace.

'I know you don't like Alan Richardson, but he's right. You'd be a target if you knew where Rupert was. Bloody people!' Ena said with exasperation. 'Damn them – the spooks and the spies!'

She busied herself collecting the empty coffee and teacups. 'I'll dump these in the kitchen and lock up. You go up to the flat. Tell Henry to pour me a large Scotch,' she called after Artie as he was leaving.

When Ena was on her own, she read the note that Alan Richardson had given her. *Urgent meeting tomorrow. PS I am assured by Colonel Smith that it will be held in a secure room.* She laughed at the postscript, flicked off the lights, locked the office door and the outside door. She went upstairs pleased that tomorrow she would be able to speak freely about Audrey Crosier.

FORTY-THREE

Ena thought she heard the main office door open and a couple of seconds later, close. She turned off the cold water tap and listened, waiting for Artie to arrive in the kitchen. When he didn't appear, she topped up the kettle and took it back to the electric point. She didn't switch it on because she wouldn't hear him above the thumping and popping sound of the kettle as it heated the water.

'I'm in the kitchen, Artie!'

When he didn't reply, Ena's first thought was that a client had come in. She straightened her skirt and tugged the bottom of her suit jacket. Catching her reflection in the stainless-steel kettle, she leaned forward and looked into it. A wide mouthed grin looked back at her and she almost laughed. It was always good to greet a potential client with a smile, it broke the ice. She looked into the room from the top step of the two that led down from the kitchen into the office. There was no one there. Then she heard a metallic click. Faint, but a click all the same.

Ena's panic button engaged and she flattened herself against the ornate door on the left of the steps and looked in the direction of the sound. A woman was bending down at the side of the filing cabinet. Without making a sound, Ena retraced her steps back to the kettle.

Why would Audrey Crosier be bending down by the filing cabinet? Why would the number one suspect in the attempted murder of Rupert Highsmith be in Ena's office at all? She smiled to herself. To retrieve the listening device that she had previously planted. Alan Richardson's charade had paid off. Audrey Crosier didn't think she was a suspect in the attempted murder of Highsmith, or she wouldn't be here, Ena thought.

She flicked the switch to put the kettle on, and while it boiled took several calming breaths. Reaching up into the cupboard she took down a mug. 'I'm having a coffee before I leave, Artie, I suppose you want one?'

'Tea for me, please.'

Although Ena had seen Audrey Crosier at the filing cabinet, she was none the less shocked to hear the woman ask for tea and dropped the mug on the countertop with a clatter. She stood it upright and held on to the counter to steady herself. When her hands had stopped shaking, she made herself a mug of coffee and a cup of tea for her visitor.

Ena's heart was pounding as she left the kitchen. Determined not to look at the filing cabinet, she turned towards her desk. Audrey Crosier was sitting at it. In a black dress that flattered her figure, and matching short jacket with a satin trim, she was taking off black gloves Not exactly appropriate for a warm September day, but very appropriate for someone who didn't want to leave fingerprints on a metal filing cabinet.

'Mrs Crosier, Audrey,' Ena said, putting a cup of tea in front of her. 'What can I do for you?' A stupid question Ena thought, but she was so taken aback at the sight of the woman – the woman who had tried to kill Rupert Highsmith, at least once, sitting on the other side of her desk and playing the role of the grieving widow that she couldn't think of anything remotely intelligent to say.

'Thank you, Ena.' Crosier nodded at the cup of tea but didn't drink it. 'I hope you don't mind me calling unannounced, but you said you would let me know if you found out anything about my husband's death in Berlin, and as I was passing...'

'Of course I don't mind,' Ena said, but thought, *passing?* Damned liar. 'I haven't had time to write the report yet,' she said, 'but I will, very soon. When I have, I'll let you know if there is anything relevant to your husband's death.'

As she took a drink of her coffee the telephone sprang into life and she almost spilled it. 'If you'll excuse me, I'm expecting a call from a client,' Ena said, putting down her mug with one hand and lifting up the telephone receiver with the other.

'Dudley Green Associates, Ena Green speaking.'

'Hello, Ena, it's Alan Richardson.'

'Hello, sir,' Ena said with a smile. 'Thank you for retuning my call.'

'Listen carefully.'

'Yes...' Ena looked at Audrey Crosier and, raising her eyebrows, put her hand over the telephone's mouthpiece. 'This won't take long,' she whispered. To Richardson she said, 'Would you mind if I called you back? I'm unable to discuss your case at the moment, as I'm with another client. I'll telephone you as soon as I'm free.'

'After thinking she'd killed Highsmith, Crosier now knows he's alive,' Richardson said.

'I'm well aware of that, sir!' Ena brought to mind the image of Crosier bending down at the side of the filing cabinet to remove the bug she had planted there; the bug Alan Richardson knew Crosier had planted, which was why he'd summoned Ena and everyone else involved in Highsmith's case to a meeting at Dudley Green Associates and not to his office or an office at GCHQ – and why he had told Ena to ask if the office was safe. He knew damn well it wasn't, but lied saying it had been swept by his men and was clean.

It took Ena every ounce of patience she had not to blow the operation wide open and give Richardson a piece of her mind in front of Audrey Crosier.

'Mr Mallory knows where the meeting is going to be held. I can send a car for you, or are you driving yourself?'

'Yes...' Ena answered in flat tones to sound bored, which was how she felt.

'Let it slip that Highsmith has been moved to a private hospital. She knows you haven't been told the name of the hospital so she won't ask. She'll have her way of finding out.'

Ena was annoyed with Richardson. The telephone call was too long. Audrey Crosier wasn't stupid. If Richardson talked any longer, Crosier would suspect something was going on. 'Sir, I'm pleased our friend has been moved somewhere safe, but could we discuss this later? Goodbye!'

Ena slammed down the telephone. 'The cheek of the man!' She looked across her desk at Audrey Crosier. 'I'm sorry. If my associate had been here he'd have dealt with that call.' She looked at her watch. 'He should have been here half an hour ago. I hope he's alright.'

'Any reason why he shouldn't be?' Crosier asked.

'Not really. It's just that he was involved in a car accident recently and there's always the possibility of concussion at a later date. I expect I'm worrying for nothing. He has probably overslept.' Ena looked at her watch again.

'Was he badly injured?' Mannered lines creased Crosier's forehead.

'No, he escaped with only a few cuts and bruises. His friend wasn't so lucky.' Now it was Ena's turn to feign concern. 'Sorry,' she said again, lifting her hand and flicking away worrying thoughts, 'I'm prattling on about something that isn't anything to do with you.' Ena took a drink of her coffee. 'Now,' she said, 'where were we?'

'You were going to tell me what you'd found out about my husband's death in Berlin.'

'I was, wasn't I. Sorry,' she said, again. She was beginning to repeat herself. Crosier turning up was unsettling. Bloody Special Branch telephoning with Crosier sitting on the other side of her desk, was unnerving.

'There was a lot of red tape, as you can imagine. There's also client confidentiality to consider. And, as I have already said, I haven't written the report yet. However,' Ena looked into Crosier's face and feigned sympathy, 'Since you are here, I feel I should tell you something of what I learned about your husband's death.'

FORTY-FOUR

Ena sat back in her chair. 'I'm sorry to have to tell you that your husband was murdered.'

Audrey Crosier took a handkerchief from her handbag. She sniffed and dabbed at dry eyes.

'I'm not at liberty to divulge my source. I'm not even sure I should be telling you what I've discovered.' Ena took a deep breath and looked at Crosier with as much compassion as she could muster. 'I believe your husband was killed by a man named Archibald Hollander. He worked for military intelligence and was in Berlin at the same time – August 1936.'

Audrey dabbed her eyes again. There were still no tears.

'There was an argument between your husband and Hollander. The landlord of the bar where they'd been drinking confirmed what was documented at MI5. I'm sorry, Audrey, but they had been drinking heavily. No one knew what the disagreement was about, but it got out of hand and what started as raised voices, ended up as a fist fight. Archibald Hollander got the better of your husband who, as you know, fell...'

'Was pushed!'

'I don't know if he fell or if he was pushed, Audrey. I can

only tell you what I was told. Your husband ended up in the River Dahme and drowned.'

'And where is this, Archibald Hollander?' Audrey spat.

'Dead. He has been dead for ten years.'

Audrey shook her head. 'His death is very convenient.'

'Convenient or not, I have seen his grave. I spoke to the parish priest who had known him for many years. He officiated at his funeral. I assure you, Archibald Hollander died ten years ago. I'm sorry, but that's everything I know.'

The two women sat in silence. Ena was the first to speak. 'I'd hoped that knowing the man who killed your husband was dead, it would give you some sort of closure.'

Crosier didn't reply, but looked at Ena with cold dark eyes. 'You won't tell me where his grave is?'

'No. What good would it do you? It doesn't matter where the grave is or even how long the man has been dead. What matters is the suspicions you had about your husband's death have proved to be correct, and that you can now get on with your life.'

Audrey Crosier got up. Without thanking Ena she made her way to the door. Ena left her seat and followed her out. Shaking hands the two women said goodbye. Crosier crossed the street to the car park, Ena watched her get into a green Ford Zephyr. She looked for signs of damage on the passenger side of the car. There was none. She waited until Crosier reversed and drove forward. With the car facing her, Ena saw no broken headlights, no damage to the bumper, no dents in the front or driver's side of the car that would suggest it had been used to run Rupert Highsmith down. But then, Ena thought, there had been plenty of time to have had the car repaired.

Ena put up her hand to wave goodbye as Audrey Crosier steered the car off the raised parking area. She didn't accelerate, but let the car roll over the pavement onto Mercer Street. Ena's heart began to pound. She turned, stepped into the entrance of

the office and pushed the door. Leaving it ajar she closed her
eyes and gulped in air. The sound of Crosier's Ford, as its tyres
rolled slowly over the edge of the tarmac onto the loose gravel
between car park and pavement, was the sound she'd heard the
night the office was broken into and she had been knocked to
the ground. The shorter of the two burglars had driven the car
in exactly the same way. As Audrey Crosier drove the Ford
Zephyr along Mercer Street, Ena closed the door and locked it.

Returning to her desk, Ena flopped down in her chair and
exhaled loudly. She now knew that Audrey Crosier was the
driver on the night the office was burgled. Was she also the
driver when Highsmith was mown down? Ena left her seat and
went over to the filing cabinet. She knelt down beside it in the
way that Crosier had done, but there was nothing. As she
thought, Crosier had removed the listening device and taken it
with her.

She heard a sound and stood up. It was the street door opening. A second later it closed. She stared at the office door, held
her breath and watched the doorknob turn. 'Artie!' She flew
across the room as he entered and fell into his arms. 'Couldn't
you have shouted hello or something?'

Artie laughed. 'I'll whistle next time so you know it's me.
How about, The Boy I love is...' He pulled a face. 'Oops! We are
being listened to.'

'Not by Audrey Crosier, but probably by *bloody Special
Branch*,' Ena said pointedly, looking up at the ceiling light.
Though where the branch's devices were she had no idea.

'Did Alan Richardson telephone?'

'Yes, I expect it was you who told him Crosier was here.'

'I rang him from upstairs.'

Ena tutted and went back to her desk. 'He was an age
instructing me. It's a wonder Crosier didn't smell a rat.' Ena

picked up her pen and, deep in thought, tapped it on her diary as if it was a drumstick.

'What is it, Ena?'

'After all the bloody running around Five in Glasgow made me do, I'm still no closer to finding out who sent Highsmith the anonymous letters and photographs.'

'Photographs taken in Berlin, or in London of Crosier and the Highsmith look-alike?'

'Berlin. Artie, think about it? Whoever sent those photographs must have been in Berlin at the same time as Rupert or how would they have got hold of them? The photographer had to be in Berlin in August 1936. But who sent him?'

'Someone connected to the failed assassination of Highsmith? Someone who was in the right-wing splinter group during Stanley Baldwin's last term in office as PM?'

'Maybe one of them was in Berlin in '36, but,' Ena said, still playing an imaginary drum, 'they wouldn't be involved in the hit-and-run. Most of them are dead now. I believe the whistle-blower is still alive, but he'd be too old. No,' Ena said, 'it's someone connected to Michael Crosier.' She stopped drumming and looked into the mid-distance as if the answer lay there.

'You've thought of something, haven't you?'

'Yes, and it is only a thought. Where was Audrey Crosier in August 1936?'

FORTY-FIVE

Ena turned onto Vauxhall Bridge Road and slowed the car to a crawl, looking for Rampayne Street, which Artie said led to Pimlico Underground Station. With signposts coming into view saying Vauxhall Bridge in a quarter of a mile, Ena realised that she had driven too far and turned onto Millbank. She then took the next left to Ponsonby Terrace – and left again to John Islip Street – where at last she was able to turn right onto Vauxhall Bridge Road.

'Rampayne Street should be on your left now, Artie. Keep your eyes peeled.'

Immediately he shouted, 'Left!'

A quick glance in the reverse mirror told Ena that there were no cars behind the Sunbeam. She yanked the steering wheel to the left and headed in the direction of the Underground.

'Left here,' Artie said.

'Are you sure?'

'This has to be the turning. The left after this one will take us to the front of Pimlico Underground and then back to Vaux- hall Bridge.'

Ena swung the car into what looked like a dead end. Leaning forward and peering out of the windscreen she could see a tall building.

'We must be at the back of it. Look, there's a sign for the car park,' Artie said.

Ena followed the sign through a narrow opening in a six-foot high wall and pulled up at the back of the building. 'This can't be the Doncaster Hotel?'

'Tradesman's entrance,' Artie said, and laughing, jumped out of the car.

Looks more like a public lavatory. Smells like one too, she thought, wrinkling her nose as she got out of the car. She looked up and counted four levels of small, frosted windows. Bathrooms, at a guess. A black iron fire escape ran from the third floor to the ground. It crossed her mind that whoever designed the hotel had made a grave error. Anyone staying on the fourth floor would have no way of escaping if there was a fire.

She grabbed her shoulder bag from the back seat, locked both the driver and passenger doors and followed Artie to what was a tradesman's entrance. A sign on the dark plastered wall said, 'Deliveries'. She followed him up two steep concrete steps to a large square slab that made a corner, and from there up a further two steps that rose at a right angle ending under an arch. Ena turned and looked back to where she had mounted the steps. She strained her eyes in the dark and saw that opposite was an arch that mirrored the one above her and Artie. She could neither see the car park, nor be seen by anyone who might be sitting in a car on surveillance. She realised then that the Doncaster was no ordinary hotel. It had rooms on three floors. Bathrooms at the back of the building were proof of that. But, Ena smiled, there would be no vacancies. The fourth floor didn't exist, except to military intelligence.

Artie knocked the door.

Ena heard the dull scraping sound of heavy bolts being pulled out of their housing before the metallic jangle of keys.

'So, this is what the spooks call going to the races.' Artie chuckled. '*Doncaster.*'

'I got it,' Ena said.

The heavy-duty door was pulled open by a man who wouldn't have looked out of place in a boxing ring with Joe Erskine. In a black suit, with shoulders at right angles to his thick neck and a black tie that stood out against a dazzling white shirt, the man nodded. 'Mrs Green and Mr Mallory?' He didn't wait for either Ena or Artie to reply. There was no need, Black-suit would have been shown their photographs. 'Follow me,' he said with an American accent.

Standing to the side to allow Ena and Artie to pass him, Black-suit pulled the door to and slid the bolts home before locking it at the top and the bottom. He put the keys in his trousers pocket and led the way along a stone corridor. Like the bottling yard at her sister Bess's hotel at Foxden, there were empty barrels, and crates of empty beer bottles and spirits. At the end of the corridor, they turned and walked along an identical corridor to a door with Kitchen written on it. Black-suit turned the heavy handle and pushed. The smell of food, the heat from large ovens and steam from boiling saucepans, met them as soon as the door opened. Ignored by the kitchen staff calling for this order or that order, they followed Black-suit to a door that was tucked out of sight behind a large boiler at the end of four sinks. Marked Private, he opened it and the cacophony of sounds made in the Doncaster Hotel's kitchen was quickly silenced as the door swung shut behind them.

'Busy kitchen,' Ena whispered to Artie. 'A lot of staff for a hotel with no paying guests.'

'There's a public bar and restaurant at the front of the hotel on Sheldon Street. It's quite smart, so I expect it's locals who come here to eat out.'

A long carpeted corridor suggested to Ena that they were now inside the hotel. The walls were cream and the carpet which was very worn was brown with an indistinguishable cream pattern. The corridors leading to the hotel's kitchen had once been outside, Ena thought. As she turned to walk down yet another corridor to another corner she tried to envisage where the back door was in relation to where she was now. Even with her photographic memory, she wasn't able to retrace her steps to the back of the hotel. She followed Black-suit and Artie around another corner and smiled. Clever, she thought. They had gone round in a circle.

Black-suit stopped in front of a lift. Not a lift that the public would use. With its scratched grey metallic doors, it looked more like a goods lift. Black-suit pressed the button at the side of the lift and the doors opened. He motioned for Ena to go in first. Artie followed and Black-suit brought up the rear.

There was one button inside which Black-suit pressed and the lift began its rocky ascent. When it juddered to a halt the doors opened and Ena and Artie alighted followed by Black-suit who directed them to a circular waiting area on the left with armchairs and occasional tables. Above the seating area there would once have been windows. Now a mural of Victoria Embankment – from the Palace of Westminster, Parliament and Big Ben – to Blackfriars Bridge in the City of London, adorned the wall.

Ena felt thick carpet beneath her feet and looked down to see a red and gold carpet with a clearly identifiable fleur-de-lis pattern. She looked at Artie and raised her eyes. The fourth floor was as spacious and smart as the ground floor had been cramped and grubby.

'Wait here, please?' Black-suit said, pointing to two chairs beneath the wall painting of the north side of the River Thames. As he knocked on the double doors, Ena and Artie sat down.

Ena's attention was taken by the lift doors opening and a man wearing kitchen whites and a chef's hat coming out of it carrying a bulky object covered with a white tablecloth.

'Looks like they're going to feed us, Artie.'

'I hope they do. I'm starving,' he said, as two waitresses in black dresses and white pinafores followed the chef the short distance along the corridor to the first of the two doors that Ena had seen when she left the lift. She nodded in agreement. She was hungry too.

FORTY-SIX

When Black-suit returned, Ena and Artie got to their feet and followed him through the double doors into a large room. The contrast between the soft lighting of the waiting area and penetrating overhead striplights gave the room a formal, sober feel. Ena blinked a couple of times until her eyes became accustomed to the brightness.

The walls were dark panelled wood from floor to ceiling. Nothing hung on them. Nothing could, there was no picture rail. Nor was there a skirting board. It occurred to Ena that the ceiling was low for a room of its size. A false ceiling hiding soundproofing material. The same for the dark wood panels. It was a secure room.

Sparsely furnished so nowhere to hide listening devices, the only furniture was a long side table that ran the length of the room on the right and a large conference table on the left. High-backed chairs had been placed around it. There were two empty. As the rest of the company were already seated, Ena assumed they were for her and Artie.

She looked around the table. Alan Richardson put up his hand in greeting and Ena nodded at the Special Branch

Inspector who she had known for several years. Alan had a clumsy way about him which, when they had first worked together, had annoyed Ena. She was Head of Cold Cases at the Home Office then, and Alan was a recently promoted Special Branch Inspector. She was used to him now, or was she? She could have happily throttled him with the telephone cable when Audrey Crosier was in her office. The call was too long. Crosier not suspecting anything was a miracle.

Ena was relieved to see her long-standing friend and ally – who her sister Claire had known during her time with the Special Operations Executive in the war – the Director of GCHQ and Henry's boss – Colonel Smith. Next to him was DI Dan Powell of Bow Street – another ally and friend. Inspector Powell had helped Ena to bring the murderer of her late colleague, Sid Parfitt to justice – when she, Artie and Sid had worked on cold cases. In return Ena had helped him to catch art thieves who were stealing paintings in Covent Garden – Ena and the inspector's home turf. The thieves running the London operation were caught. In Paris the con was still being worked.

Artie and Ena crossed the room to the conference table. Artie walked round to a vacant chair next to DI Powell – Ena took her seat at the opposite end of the table to Colonel Smith.

As Artie, an ex-employee of GCHQ, sat down, Colonel Smith welcomed him with a nod. To Ena he smiled. 'I'm glad you could make it, Ena, Mallory.'

'Sir!' Artie acknowledged.

'Thank you,' Ena said, smiling at the colonel. She put her shoulder bag on the floor beside her chair and looked around the assembled group of SIS and other military intelligence personnel, and said hello to Gordon Giles of MI5. In his late fifties, Assistant Director Giles was around the same age as Colonel Smith and some ten years older than the other men at the table. Old school, Gordon Giles was an amiable chap who was nicknamed 'Mother's Ruin' by the foot soldiers at MI5.

Next to AD Giles was a miserable looking Max Drew, Director of Operations at MI6 who no one would dare to call anything but Sir. After greeting both men, Ena's eyes settled on the only member of the esteemed group that she didn't know and the only other woman at the meeting.

'Pamela Beha!' A woman in her mid-forties, with short straight blonde hair, stood up and offered Ena her hand. 'Pamela!' she said in a mid-Atlantic, slightly south-eastern American accent. 'It's good to meet you, Ena. I've heard some great things about you.'

'Pleased to meet you, Pamela,' Ena replied, shaking her hand, embarrassed that the CIA agent had been told about her, but no one had thought to tell her that there was going to be a CIA agent present. Ena knew who Pamela Beha was, not only by her accent, but she had read a copy of the press release of the forthcoming defection of two US cryptologists, which she knew Beha and Highsmith had uncovered. Ena smiled at the female agent. There were more women working in the intelligence services these days, although not enough. The SIS was still very much a man's club.

'Agent Beha is the CIA agent who Highsmith was working with until his... *accident*,' Alan Richardson informed Ena.

'It wasn't an accident from what I hear, huh, Ena?'

'No, Pamela, it wasn't.'

With her elbows planted firmly on the table, Pamela Beha, leaned forward, her intelligent eyes were bright and inquisitive. 'Do you think Audrey Crosier had anything to do with the *accident*, Ena?'

As she opened her mouth to reply to the CIA agent, Alan Richardson cut in. 'I had it written up for you, Pamela,' he said, pointing to several pages of A4-typed notes.

Pamela Beha lifted up her copy of the transcript detailing

conversations between Ena and Audrey Crosier, and said, 'Alan, I don't mean to butt in, but I was only invited to join you a few hours ago and have only just been given a copy of the meetings between Ena and Crosier.' The CIA agent looked at Ena and raised her eyebrows before turning back to Alan. 'Would it be okay with you if Ena went through the Crosier issue from the get-go, to bring me,' Beha looked around the table, 'and our colleagues up to speed?'

The nodding of heads told Ena that Agent Beha had got her way.

Richardson gave the CIA agent a sharp nod by way of an agreeing with her.

'I want to know as much about the woman who was married to the East German agent, Michael Crosier, as you do.' She turned from Richardson and looked at Ena. 'I'm particularly interested in anything you think might be relevant to the work Rupert and I have been doing recently.'

'I haven't been briefed on Highsmith's work with the CIA,' Ena lied. She had been briefed, but it was by her husband and it was unofficial. It wasn't by Colonel Smith or anyone with the authority to share top secret information that came from GCHQ. Feeling her cheeks growing red with embarrassment, she said, 'If you'll bear with me, Pamela.' Ena looked around the table. 'For those here that don't know all the facts, I would like to begin with a break-in at the offices of Dudley Green Associates some months ago. At the time I had no idea who it could have been, but new evidence has come to light and I now strongly believe that Audrey Crosier and the gorilla who impersonated the police officer guarding Highsmith at St Thomas' hospital – where a second attempt was made on his life – were the two who broke into my office.'

She looked across the table and addressed Inspector Powell. 'And, I believe it was Audrey Crosier who ran Rupert Highsmith down. If you have her car examined, Inspector, you'll find it has a new bumper, right wing, headlight and probably several other new fittings. And,' Ena said, focusing on Pamela Beha, 'we know it was Audrey Crosier dressed as a nurse who tried to kill Highsmith in the hospital.'

Ena cast her eyes around the table again. She looked first at Gordon Giles of MI5 and then at Max Drew, MI6. 'I have as many questions as I do answers. Firstly, I would like to know where Audrey Crosier was when her husband Michael was in Berlin in 1936?' All eyes were on her, but no one spoke. 'Alright, as you can't, or won't, tell me,' Ena said, 'let me tell you.' She was about to break client confidentiality, or at least push the bar. She looked at Artie for approval. He gave it with a wink. 'I believe Audrey Crosier was in Berlin with Michael Crosier in 1936. Whether they were man and wife then I have no idea. What I do know is, Audrey Crosier took photographs of Rupert Highsmith in pseudo compromising situations with a Jewish boy. I say *pseudo* because although Highsmith took a Jewish boy back to his hotel, it was to save the boy's life after his family had been taken away by Nazi soldiers. There are photographs of Highsmith handing over money to a dishevelled looking dark-haired man. The man was a member of a Jewish resistance group. Highsmith gave him money to get the boy out of Berlin and to safety in the country.' She looked again at Pamela Beha. 'The resistance man was known to the night manager of the hotel who was an MI5 agent working undercover.'

'So,' Pamela said, 'Crosier's wife was part of the conspiracy to assassinate Highsmith in '36?'

'Was she the backup, in case her husband didn't succeed in killing Mr Highsmith?' DI Powell asked.

'No,' Ena said, taking in both Pamela Beha and the inspector. 'Audrey was a sleeper. She was sent to Berlin at the same time as her husband as his shadow, but not as backup. Until '36 they were both sleepers. I suspect they were originally from

Berlin, working for the Russians. They lived ordinary lives in London until they were activated. In Berlin, Audrey Crosier had her own orders.' Ena looked at DI Powell. 'They were not to kill Highsmith in the event of her husband failing to do so. I believe Audrey Crosier's orders were to take compromising photographs to discredit Highsmith.'

'Mrs Green, you cannot be sure of this?' It was Gordon Giles of MI5 who spoke.

FORTY-SEVEN

Ena glanced at Gordon Giles of MI5, but spoke to DI Powell. 'You see, Inspector, the world of spies is a dirty world. Loyalty is demanded of those in the lower ranks, those who risk their lives in the field, but not from those in high places. They don't have to adhere to such mundane allegiances as loyalty. When an agent is discredited, the intelligence services is informed of the agent's *indiscretions*. If the agent is killed and his body disposed of, which in the case of Rupert Highsmith was the plan, there would be no need for his past indiscretions to come out. A *cleaner* would be sent to clear up the mess and there would be no enquiry into the agent's death. The photographs Audrey Crosier took were a *backup* in the event that Highsmith's body was found. Even the murder of a *loyal* agent like Rupert Highsmith would be ignored if he'd been caught in a compromising position with another man, or in the case of the Berlin photographs, a boy. An agent's indiscretions – real or false – would be swept under the carpet and there'd be no investigation into his death. That is as long as no shame or blame could be attributed to the intelligence services.'

'Which didn't happen to Highsmith,' AD Giles from MI5 said.

'Only because in 1936 Rupert also worked for the Prime Minister, Stanley Baldwin,' Artie corrected.

'When agents are discredited they are disowned by the intelligence services that they had worked for, so their misconduct doesn't reflect badly on the service and they don't lose face with their friends across the pond.' Ena shot a look at the CIA agent. She could have bitten off her tongue. 'Sorry, Pamela, I didn't mean to...'

Pamela Beha accepted Ena's apology with a shrug of the shoulders and a smile. 'It was an emotive time, Ena.'

MI6's Max Drew cleared his throat. 'It isn't about losing face, Ena, it's about damage limitation. Not letting our enemies know they have won. Or that they have got the better of us. In Rupert Highsmith's case, they never did.'

'And they never would,' Ena said.

At that moment there was a knock at the door. Colonel Smith who was closest got up and opened it. Welcoming two women, he pointed to the side table that ran half the length of the secure room. Thanking them he returned to his chair and announced, 'We'll take a short break for refreshments.'

Mutterings of good idea and I'm ready for a drink floated around the room. The colonel made a joke about non-alcoholic drinks only and everyone laughed.

One of the women wheeled in a catering trolley laden with sandwiches, Scotch eggs, wedges of pork pie, cakes, crockery and napkins. The other pushed in a trolley containing a large teapot, and an even larger coffee jug, cups and saucers. Without speaking, the women laid out enough food to feed a small army. When they had finished they turned to leave.

To the last caterer, Colonel Smith said, 'We shouldn't be more than half an hour, Ida.'

Ida nodded and without speaking, left.

Ena took her cue from the colonel. When he stood up, she followed. At the far end of the long table was the tea and coffee and the cups and saucers. Nearest was the food, plates and napkins.

There was a variety of sandwiches. Ena was pleased to see that the sliced bread still bore crusts. She was ravenous. She hadn't eaten since breakfast and helped herself to a round of cheese and tomato, and one of tinned salmon and cucumber. She gave the cake a miss, although it did look delicious. Taking her plate of sandwiches to the conference table she sat down and began to eat hungrily.

'Richardson's a bit quiet,' Artie whispered, joining her.

'He is, but the meeting isn't over yet. Give him time.'

When they had finished eating, Ena and Artie returned to the side table.

'Tea or coffee?' Artie asked.

'We'd better have tea. Looks like everyone else is on coffee. We don't want it to run out.'

'I thought Henry would be here,' Artie said, pouring Ena and then himself a cup of tea.

'I'm glad he isn't. I can speak more freely when Henry isn't listening.'

'Which you did,' Artie said, giggling.

Ena picked up her cup and whispered, 'Now I've had my say, I'd better be less... What was the word Pamela Beha used?'

'Emotive. "*It was an emotive time, Eeenah,*"' Artie said, in a Southern American drawl, which sounded nothing like the CIA agent's accent.

'And she was right. It was an emotive time. It still is.' Taking a sip of her tea, Ena looked over the top of her cup. 'I'm finding it hard to imagine Highsmith paired with her,' she said, putting the cup in its saucer. 'They are chalk and cheese. Rupert's as tall as Beha is short,' she mused.

'Not the most likely couple, I'll give you that.'

'Beha is no spring chicken, but she's an attractive woman. How old do you think she is?'

'Mid-forties,' Artie replied.

'They wouldn't blend in as a married couple on a covert op. Neither of them look ordinary enough.' Ena glanced over to where Pamela Beha was sitting and quickly looked away. The CIA agent was watching her. Ena turned her back on the gathering and refilled her cup. When she had added milk, she said, 'What do you make of her?'

Artie sniffed. 'She looks like butter wouldn't melt, but Rupert said she's a tough cookie with a razor-sharp mind and a memory like an elephant. He said he wouldn't want to get on the wrong side of her. She can be a hard B.'

'Shush, she'll hear you.'

Artie pressed his lips together and looked to the heavens. He followed Ena back to the conference table and took his seat next to Inspector Powell.

FORTY-EIGHT

As if by magic, exactly half an hour after the caterers had left there was a knock at the door. Ida and her assistant entered to the sound of clinking cups as they were put down in their saucers, and a flurry of napkins as mouths were dabbed. The diligent waitresses began to work. Ida cleared the conference table quickly and quietly, while her assistant made short work of removing the pots and crocks from the side table. When they left, the meeting resumed.

'Ena, you know more about the anonymous letters and the pornographic photographs than anyone else at the table?' Alan Richardson said.

Ena shot the Special Branch director a harsh look. 'That isn't true, Alan. Mr Highsmith was Artie's client. It wasn't until after the hit-and-run that I assisted in the case. Neither is it true that the photographs of Mr Highsmith in Berlin are porno-graphic. As I said, the photographs had been taken to look as if lewd behaviour was taking place. It was not.'

'I understand you were also injured in the hit-and-run, Mr Mallory?' AD Giles said.

'Yes, but only cuts and bruises. Rupert pushed me out of the path of the car.'

'And so it was you, Ena, who went up to MI5's office in Glasgow?'

'I didn't actually go to the office in Glasgow, but yes, the investigation took me to Scotland. As Artie was injured, although not as badly as Mr Highsmith, I took over the case. Also, because at the time we didn't know who was behind the attempt on Highsmith's life, I was worried that Artie would be in danger if he went to Scotland asking questions.'

Ena glanced at Gordon Giles. He would know why she went up to MI5 Scotland. Her meeting with Fraser would be a matter of record at Five by now. She felt her cheeks getting hot and cleared her throat. Picking up the water jug, Ena filled the nearest glass and took several sips.

'Thank you for explaining, Mrs Green.' Gordon Giles looked from Ena to Artie. 'I'll ask you both. Do you think the threatening letters and photographs that Highsmith received were an act of revenge?'

'No!' Ena and Artie said at the same time.

'It's been twenty-four years since Michael Crosier was killed. Why would Audrey wait until now to take revenge for the death of a husband who, as far as we know, was in name only,' Ena said.

'She had been dormant for almost a quarter of a century,' Artie added. 'She'd have acted sooner if it was revenge. She knew when her husband was killed that Rupert was in Berlin.'

Ena looked at the CIA agent. She was nodding. 'I think Pamela would agree that Audrey Crosier may have blamed Rupert Highsmith for her husband's death, if he was her husband then, but I don't believe that was her motive for attempting to kill him now.'

Gordon Giles shrugged his shoulders and looked down at his notes.

'No,' Ena said again. 'In my opinion, attempting to kill Rupert Highsmith in a hit-and-run, and later with ketamine in his plasma tube was not a twenty four-year-old revenge hit!'

'We've had a file on Michael and Audrey Crosier, or, to give them their East German names, Rolf Muller and Angela Schulz, since they arrived in England in 1930,' Gordon Giles, said. 'Muller aka Michael Crosier was activated immediately. As you know he worked for MI5 until his death in Berlin in '36.'

'Thank God Crosier was taken out before he could kill Highsmith,' Pamela Beha said.

Assistant Director Giles nodded. 'The intelligence services knew Michael Crosier was an East German agent when he applied to work for MI5. Five gave him a job to keep an eye on him.'

Pamela Beha laughed. 'Keep your friends close and your enemies closer, huh, Gordon?'

'Something like that, Pamela.'

'He spent his MI5 career behind a desk. The Olympic Games in '36 was his first field assignment, and he wouldn't have got that if it hadn't been that MI5 and Six had eyes on him at all times.'

Drew nodded. 'We hoped he might lead us to bigger fish in Berlin. He didn't unfortunately. Nor did he do anything without the security services knowing about it.'

'What we didn't know at the time was whether Audrey Crosier was working with her husband or independently of him.'

Alan Richardson blew out his cheeks. 'That was a bit risky, wasn't it? If Crosier hadn't been killed in Berlin, God knows what would have happened to Stanley Baldwin and his cabinet.'

Giles nodded. 'The fallout would have been immense. With Hitler growing in popularity and...' The MI5 AD shuddered. 'It would have been a disaster.'

'A bad day for Britain,' Drew said.

'For the world,' Pamela Beha corrected.

'On the other hand, you might have turned him. Got him to work for you as a double agent,' Richardson said.

'We weren't interested at that point. The only thing that mattered to the British intelligence services was stopping the assassinations of Rupert Highsmith and Prime Minister Baldwin.'

A heavy silence fell among the people around the table. It was Pamela Beha who broke it. 'After Crosier *drowned*, did you look further into his background?'

'Yes, Rupert Highsmith was the chief investigator. Michael Crosier had stated on his job application form for MI5 that he was born and brought up in Slough. He had passed the eleven plus and had attended Upton Court Grammar School before going up to Cambridge. Highsmith looked up his old Master at Cambridge and went down to see him. He spoke of Michael in glowing terms. He said he had excelled in everything. He was popular and had a lot of friends. He was an energetic student, involved in the Student Rag and the Student Union. And he was not only academic, he was a sportsman, excelling at rugby, tennis and cricket. His death had shocked everyone. To die so young, with your whole life ahead of you. Tears had filled the old master's eyes.

Highsmith asked him how Michael had died and he told him that the weekend after getting his degree he was out celebrating with chums on Saturday night and was killed in a car crash.'

Pamela Beha's eyes narrowed. 'So, the KGB got hold of copies of young Michael Crosier from Slough's birth certificate, school reports, college certificate – not difficult to do as we all know – and the deceased Michael Crosier came back to life and Rolf Muller was killed off. And Audrey?' Pamela asked.

'Audrey, as Ena said, was a shadow sleeper, Michaels'

shadow. She'd have been given the identity of some unfortunate woman who was also deceased.'

'And Audrey Crosier, the perfect shadow,' Ena added, 'was in Berlin when Michael was there in '36.'

'But she couldn't have known in advance about the boy.'

'No, she wouldn't have. The boy was a lucky find,' Ena said. 'If Highsmith had been *killed by Michael Crosier*, and if there had been an investigation, Audrey would have sent those photographs to MI5, Six, GCHQ and Stanley Baldwin. She'd have sent them to Old King Cole if she'd had to.'

The CIA agent nodded that she understood. 'As you said, Ena, discrediting an agent's name after they had been killed was the best way of keeping the intelligence services from investigating the agent's death. His killer would be known to the service, but he would never be brought to justice.'

'There'd be a small funeral somewhere in the country, only close friends attending, and the SIS would in all probability brush what the agent had been working on under the carpet.'

'I can see that, but why activate her now?' DI Powell asked.

'To discredit Rupert who has been working with me,' Pamela Beha said. 'Some of Rupert's past associations with men have been questionable. Two consenting adults is of no interest to the CIA, but a man and a boy? There would have been every chance, if the photographs had been real, that the CIA would have taken him off the investigation. However, what Audrey Crosier's people didn't take into consideration was Highsmith's working reputation with the agency. Rupert is greatly respected by the CIA.'

FORTY-NINE

'The plan, as far as we know, was to take Highsmith out, which the East Germans believed they had done until you had a visit from Audrey Crosier,' Alan Richardson said to Ena.

'After the charade over the telephone, who knows what they now think?' Ena couldn't help herself but have a dig at Alan. 'What I don't understand is why go to the trouble of saying Highsmith had died in St Thomas' after Crosier had offloaded a syringe of ketamine into his saline drip, only to tell her, and whoever was listening to the conversation, that he wasn't dead?'

'To buy time. We needed to get Highsmith away from St Thomas' and get the Americans onside. Mr Mallory letting us know that Crosier was in your office gave us the perfect opportunity to telephone you while she was there and plant the idea that Highsmith was alive and in a private hospital.'

'But there are several private hospitals in London,' Ena questioned.

'The CIA will leak which hospital it is,' Pamela Beha said. 'I believe the attempt on Rupert's life was because of the work he was doing with me.' Agent Beha looked at each member of the security services in turn. 'What I'm about to tell you is for your ears only and should not go beyond these four walls,' she said. 'We received intel that two of our guys, two American cryptologists, were working for the Russians. Rupert had been digging into the possible defections of the cryptologists for months. He was about to scupper their plans of a press release which, if the two men had gone public, would have blown the CIA and MI6 out of the water. Like Alan, the CIA needed time. Because of the hit-and-run and Rupert being hospitalised, the defection of two cryptologists is back on schedule. The two traitors will have their press release before they defect to Russia and the Bear will have its day in the political arena. It's just another attempt to show the West how clever and powerful the East is.'

'What about Western sigint activities?' Colonel Smith asked.

'NSA has been working on sigint. Information has been changed. It'll take the Russians months to sort it out.'

'And by then it will be out of date.'

'Exactly, Ena.'

'Was it Audrey Crosier behind the wheel of the car that hit Highsmith?' Ena asked Beha.

It was DI Powell who answered. 'No, it was the chap who impersonated the PC at St Thomas.' It was the first time for a while that the inspector had spoken.

Ena had a sudden thought. 'Colonel, is Audrey Crosier's son or daughter-in-law involved in any of this?'

'Not as far as we know. We've looked into the son and his wife and we're sure that neither of them knew anything about Michael or Audrey Crosier's past lives. I went to see Matthew and he's devastated. At first he wouldn't accept that his parents were Soviet spies. It will take him some time, maybe years, to come to terms with what he has learned about them.'

'If he ever comes to terms with it.'

'I think he will. He seems like a fairly strong character, his wife too. She'll help him to get through it. No one outside this room knows who his parents really are, and no one will. There is no reason why he should hear from any of us again.'

'What about the hospital staff? The doctors and nurses who looked after Rupert?' Ena asked. 'The doctor I sent in to High-smith knows he'd been poisoned. Others must know.'

Colonel Smith nodded. 'They were told the woman posing as a nurse was mentally ill. She had tried to kill Mr Highsmith because she blamed him for the death of her husband who was killed in a car crash in which Mr Highsmith was driving. They seemed to accept what they were told. To be honest they were all too busy to look for flaws in the story.'

FIFTY

'Ena! Henry! Come in.' Ena and then Henry entered the spacious hall of the Galbraith's London home. Their host, Charles Galbraith, kissed Ena on her cheek and shook Henry's hand.

'How's Priscilla?' Ena asked.

'Excited. Fussing over the food, the table settings, flowers.' Charles rolled his eyes.

'Have you told her about Mary, yet?'

'No. She's just happy that you and Henry are able to join us tonight.'

'And you?' Ena asked. 'How are you?'

'Nervous!'

'Nervous?' Ena said, to which she and Charles both laughed.

Charles held up his hands in a gesture of surrender. 'After the disappointment of last year,' he said, turning to Henry to include him in the conversation, 'I'm more than a little apprehensive as to how Priscilla will take the news that Ena has found her daughter.'

Hanging up Ena's coat, Charles shouted, 'Our guests have

arrived, darling.' To Ena he whispered, 'I'm also very happy to see you two.' And then in a normal voice, 'Come through to the sitting room. Let me get you both a drink. Whisky?' he said to Henry. 'And what about you, Ena?'

'I'll have a small whisky, thank you, Charles.'

Priscilla, almost gliding into the room, was wearing an elegant silk turquoise dress with a V-neck, chiffon overlay and chiffon sleeves. Around her neck was a fine gold chain with a single pearl. It reminded Ena of a teardrop. Ena admired the way her friend dressed and, because she was going to Jeanie McKinley and Gerry Cooper's engagement party later in the month, she had pushed the boat out and bought a new dress that the assistant in the clothes shop said would look perfect at a dinner party, cocktail party, or a wedding. Well, she wasn't going to a wedding, but her new dress would suit the Galbraith's dinner party and Jeanie and Gerry's engagement party.

Ena often felt dowdy next to her friend Priscilla, but not tonight, not in her new black sleeveless dress with its boat neck, nipped in at the waist with a diamanté buckle, and a black silk kaftan style jacket made of fabric that was so fine it wafted behind her when she walked. She loved the feel of the contrasting loose style of the kaftan over the fitted dress.

'Ena, I'm so pleased to see you,' Priscilla said, kissing her on both cheeks. 'It's been too long.' Priscilla then turned, threw her arms around Henry and kissed him on both cheeks.

'Well, if you will spend half your life in the south of France,' Henry said, accepting a glass of whisky from Charles.

'And it was wonderful, wasn't it, darling?' Charles smiled. 'You must come next year,' Priscilla said, not giving her husband time to reply. 'It's such fun. We've made some good friends over the years, and they would love you. And,' she said, barely taking a breath, 'there's plenty of room in the villa. Say you'll come,' she said, appealing first to Henry and then to Ena. 'Please.'

'Of course, we'll come. We'd love to, wouldn't we, darling?'

'Yes,' Ena said, her eyes wide with surprise that Henry agreed to the holiday. She knew the south of France was the last place Henry would want to spend time.

Mrs Doyle, the Galbraith's housekeeper who was also an amazing cook, knocked before poking her head around the sitting room door.

'Battle stations. Mrs Doyle needs me in the kitchen,' Priscilla said, jumping up and following the housekeeper.

'My heart leaps with joy to see Priscilla so happy,' Charles said, when his wife had danced out of the room.

'Good Lord, look at the time. It's well past the time we asked Mrs Doyle to stay on this evening. Would you excuse me?' Priscilla said, getting up from the table.

'I'll go out and flag down a taxi. If you'll excuse me,' Charles said, leaving the dining room as Priscilla returned.

'I thought Mrs Doyle was your housekeeper?' Ena said.

'She is. Goodness knows what we'd do without her.'

'Didn't she used to live in?'

'Yes, until recently. Her sister came over from Ireland. She had the most awful marriage. The man took everything she had and left her without a penny.' Priscilla shook her head. 'She had nowhere to live. I don't want to sound unkind, but Mrs Doyle's rooms weren't big enough to accommodate two adults, so Charles bought a small mews house for Mrs Doyle and her sister lives with her.'

'Like a retainer?'

Priscilla thought for a moment before saying, 'I suppose it is like a retainer. Mrs Doyle will live there until she wishes to leave, returns to Ireland, or... Well, she can live there as long as she wants. Charles is happy that, with house prices soaring, he has a good investment and Mrs Doyle and her sister are happy because they have a nice house to live in. It's a ten-minute bus ride for Mrs D to get here in the mornings, and the same to get home at night. If she stays on and cooks for us, Charles puts her in a taxi.'

'And it isn't usually this late,' Charles said, coming into the room. 'Mrs Doyle is a gem,' he said, picking up his glass but not taking his seat. 'Why don't we take our drinks through to the sitting room? We'll be more comfortable.'

The sitting room was bigger than the dining room by half again. Charles refreshed their glasses from crystal decanters on the sideboard. After giving Priscilla a brandy, he patted the cushion next to him on the long settee. When she was seated, and had taken a drink, she put her glass on the occasional table next to the arm of the settee. Smiling fondly, Charles took hold of his wife's hands and kissed them. 'Darling, Ena, and I have something to tell you.'

Ena could feel her heart drumming as Priscilla looked from Charles to her with an excited grin on her face.

'Well?' Priscilla said, her eyes searching her husband's eyes. 'What is it?' she asked before Charles had time to speak. 'Charles?'

Charles looked at Ena, she nodded and he cleared his throat. 'A young woman wrote to me some time ago—'

Priscilla took a sharp breath. 'Was it? Charles, darling, please tell me if she is—?'

Charles put his arm around his wife and pulled her gently to him. 'Yes,' he whispered.

'Are you sure?' Priscilla asked, her voice muffled as she pressed her face against his chest.

'Yes,' Ena said. 'We're sure that the young woman I met is your daughter.'

Priscilla lifted her head and looked lovingly into Charles' face. Then she turned to Ena. 'You met? Where is she? Can I meet her? Does she know I didn't want to give her away?'

'Yes, she knows everything. Her mother too.'

'Her mother? Yes, of course. She has a mother...' Priscilla said, her voice trailing off as the realisation that the girl had a mother, dawned.

'She's a beautiful girl,' Ena said. 'She has your eyes and titian hair.'

'I had titian hair when I was young.'

'She's tall and slender, and very bright.' Charles took a photograph from his pocket. 'She looks like you when you were her age,' he said, handing her the photograph that Ena had taken of Mary Hornsby.

Priscilla took the photograph with shaking hands. 'She does, doesn't she? Look like me,' she said laughing through her tears. 'What's her name?'

'Mary.'

'Did she know she was adopted? I mean, before you met her?'

'Yes, her mother had told her.'

'Mary,' Priscilla said. She put the photograph down on the table in front of her, but didn't take her eyes off it. 'Mary,' she said again.

Then she asked the question Ena knew her friend would ask. A question for which there was as yet no answer.

Priscilla looked pleadingly into Charles eyes. 'Can I meet her?'

Charles didn't answer. Ena could see that he was struggling to explain the situation for fear he would hurt Priscilla.

'Doesn't she want to meet me?'

'Yes!' Ena said. 'She wants to meet you very much, but she needs a little time. She's going to write to Charles and arrange a time that's suitable for you both. I didn't push her because I could see that although she wanted to meet you, she didn't want to hurt her adoptive mother.'

'You must be patient, my love,' Charles said.

'I will.' Priscilla smiled at Ena, her hazel and green eyes sparkling as Mary Hornsby's eyes had done when she smiled.

Ena told Priscilla about the first time she saw Mary when Mary was going to college with her friend in Liverpool. She told her how beautiful Mary was and that she was fashionable in a classical way. She also told Priscilla about Mary's mother, Mrs Hornsby, who had been the wife of her old landlord, Reg Addison.

'Mrs Hornsby believed that her husband had privately adopted Mary. She had no idea about Mary's birth until many years later when Addison left her for another woman. It wasn't until she found old rent books, names and addresses – and Mary's birth certificate – that her husband had left behind, that she knew he was Mary's father. She told me that she had no reason to believe Mary's real mother wanted her because she believed the lies that Reg Addison told her. By the time she knew the truth, she had formed a loving bond – a mother's bond – with his child. Some years later when Mary needed a passport, Mrs Hornsby, which is her maiden name, told Mary that she was adopted and that she now believed her real mother hadn't given her up for adoption voluntarily.'

FIFTY-ONE

'Telephone!' Ena shouted from the cloakroom.

'Got it,' came Artie's reply.

'It's time we got some business in,' Ena said to Artie as he brought two mugs of coffee in from the kitchen. He put one on Ena's desk and took the other to the conference table.

'We'll put an ad in The Times.'

Ena nodded that she agreed. 'Who rang when I was in the toilet?'

'Audrey Crosier. She wants to see you. She said she has something important to tell you.'

'I wonder what it could be? What time did she say she'd be here?'

'She didn't. She wants you to go to her flat.'

Ena took a gulp of her coffee and put the mug down with a thud. 'Something important?' she said, getting to her feet. She picked up her bag and headed for the door.

'Hang on, Ena. Audrey Crosier is dangerous, I'm coming with you,' Artie said, 'I don't trust that woman.'

Ena didn't argue. She didn't trust Audrey Crosier either.

She had tried to kill Highsmith – twice. Who knows what the woman was capable of?

Ena parked opposite Audrey Crosier's maisonette, as she had done before. She got out of the car, locked her door and went round to the passenger side. When Artie was out of the car she locked the passenger door and led the way to number one.

Approaching the gate, Ena saw the near side front curtain swing into position. She turned to Artie and flicked her head sideways. He nodded that he had also seen the curtain. As they neared the front door, they saw it was slightly open.

'Crosier knows we're here, she's just seen us,' Ena whispered. 'Why hasn't she come to the door?'

Artie shrugged his shoulders, and didn't comment.

Ena knocked on the door and called, 'Hello?' When there was no reply, she pushed the door with the toe of her shoe. It opened a little wider. She called 'hello' again. Again, there was no reply. She turned to Artie, whispered, 'Come on,' and stepped over the threshold.

Artie tapped her on the shoulder and she jumped. 'What the hell...?' she hissed.

'Don't you think we should wait for her to let us in?'

'Why? She knows we're here.'

'She might not like it because I'm with you.'

Ena shook her head. 'She must have seen you with me when she was at the window. If she didn't like you being here, she wouldn't have left the door open.' As Ena turned back to the door there was a loud bang, a door somewhere in the flat had slammed causing a current of air to tug at the door she was holding.

'What the—?'

'The back door,' Ena whispered.

Artie remained silent, listening for sounds of movement in the flat. 'It's very quiet,' he said after some time.'

'Too quiet. What the hell is she playing at?'

'I tell you, it's a trap. I bet you—'

'Why would she want to trap us?' Ena whispered. 'She has no idea that we know who she really is. And when she came to the office, I told her what she wanted to know and we parted on good terms. No—'

Close by the engine of a car was gunned. Ena and Artie turned at the same time. The engine was being revved loudly.

'Here.' Ena gave Artie the keys to the Sunbeam. 'Follow her. I'll go in and have a look around.'

Artie ran down the path and through the gate to the corner of Telford and Tolgarth Avenue. As he jumped into the Sunbeam, Audrey Crosier's green Ford Zephyr roared off. He ignited the engine and pulled away from the kerb slowly. Staying two cars behind the green Zephyr, Artie followed Audrey Crosier along Tolgarth Avenue and onto Streatham High Road.

To enter someone's property without an invitation was breaking the law. However, if Crosier had just driven off, she wouldn't know. And, if it wasn't Crosier driving her car, she may be in trouble and need help. If she was asked, Ena would tell the truth. Audrey Crosier had telephoned Dudley Green Associates asking to see Ena. The door was open when she arrived, she heard a bang and, as a concerned citizen doing her civic duty, Ena entered the flat to investigate. She stepped into the hall.

Pulling the door to behind her, Ena walked along the corridor. The carpet was thick. Her tread made no sound. The door to the kitchen was wide open. The study door was ajar, as it had been the first time Ena was in the flat, the day she interviewed Audrey Crosier about her husband's connection to Rupert

Highsmith in Berlin. She poked her head into the kitchen. The back door was shut. She assumed it was the back door she'd heard slam before Crosier's car drove off. With no sign of life in the kitchen, she backed out into the corridor and turning, pushed the study door. Something was stopping it from opening fully. She pushed harder, the obstacle gave way and she entered.

Audrey Crosier lay on her back. White crystals forming in the saliva at the corners of her mouth suggested to Ena that she had been poisoned with cyanide. Her left arm, from the shoulder, was at a right angle to her body. It looked broken. And her brown eyes, dull and unfocused, were open but there was no life in them. Kneeling beside Crosier, Ena lifted her hand. It was still warm. She felt her wrist for a pulse. There wasn't one.

Since the woman was dead, telephoning for an ambulance wasn't urgent. It was the police Ena would telephone, but not until she'd had a good look around. A letter protruded from the top of the typewriter. Using her handkerchief, Ena lifted the overhanging paper and read, *Dear Matthew, I'm sorry you had to find out about your father the way you did. He was a good man. He loved you very much, as I did.* 'Did,' Ena said aloud and quickly read on. *Now that I have gone, you will be told things about me that I wish I had told you myself. I'm sorry you'll hear about the worst of me, not the best. But it is too late for regrets. Son, whatever you're told about me, please know that I have always loved you. I am not a traitor; I am a loyal patriot. My reward for this is also my punishment. I shall spend the rest of my days alone in*

'In?' Where was Audrey Crosier planning to go... With her handkerchief wrapped around the fingers of her left hand, Ena pulled open the drawers of Crosier's writing desk one by one. There was little of interest in any of them. Pens, a notepad with nothing written on it, blank sheets of paper. In another, receipts for household appliances. Mostly white goods for the kitchen. In the bottom drawer was a cash tin. Ena estimated the notes to add up to around ten pounds. She was hoping to find a passport, or letters from abroad, but there was nothing to shed light on Crosier's plans. She closed the last drawer. She glanced through a pile of envelopes on the left of the desk. Bills – electricity, gas, rates – nothing out of the ordinary.

Ena stepped over Crosier's body and squeezed through the door. The kitchen she had been in, but it was the sitting room and bedroom, both at the front of the maisonette, that interested Ena the most. She went to the sitting room first, nudging open the door with her elbow. It was neat and tidy with plain dark blue curtains and carpet, and a matching blue rug with a gold leaf pattern in front of the fire. Above it, a wooden surround and above that, a gilt mirror. The furniture, while plain, was good quality. Behind the door a dining table and six chairs were tucked into a spacious arched recess. Silver candlesticks, one at each end of the table, caught the sun as it shone through a tall single window.

Ena walked around the table and stopped to look out of the window. There were more cars parked along the avenue than there had been when she arrived. She looked at her watch. She had been in Audrey Crosier's flat half an hour. Leaving the dining area, Ena carefully opened the door of a Welsh dresser. Apart from a bottle of sherry and one of port, there was nothing to see. A pale blue and white China dinner service, a design that Ena didn't recognise, was neatly placed on the shelves. Reaching up, she ran the flat of her hand along the top of the dresser. She found nothing, not even dust. Audrey Crosier wasn't only meticulously tidy, she was scrupulously clean.

Ena wondered what was in the sitting room the first time she came to the flat. There was definitely something her host didn't want her to see. She looked from the door to bay window, and from fireplace to dining table. Whatever it was, it wasn't there now.

Next to the dresser, before the bay window, was a walnut

bureau. She looked closely at the narrow space between the body and the lid of the bureau, and gave it a gentle tug. It was not locked. It pulled down to make a writing desk.

As she began to search through envelopes and papers in their narrow compartments, Ena heard a click. It sounded like the front door. Someone was in the hall.

FIFTY-TWO

Without making a sound, Ena crossed to the dining table and picked up a silver candlestick. It was heavy enough to floor anyone wishing to do her harm. Pressing her back against the wall, holding the candlestick above her head, she squeezed into the narrow space behind the sitting room door, and waited.

Concentrating on the narrow gap between the door's hinges, Ena waited for whoever had broken in to pass along the corridor. Her arm began to ache. It felt like an age that she had been standing there with the heavy candlestick raised above her head. She was inches away from whoever was outside the door. She held her breath. Her heart was pounding. One step more, she willed, just one step and she would see who was there. Hardly daring to breathe in case the person on the other side of the wall heard her, she reached up and with both hands gripped the candlestick more tightly. If he, or she, came into the sitting room they would feel the weight of it on their head.

'Ena?'

Losing her balance with the shock of hearing Artie calling her name, Ena toppled forwards, giving way to the weight of the candlestick. It cracked against the round ornate glass window in the door before flying out of her hands and falling on the floor, missing her feet by inches.

'What the hell are you doing creeping about,' Ena scolded.

'I could ask you the same thing,' Artie said, picking up the candlestick and moving his arm up and down, as if he was weighing it. 'You could have brained me with this thing.'

Ena hadn't realised she'd been holding her breath and exhaled loudly. 'Sorry,' she gasped when she had recovered from the shock of seeing Artie and was breathing normally. 'I didn't expect you back so soon. I thought Audrey Crosier's killer had returned.'

'What?'

'She's in the study at the end of the passage.'

'Have you called the police?'

'No. I was going to when I'd had a mooch around.'

Artie took his handkerchief from his pocket, wiped his and Ena's fingerprints from the candlestick and put it on the dining table, before heading down the passage to the study, leaving Ena to look through the bureau.

'She's still warm,' he said on his return.

'You didn't touch anything, did you?' Artie gave her a look of incredulity and tutted. 'Did you read the letter?'

'Yes. She was saying goodbye, not because she thought she was going to die, but because she had planned to leave London. Her *reward and her punishment was to be on her own,*' Artie mulled over what Audrey Crosier had typed and then said, 'I wonder where she was going?'

'That we may never know.'

'Unless we find out who killed her. My money's on the Russians.'

'She came from East Berlin. Her killer is most likely the driver of her car. Were you able to follow it?'

'Oh, yes. All the way to Orpington Road.'

Ena shot Artie a look of utter surprise. 'Matthew Crosier's house? I can't see Matthew killing his mother.'

'It wasn't him driving. Unless Audrey had him when she was ten.'

'Who then?' Before Artie could answer, Ena said, 'The oaf at the hospital with Crosier, posing as a copper.'

Closing the lid of the bureau and pushing the drawers to, Ena said, 'Come on. We need to find something, anything, that will tell us who killed her? I haven't found her passport. Unless it's in here.'

Artie followed Ena into Audrey Crosier's bedroom. 'It's all very...' he searched for a word to describe how neat everything in the flat was.

'Well-organised?'

'Too well-organised if you ask me.'

Using his handkerchief Artie opened the wardrobe doors while Ena opened the drawers of the tallboy.

'Nothing. Only clothes. I'll have a look in the spare bedroom.'

'Only clothes here too,' Ena said, pushing the drawers of the tallboy back into the unit before crossing to the dressing table in the bay window overlooking the small garden.

'Check the bathroom,' Ena shouted, hearing Artie leaving the single bedroom that was situated between the bathroom and kitchen.

In the middle of the dressing table was a silver backed brush, comb and hand-mirror and behind them a bottle of Chanel No 5. On the left, a silver frame with a photograph of her son Matthew and his wife on their wedding day and on the right, a matching frame with a black and white photograph of a young Michael and a young and very beautiful, Audrey.

When Ena met Matthew, he asked her not to call on his mother until he'd spoken to her, told her who Ena was, and explained why she wanted to speak to her. He obviously loved his mother very much. With a heavy heart Ena turned away from Audrey's photograph, grateful that it was not her who had to break the news to Matthew Crosier that his mother was dead.

'Now, we can telephone the police,' Ena said, joining Artie as he was putting packets of indigestion remedies, Aspirin and other harmless medicines back in the bathroom cabinet.

'Nothing in here,' he said.

'Shush!' Ena put her forefinger up to her lips. 'Did you hear that?'

Artie nodded and followed Ena out of the bathroom. Together they turned to the front door. 'Voices? Could be neighbours?' Artie whispered.

'Whoever it is, they're right outside the door.' Ena focused on the doorknob, waiting for it to turn. It didn't. Instead, the door crashed open and two men stumbled into the hall – one charged at Ena, the other at Artie.

The man first through the door grabbed Ena's hands and forced them behind her back. The other man, younger than the first, did the same to Artie.

Neither Ena nor Artie offered resistance.

'We have reason to believe you broke into this flat. What's your name?' the older man who had hold of Ena barked.

'Ena Green—'

'And you?' he shouted at Artie.

'Mallory—'

'Ena Green, I am arresting you on suspicion of breaking and entering.' He looked at Artie.

Before he had time to arrest Artie, Ena said, 'We didn't break in. The door was open when we got here. We entered the flat because Mrs Crosier didn't answer the door when we knocked. Nor did she reply when we called her name. If you'd care to look in my pocket,' Ena said, motioning with her head to the left pocket in her jacket, 'you will find my card.'

The older policeman nodded to the younger who

forced his large plate-like hand into Ena's pocket. He brought out a business card and read, 'Dudley Green Investigations.'

'We are private investigators. Mrs Crosier was our client,' Ena said, stretching the truth. 'We are here at Mrs Crosier's request.' The smirk on the younger policeman's face told Ena he didn't believe her. The older policeman looked down his nose and frowned.

'If you need confirmation, I suggest you telephone Detective Inspector Powell at Bow Street Police Station.' Ena would have liked nothing more than to back up her suggestion with, 'our agency *often works with him.*' But as most of the work she did with Dan Powell was unofficial, she ended with, 'DI Powell, will vouch for us.'

The detectives looked at one another. The older one said, 'Ask the neighbour if you can use her telephone. Ring the station and get someone to phone Bow Street.'

'Sir!' The younger policeman let go of Artie's hands and left.

Releasing Ena, the older detective said, 'So, Mrs Crosier wasn't here when you arrived?'

'I didn't say that,' Ena corrected. 'I said the door was ajar and when I knocked she didn't answer.'

'But you believed her to be here?'

'Of course. She had left a message for me saying she'd be here. Look, you know who I am. You might at least have had the courtesy to introduce yourself before arresting me and almost breaking my arm.' Ena waited for the plain clothes policeman to give her his name and rank.

'Detective Inspector Thorn, Streatham.'

'Detective Thorn, my associate and I entered the flat because, after knocking several times, Mrs Crosier hadn't come to the door. We heard a loud noise, a bang, which we subsequently learned was the back door slamming. We didn't know it was a door slamming at the time and were worried that she might be in need of assistance.'

'And was she?'

Ena looked at Artie and raised her eyes. She was about to make the situation a whole lot worse but there was nothing she could do about that. If she didn't tell the DI that Audrey Crosier was dead, she and Artie would be in real trouble. 'We were too late. Mrs Crosier is in the study,' she said, pointing to the door at the end of the passage.

The inspector's eyebrows met in the middle of his forehead in a frown.

'She's dead!'

FIFTY-THREE

The door opened and the younger detective came into the hall. Closing the door, he handed the inspector Ena's card and nodded.

'Thank you, Sergeant. Go back to the neighbour and ask to use the phone again. We need forensics and fingerprints up here, as soon as! Then hang about outside until they get here. We may have a crime on our hands. We don't want all and sundry coming in.'

'Sir!' the sergeant said and left again.

'Right then,' the inspector said. 'Let's have a look at the body.'

Ena and Artie followed the inspector to the study.

The first thing he did was crouch down and feel for Audrey Crosier's pulse. 'She's dead alright.' He stood up and turned to Ena and Artie, who were huddled in the doorway. 'How long did you say you'd been here?'

Ena felt the colour rise from her neck to her cheeks. 'Not long. Ten, maybe fifteen minutes,' she lied.

'Have you touched anything in here?'

Artie shook his head and Ena said, 'No.' Taking the focus

away from touching anything, she said, 'There's a letter in the typewriter you might want to read, Inspector. It alludes to her leaving London.'

The inspector went over to the typewriter and, using a pencil that he took from his top pocket, lifted the overhang of paper. He made several muttering noises and when he had finished reading let the letter fall back into place. 'Any idea where she might have been going?'

Back to East Berlin, or to Russia, Ena thought, but had no intention of saying. It was hard to believe she'd go anywhere if it meant leaving her son.

'Mrs Crosier gave no indication that she was leaving when she telephoned the office,' Artie said.

'Nor did she tell me she was planning to leave when she last came to the office.' Ena glanced at the typewriter. 'She says she's leaving in that letter, but anyone could have typed it. There's no signature to prove Audrey Crosier was the author of the letter.' A sudden thought flashed into Ena's mind. She hadn't had time to type up Michael Crosier's notes when Audrey came to the office. She did it later and posted it the following day, to this address. The envelope wasn't here. If it had been, she'd have seen it.

'Mrs Green?'

Ena looked up. 'Sorry. Er... No. If she was planning to leave London, I have no idea where she would have gone.'

'You said she came to your office some time ago? Why was that?'

'As she's dead, I suppose I can tell you. I interviewed her about a case I was working on that involved her late husband. I was not at liberty to discuss the case as it would have been a breach of client confidentiality, but I'd agreed to let her know if anything came up that involved her husband.'

'And did it?'

Ena was careful not to say more than was absolutely necessary. 'No. There was nothing remotely suspicious about her husband's death. He drowned. It was a tragic accident, nothing more. There was no reason for us to meet again.'

'If that was the case, why would she telephone you today and ask you to come here?'

Ena looked down at Audrey Crosier's dead body. 'I wish I knew.'

'Mr Mallory?'

Artie shook his head. 'All she said on the telephone was that she wanted to see Mrs Green. She didn't say why.'

'Well, that's it then!' The inspector looked at his watch. 'The fingerprint boys will be here soon. I don't suppose whoever killed Mrs Crosier has been careless enough to leave us a set of prints. We could get lucky, I suppose,' he said, looking at Crosier's body. 'What's that?' He knelt down on one knee and looked closely. 'White crystals dried in the corner of Mrs Crosier's mouth. Looks like she's been poisoned,' he muttered.

Ena looked at Artie, put her up a hand and wiggled her fingers. 'Prints,' she mouthed. He rolled his eyes and nodded. 'Inspector?'

'Huh?'

'My colleague and I were wondering...?'

'Yes, you can go,' he said, still focusing on Audrey Crosier. 'Someone will telephone to arrange for you to come down to Streatham Station to give your statements.' He stood up with a breathy, 'Huh! Will you be in your office tomorrow?'

'Yes, one or other of us will be.' Neither Ena nor Artie attempted to leave.

'What is it?' the inspector asked.

Ena could feel her cheeks growing red. 'Your fingerprint people might find... will probably find mine and Mr Mallory's fingerprints in some of the other rooms.'

The inspector glowered.

'I thought I should tell you so you can eliminate us. We were very careful—'

'Mrs Green, you had no business going into any of the rooms, especially once you knew a crime had been committed.'

'I don't mean to contradict you, Inspector, but I believe I had every right. Mrs Crosier asked me to come here today. In between her telephoning the office – and me arriving here – she was killed. That gives me the right!' Ena slammed her fist on the desk. She knew she was talking out of her hat, but held herself ram-rod straight.

The inspector straightened up too. He looked at Ena with a confident grin. 'See the white powder in the corner of the deceased's mouth?' Ena nodded. 'It's possible that is poison. In which case she may not have been killed, but took her own life.'

'Suicide?' Ena bit her lip to stop herself from saying what a ridiculous notion that was. 'But, Inspector, if Audrey Crosier had planned to commit suicide, she wouldn't have written a letter saying she was leaving.'

FIFTY-FOUR

Ena looked up as the door to her office opened. 'Hello?' she said. 'This is a surprise. How lovely to see you both. Artie,' she called over her shoulder, 'we have visitors.'

Artie poked his head around the kitchen door. 'Good God!' he exclaimed; his eyes fixed on the younger of the two women as he left the kitchen for the office. 'This young lady looks so much like you, Mrs Galbraith, she must be your sister.'

Priscilla roared with laughter. 'You flatterer. This beautiful young woman is my daughter,' she said, pride bursting from her.

'Come in. Sit down.' Ena ran to the conference table and pulled out two chairs. Sitting on the opposite side of the table, Ena shook her head and, laughing, said, 'I can hardly believe my eyes. I knew when I met Mary that she looked like you. Well, how I imagined you had looked when you were her age, but seeing the two of you together...'

'You're like two peas in a pod,' Artie said, joining the women at the table, but not sitting down.

'Radiant, was what I was going to say, but Artie's right, you are very alike.'

'Who wants coffee?'

'Not for me,' Priscilla said.

Artie looked at Mary.

'No, thank you. We had cappuccino in Soho when we finished shopping in Carnaby Street,' Mary said, her eyes sparkling with excitement.

'Carnaby Street?' Artie exclaimed. 'I love shopping in Carnaby Street.'

'We went to the Kings Road too,' Mary said.

Artie shook his head playfully. 'And what did you buy from the King's Road?'

Mary, enjoying the fun she was having with Artie laughed and said, 'I bought a dress from Très Chic. That's a boutique on the Kings Road, in Chelsea. It's at the opposite end of the road to Mary Quant's shop, Bazaar. We looked in there, but...' Mary sucked air through pursed lips. 'It was very expensive. Mum would go mad if—' She stopped speaking, turned to Priscilla and bit her lip. 'I'm sorry, I didn't mean...'

Priscilla smiled lovingly and said, 'And, I would agree with your mum. The dress you decided upon is every bit as lovely as the one we saw in the window of Bazaar. I'm sure your mum will love it on you. She'll love what you bought her too,' Priscilla said, crunching up her shoulders and winking conspiratorially.

'She will, won't she? Right!' Mary said, turning back to Artie, 'I have a dress from Kings Road, and shoes and records from Carnaby Street. Oh, and I bought a pair of earrings for my friend who I go to college with in Liverpool and a pretty scarf for Mum.'

'Come on then!' Artie ordered. 'Let's have a look at your new dress.'

Ena could see that the delightful young woman was trying not to laugh. She rolled her eyes at Artie and tutted. She was clearly enjoying him pulling her leg. She leaned sideways and picked up a carrier bag with the name Très Chic on it. The name was in swirling blues and pinks, the dress inside was navy blue. Mary stood up and held the dress against her. It was short, but not too short. It was the length a modern girl would wear and a modern mother would approve of. It had big round white buttons down the left side and a white collar. 'And these,' she said, taking white patent shoes from a Ravel box, 'are to go with the dress. I didn't need a white handbag; I have one at home.'

Artie clapped. 'You will look a stunner in that outfit.'

'Yes, you will,' Ena agreed. 'I still can't believe you're here,' she said, reaching out and giving Mary's hand a squeeze.

'Mrs Green, I thought about what you told Mum and me when you came to see us in Liverpool. When you left, we discussed what you'd said, as well as everything that had brought us to this point in our lives and we both agreed that, as long as me coming to meet Priscilla didn't cause any upset,' Mary looked at Priscilla who, smiling, shook her head, 'it was the right time for me to come.'

'I am so pleased for you, for you all. Thank you for bringing Mary to see Artie and me,' Ena said to Priscilla.

'Not only did Mary want to see you, but Mrs Hornsby hopes to see you too. Neither she nor Charles wanted to come shopping, so we sent them to the Victoria and Albert Museum. We're meeting them for lunch at Café Rouge on Marlborough Street, at one thirty. Please say you'll join us. Well? Come on, you two. You have to eat, so why not with us?'

Ena took some time to answer her friend. She might have told Priscilla about Audrey Crosier, had she been on her own, but she wasn't going to say she and Artie had found a dead spy the day before in front of Mary. 'The thing is,' she said at last, 'while Artie and I would love to join you for lunch,' Ena smiled at Mary, 'there has been a problem with an investigation.'

'It isn't anything to do with us really,' Artie interjected, 'but we said we'd help the police with their enquiries.'

'We can't really get out of it,' Ena said, as Artie interrupted. 'It isn't something we can put off.'

Ena continued. 'I'm due at Streatham Police Station in half an hour, Artie sometime later. The timing isn't good. I'm afraid.' Ena hoped Priscilla would understand the importance of a meeting taking place at a police station. 'It's a sandwich for us today. But another time?' Ena said, taking in both women.

Priscilla nodded, pushed back her chair and stood up. Mary did the same. 'Of course, we understand,' Ena's friend said. 'I'm going to show Mary round Covent Garden, then we'll saunter down to Marlborough Street. If you can make it, we'll be there until three o'clock.'

'Mum will be disappointed not to see you, but we'll be coming to London again.'

FIFTY-FIVE

Ena brought the Sunbeam to a halt on Streatham High Road, a few yards from the entrance to the police station. The desk sergeant told her she was expected and seconds later a door marked Private at the side of the public waiting area was opened by a young WPC who introduced herself as WPC Horton. She then showed Ena into an interview room at the far end of the corridor.

'Mrs Green, sir,' the WPC said to Inspector Thorn, the DI Ena had met in Audrey Crosier's flat on the day she was murdered.

DI Thorn stood up and offered Ena his hand. 'Mrs Green, thank you for coming in today.'

Ena shook the inspector's hand but felt no need to comment. As Audrey Crosier was killed in the Streatham area, she had expected to be called into Streatham Police Station to give a statement – and today was the day. She smiled.

WPC Horton pulled out a chair for Ena.

'Thank you,' she said, before sitting down.

'Mrs Green, Alan Richardson of Special Branch has taken

me into his confidence. He has explained your involvement in the Crosier case.'

'I see,' Ena said, wondering how much Richardson had told Thorn.

'I am up to speed with what happened at the hospital, but if you would go through what happened on the day you found Mrs Crosier's body – make sure we haven't missed anything – we can wrap the case up.'

'I'm sorry,' Ena said. 'Do you mean leave the investigation to Special Branch?'

DI Thorn looked down at the table. 'Yes,' he said.

'Right! Well!' Ena said, unable to stop herself from being angry and not caring if it showed in her voice. She looked at WPC Horton who picked up her pen to write down Ena's statement. 'Where would you like me to start?'

'With the telephone call Mrs Crosier made to your office, if you will?'

In monosyllables Ena repeated almost verbatim what she had told DI Thorn on the day she found Audrey Crosier dead. When she had finished, she waited for the WPC to finish writing – and signed the statement. 'I take it you're done with me?'

'Yes, thank you, Mrs Green.'

'Do you need my associate, Mr Mallory, to come down to make a statement? He wasn't there when I found Crosier.'

Thorn shook his head. 'No. I think what you have said covers all we needed to know.'

'Good. So,' she said, getting up from her chair, 'if you don't mind, I'll be going. I have *important* work to do at the office.' Not giving a damn about Thorn, but not wanting to appear rude to the WPC – after all the charade wasn't her fault – Ena gave her a warm smile and said, 'Thank you.' To the inspector she said, 'Good day!' and left.

* * *

Ena pulled into a Dudley Green Associates parking space on Mercer Street and parked next to DI Powell's black Wolseley. She ran across the road and after hanging up her coat in the cloak room, and putting a comb through her hair, she entered the office. Inspector Powell was sitting at Artie's desk.

Seeing Ena, the inspector left his chair and walked to her with his hand outstretched. Meeting in the middle of the room they shook hands.

'Hello! Am I pleased to see you,' Ena said.

'How did it go with Inspector Thorn?'

Ena gave her friend Dan Powell a look of incredulity.

'That good, was it?' the inspector said, laughing.

'It was a waste of time.' She smiled at Artie. 'What is it you say? *That's an hour of my life I won't get back?*' She shook her head. 'Why Inspector Thorn insisted I went down to Streatham Police Station and give a statement, Lord knows.'

'I suppose it was to see if you had remembered anything else about the day you found Audrey Crosier's body.'

'I'd understand if it was that, or anything else to do with the case, but he didn't ask me anything he hadn't already asked me.'

'Did he tell you Special Branch have taken over the investigation?'

'What?' Artie interrupted.

'Alan telephoned me this morning. Special Branch have taken the case in-house. Any further investigation is to be done solely by them.'

'How do you feel about Special Branch taking over?' Artie asked the inspector.

'Me?' DI Powell chuckled. 'Mr Highsmith being run down on Floral Street and the attempt on his life at St Thomas' Hospital were both on my patch. And, in both cases, Audrey Crosier was my main person of interest—'

'Guilty as hell!'

'No proof of the former, but yes, because she had attempted to kill Mr Highsmith in the hospital, I'd have had a strong case to charge her.' He looked at Ena. 'I wish we'd got her that night.'

'The good news is Rupert is alive and recovering from the injuries Crosier inflicted in the hit-and-run, and the damn woman is dead.'

'She is, and she was not murdered on my patch. I couldn't give a fig about Mrs Crosier's murder or the Russian spy who was holed up at Matthew Crosier's house. They are Nick Thorn and Alan Richardson's problems.'

'Thorn got the Russian? He didn't say.'

Inspector Powell shrugged. 'He wouldn't have if Artie hadn't followed him to Matthew Crosier's house.'

'Has he confessed to killing Audrey Crosier?'

'No. He denied it.'

'But he was in her flat. We heard him leave, saw him drive off. What about impersonating a police officer? And he's an accomplice to attempted murder.'

Dan Powell laughed. 'He has a rock-solid alibi for the time Crosier tried to kill Mr Highsmith.'

'He can't have, I saw him.'

'He told Alan Richardson he was at the Russian Embassy sorting out his out-of-date visa.'

'And Richardson believed him?'

'He had no choice. The Russian has several witnesses that will testify to him being there.'

Ena looked at Artie. 'Visa?' She turned her attention back to the inspector. 'Don't tell me.' She threw her hands up in the air. 'A new visa couldn't be arranged in time, so they are sending him home to Russia. When?'

'Today,' DI Powell said.

'At least he'll no longer be a threat to Mr Highsmith. Or to Matthew Crosier and his wife.'

'No, thank God. Matthew went to Streatham to see Thorn yesterday afternoon after CID had picked the Russian up. Matthew didn't like the Russian, said he didn't trust him. But the big Muscovite spun him a right old tale about his father and Matthew's father being best friends when they were teenagers. He said his father had saved Matthew's father from drowning when they were set upon by local thugs while fishing and Michael had fallen into the river.'

A cold shudder ran the length of Ena's spine. 'Strange,' she said. 'Matthew's father, Michael Crosier, drowned in a river on the outskirts of Berlin in 1936.'

'A coincidence?'

'No,' Ena shook her head. 'The bastard was playing mind games, trying to get Matthew to trust him.'

'I can't believe Matthew Crosier believed that the son of his spying father's friend, from all those years ago, turned up on his doorstep out of the blue?'

'It wasn't out of the blue, Artie. He told Matthew that he was the attaché to the Third Minister for Urban Development, and that he had been sent to England to work at the Russian Embassy for six months. His job was to learn all he could about rebuilding houses in urban districts like the East End.'

'If that's true, he'd have diplomatic immunity,' Ena said. 'So why kill Audrey Crosier?'

'Maybe the Kremlin wanted their shadow sleeper put to sleep permanently.'

'There can be no other reason,' Ena said.

'The Russian told Matthew that he wanted to get in touch with Audrey to pass on his father's condolences.'

'What? And Audrey just said, "Come round?"'

'That's what the Russian said.'

'Which is a load of rubbish.' Ena looked at Artie. 'When she telephoned here, she said she had something important to tell me. I think she was going to give the Russian up. We'll never know now, but I'm damn sure she wouldn't have asked me to go to her flat if she knew the Russian would be there.'

'She may have been going to frame him for the hit-and-run. Say he'd coerced her and threatened her son's life if she didn't kill Highsmith in St Thomas'. And, because she didn't succeed, she could say she was only going through the motions and had never intended to kill Highsmith.'

'Whatever she said would have been lies. The Russian had been Audrey Crosier's accomplice from the minute he arrived in England. Probably the reason he was sent here.'

'Activating a sleeping agent after so many years dormant, how could they be sure she'd get the job done? She'd been a housewife and a mother most of her adult life.' A thought struck Ena and she caught her breath.

'What is it, Ena?'

'We got it wrong. *I* got it wrong. The Russian *was* the killer! Audrey Crosier was a scapegoat. She didn't know it, which is why she wrote the letter she left in the typewriter. She wasn't going to kill herself, she thought she'd be leaving to go back to Berlin, or to Russia. The white substance in the corner of her mouth was potassium cyanide.'

'You're saying she committed suicide? A cyanide capsule in a false tooth which she crushed—?'

'No. She'd been in England thirty odd years. It would have meant she'd never have been able to go to the dentist. The Russian killed her and made it look like suicide. He killed one of his own.' Cleaning house, Ena thought. Like Archibald Hollander had done when he killed Michael Crosier in Berlin in 1936, Audrey Crosier's accomplice had killed her; had cleaned house. Twenty-four years had passed but nothing in the world of the spies and spooks – in the West or the East – had changed. Just a different cleaner, a different country, a different war.

'Does Inspector Thorn want me to go down to Streatham Police Station to give a statement, Ena?' Artie asked.

Ena was deep in thought. Then, as if she had only just heard his question she said, 'No. We're officially off the case. Alan Richardson's orders.'

'After all the legwork you've done?'

'And believe me there was a lot of legwork in Scotland and Shetland. Bloody Special Branch!' Ena couldn't help herself and burst out laughing. 'My nose has been well and truly put out of joint.'

The two men laughed with Ena. 'I think we should celebrate,' she said. 'Come on, you two.' She looked at the clock. 'We have time to get to Marlborough Street and have lunch with the Galbraiths. Enjoy a happy occasion, a beginning not an end. Let's have something to eat and a glass of wine to celebrate Priscilla being united with her daughter and Detective Inspector Thorn solving the Crosier case!'

'But he didn't,' Artie said, 'you did. The cheeky bugger.'

'You know that and I know that. On the plus side, we won't have to go to court,' Ena said, 'which is another reason to celebrate. Oh, I almost forgot. Henry's working in London today and said he'd be home for lunch. So...' Ena picked up her notepad and pen, scribbled a message to Henry telling him that she, Artie and Dan Powell were meeting the Galbraiths for lunch at Café Rouge, Marlborough Street – and asked him to join them. 'Look sharp,' she ordered, tearing the sheet of paper out of the pad, 'I'm famished.'

Artie jumped up and followed Ena and DI Powell out of the office. Ena pushed the note she'd written to Henry through the letter box of number 8a and buttoned up her coat against the chill wind of early October.

When Artie had locked the outer door, Ena put one hand through his arm and one through the arm of Inspector Powell and the three of them marched along Mercer Street.

FIFTY-SIX

It was mild for November. The sky was blue-black with an array of bright stars. The tall shrubs that had once hidden the house from the road had been cut back allowing the streetlight to show Ena the way. She turned into the half-moon shaped drive that led to Mrs Thornton's Victorian villa. With the curtains not yet drawn, lights shone brightly from every window. Ena parked next to Jeanie McKinlay's car. The old green Morris Minor had been a life saver earlier in the year. Ena and Henry got out of the Sunbeam and Ena locked it. An ice-cold shiver ran up her spine. But for Jeanie McKinlay's quick thinking there might have been two murders at the Willows residential home instead of one, and one here too.

Jeanie had told Ena that Mrs Thornton had a grandson and Ena came to the house to find out whether the boy was in cahoots with his sister, Andrea, in trying to kill their grand-mother. When she arrived, Ena rang the front doorbell but there was no reply. She followed the path along the side of the house to the back door. She peered in to a sparsely furnished kitchen and recoiled in horror. A boy in his mid-teens, bound to a wheelchair, stared back at her. Ena knew then that the boy had to be Mrs Thornton's grandson, Andrea Thornton's brother.

The boy's name was Rory. Jeanie McKinlay had spoken of him in a recent letter.

'Ena?'

She looked up. Henry was calling her from the open door of the villa. Standing next to him was Rory.

Ena ran up the steps. 'Rory!' she exclaimed.

Rory beamed her a smile and leaning on his left stick, lifted his right hand to shake Ena's hand. 'Mrs Green.'

'Call me Ena, please.' She held the hand of the young man who she had last seen in soiled clothes, bound to a wheelchair. 'You look well, really well.'

'I feel well,' he said. smiling. 'I no longer need the wheelchair.'

'I can see that,' Ena said, letting Rory lead her and Henry into the house. Rory walked with the aid of two sticks, but he was walking.

The house was bright and cheerful, the rooms had been decorated in light colours and the furniture was no longer hidden beneath dustsheets.

Mrs Thornton greeted Ena and Henry warmly and led them through to the kitchen. The back door was open. Beyond it a dozen or more people stood around a bonfire. Ena saw Jeanie running across the lawn towards her followed by a good-looking man, a little older than Jeanie, with sandy coloured hair.

Jeanie threw her arms around Ena and hugged her as Henry and Gerry shook hands.

Jeanie looked over Ena's shoulder into the kitchen. 'Where's Mr Mallory?' she asked, walking into the house.

'His friend was released from hospital today, so he's getting him settled in at home. He sends his love and wishes you a happy engagement party.' Ena gave Jeanie two prettily wrapped parcels. 'From Henry and me. And, this one is from Artie.'

Before Jeanie had time to open her engagement presents, Mrs Thornton joined them. 'There's mulled wine on the stove.'

Jeanie took Gerry's hand and said to Mrs Thornton, 'May I tell Ena?'

Mrs Thornton laughed good heartedly. 'Of course you can.'

Jeanie took a deep breath and smiling said, 'Mrs Thornton has had the old summer house converted into a private physiotherapy practice.'

'My grandson Rory wants to resume his education, which would not have been possible without the hard work of these two young miracle workers,' Mrs Thornton said, looking from Gerry to Jeanie. Blinking back her tears she said, 'Show Ena and Henry the work that has been done, while I get them mulled wine. Take care,' she said, 'the paint may not be dry.'

Ena and Henry followed Jeanie and Gerry into the garden where they were met by Rory. Jeanie ran ahead to the summerhouse. With a red and blue brick exterior the summerhouse looked more like a bungalow. Jeanie opened the door and ushered them in.

Ena gasped with surprise. 'It's amazing.'

'It has everything,' Rory said. 'Even my old parallel walking bars.'

'This is reception,' Gerry said. 'It will have a desk and seating. And this,' he continued, opening the door on his right, 'is the massage room. Back, legs and other muscle problems in here. Sturdy padded beds will be bolted to the floor. They're arriving on Monday.' Ena and Henry looked into the room. The walls were a soft dove grey and the lighting was subtle. And this room,' he said, crossing to the room opposite. 'This is the main physical therapy and exercise room.' Ena and Henry stood inside the door while Gerry described the equipment needed. 'Parallel bars, dumbbells and kettlebells.

There'll be other equipment when we need it. For the time being, our job is to get people's muscles built up and get them walking – once they're strong enough. I shall carry on working at St Thomas', Gerry said, leaving the room and closing the door behind Ena and Henry. 'It will be a private consultancy,' he said. Turning, he held out his hand and Jeanie took it.

'When the building is ready and the equipment has been installed, give Artie a ring at the office. Rupert I'm sure would be grateful for any help you could give him to speed up his recovery,' Ena said. She looked at Henry. 'What do you think, darling?'

'I think that's a splendid idea. He's adamant he's returning to work. If he's going to be fit enough, he'll need all the help he can get.'

Ena heard Rory calling Gerry from the back door. 'Come on, it's time for the firework display.'

Jeanie left her fiancé and walked into the kitchen at Rory's side.

'Bring me down a cup of mulled wine, will you, Jeanie?' Gerry called.

'Will do.' Jeanie turned to Ena, her eyes sparkling with happiness. 'The fireworks are at the bottom of the garden in an old Anderson shelter,' she said. Taking a long-handled ladle, she started spooning spicy red wine with sultanas and chopped up clementines from a large saucepan into two thick, jug style glasses. 'Rory,' she said, 'bring Ena and Henry out when they've got some wine, will you, love?'

Rory lifted a stick in acknowledgment and Ena spooned mulled wine into three glass mugs. She gave Henry his wine in the kitchen and carried her own and Rory's outside. Rory, leaning on a wooden post that supported the roof of the ornate

garden shed, stood his sticks against the wall and took his glass
from Ena.

The combination of burning wood from the bonfire and
cinnamon from the hot mulled wine filled the air. Ena looked
about her at the friends of Jeanie and Gerry, Mrs Thornton and
her grandson, Rory. As she watched the assembled crowd chatting and laughing in anticipation of the firework display, Ena
caught the eye of Mrs Thornton. She waved and Ena raised her
glass. Life was at last working out for the kind old lady. She had
lost so much when her daughter and son-in-law were killed in a
car crash. Ena observed Mrs Thornton waving to Rory and
turned to see the young man wave back at her. What a difference six months of being loved and cared for had made.

When Ena first met Rory it was not only his legs that had
been broken, his spirit had been broken too. Now, after just six
months of physiotherapy treatment he had gone from a boy in a
wheelchair to being strong enough not only to stand up, but to
walk with the use of sticks. Gerry and Jeanie had done a good
job with him. Ena hoped they would be able to do an equally
good job with Rupert Highsmith.

Ena's thoughts were interrupted by a rocket zooming high
into the sky. It made a whizzing noise before bursting into silver
stars. Immediately afterwards a second rocket whirred into the
air, this time leaving a trail of gold stars. A third missile left a
smoky trail behind it before showering the area with red and
green shooting stars. Loud cracks and bangs made everyone
jump, which was followed by a great deal of laughter and
squeals.

Jeanie and Gerry appeared from the right side of the bonfire
and while Jeanie passed around sparklers, Gerry, from a safe
distance, lit the touch paper on cartwheels, jumping jacks and
Roman candles.

Watching the array of colourful fireworks, Ena pulled up
the collar of her coat, wrapped her hands around the hot glass

and sipped her mulled wine. From being an unusually hot summer that had lasted until late September, October came and went in a flash leaving a cold and damp November that had taken everyone by surprise.

Henry put his arm around her shoulders and she leaned into him to watch the last of the fireworks.

When the firework display came to an end, Gerry raked the embers of the bonfire before dampening what remained of the ashes, and Jeanie and Mrs Thornton ushered everyone into the house for more mulled wine, sausages in bread rolls and baked potatoes that had been cooked on the bonfire. Walking casually at Rory's side, Jeanie beckoned Ena and Henry to follow.

'I love you, Ena,' Henry said, catching up with her.

'Hu-huh!'

'Did you hear me?'

Ena put her hand through her husband's arm and pulled him to her. 'Oh, yes, I heard you.'

A LETTER FROM THE AUTHOR

Dear reader,

Thank you for reading *Justice*. I hope you enjoyed Artie Mallory's journey: escaping death after the hit-and-run incident that almost killed his partner, Rupert Highsmith. And I hope you enjoyed meeting, again, one of my favourite characters, the lovely, generous, and zany Pricilla Galbraith.

If you enjoyed *Justice*, and I hope you did, would you like to join other readers to hear about my new releases and bonus content? I have both fiction and non-fiction ideas waiting to burst onto the page. A Christmas story for 2024, a collection of... Oh, but to tell you now would give the game away. Why not sign up for my newsletter? I would love it if you did.

www.stormpublishing.co/madalyn-morgan

Also, if you could spare a few moments to leave a review, I would appreciate it. Even a short review, if it is positive, can make all the difference in encouraging other readers to discover my books for the first time. Thank you very much!

The inspiration to write *Justice* came from the plots and storylines of earlier novels. It's that thing about tying up loose ends and seeing justice done. Oh, and Shetland. I couldn't get Shetland out of my head. Ena just had to visit that beautiful, wild and windy island.

At the end of the last novel, *Confessions*, Ena's associate, the lovely Artie Mallory, has fallen for Rupert Highsmith. Ena thought Highsmith arrogant – and with good reason. All Ena wants is for Artie to be happy. But will he be? I love it when ideas flood my mind – and one particular idea came to me like a tsunami. Highsmith had a chequered past. He worked for MI5, never played by the rules, and had made many enemies. Something was niggling me – an event, a place, or maybe a problem that hadn't been resolved. Berlin!

That night, I woke up thinking about Highsmith in Berlin in '39 with Ena's old friend Sid. Then, suddenly, a gem of an idea came into my head. Inspiration came while I was writing *Justice* in the same way that it had come to me when I wrote my last novel, *Confessions*. I grabbed my notepad and pen from the bedside table and, with my small torch between my teeth, I wrote down several ideas. The most exciting was an attempt on Highsmith's life. I knew if I didn't write it down, I would forget it by the morning.

I also wanted justice for Priscilla Galbraith. I wanted readers to understand her. My challenge when I wrote Priscilla's character history was to make a thief married to a rich, older man likeable. It is our upbringing and our experiences as children that shape us and make us who we are as adults. As an actress, I wrote biographies for every character I played. Characters in a play are not born when the curtain goes up on the first night, nor are characters in a book born on the first page: they have histories and backstories. It is the life already lived that makes us who we are – and it makes fictional characters real and believable.

With someone like Priscilla, people make judgements. They assume the worst. I wanted to prove them wrong. I wanted Priscilla to grow despite all she had been through. I wanted her to find happiness – and she did.

With characters like Priscilla, there would be underlying reasons for her behaviour, which I knew I could work on.

Priscilla developed on the page and grew into someone endearing. Well, for me, she did. I hope she did for you, too.

Thank you so much for being part of my writing journey. I have loved writing about what inspired me to write my novels. Sadly, *Justice* is the last book in the Sisters of Wartime England series – for the moment. Please stay in touch, as I have many more stories and ideas to share with you, including a standalone sequel to *Destiny* and a Christmas love story with an Ena Dudley investigation.

Best wishes and happy reading,

Madalyn x

madalynmorgan.wordpress.com

 facebook.com/madalyn.morgan1

twitter.com/ActScribblerDJ

 instagram.com/madalynmorgan1

 pinterest.com/madalynmorgan

ACKNOWLEDGMENTS

Thanks to best-selling author Michael Jecks for his wonderful endorsement, and to Rebecca Emin, Maureen Vincent-Northam, Cathy Helms, Fran Netherway and Pamela Beha for their help and support. And, special thanks to, Children In Read and The Authors' and Illustrators' for giving me the opportunity to donate this, and other novels, to be auctioned for the charity Children In Need.

Printed in Great Britain
by Amazon

56433920R00179